Garden
Plot

Garden Plot

a mystery rooted in humor

by

Kristen McKendry

Covenant Communications, Inc.

Cover image: *Vegetable Garden* © dfli, *Hunting Rifle* © Nicemonkey, courtesy iStockphoto.com.

Cover design copyright © 2011 by Covenant Communications, Inc.

Published by Covenant Communications, Inc.
American Fork, Utah

Printed in the United States of America
First Printing: August 2011

17 16 15 14 13 12 11   10 9 8 7 6 5 4 3 2 1

ISBN-13: 978-1-60861-236-9

To my boys, who are the best part of the story

Acknowledgments

Thank you once again to Samantha Van Walraven and all those at Covenant for doing a terrific job. Thank you to Tom McNamara and Jake Poranganel for the information about police procedures (even though Erin tends to disregard them). Thank you to the Ontario Therapeutic Riding Association for the important work they do. Thank you to Shiromi Perera for letting me dump all over her on a daily basis. Thank you to my mom, my personal promotions manager at home and abroad. Thank you to Kaylene Nielsen and Brian Garner for controlling crowds and sorting M&Ms. Thank you to Albert and Joyce Stumphy for a wonderful dinner, a beautiful view, and the Goldwyn Girls. Thanks to David Lougheed for the jealous cow. Thank you to Trevor D'Angelo for letting me use his name. And, as always, thank you to my husband ("He Who Shall Not Be Named") for his incredible patience. If a homicide detective is impossible to live with, a writer is even worse.

Chapter One

It couldn't be good for business to have a guest drop dead in the vegetable garden.

I'd had one fall off the wagon, dance on the lawn in her nightgown, and have to be shipped back to detox. We'd had a fistfight or two. Once, we'd had a slightly unstable kleptomaniac who thought he was a raccoon and kept pocketing the silverware. But I'd never had anyone peg out in the yard before.

My first impulse was to roll the body tidily under the privet and hope that no one would notice. But, no, he was bound to be found sooner or later, and there was likely some law against hiding bodies in the bushes. With more irritation than alarm, I headed for the house. Maybe the police could get him bundled away quietly without the rest of the guests—we always carefully referred to them as guests instead of patients—finding out.

It wasn't to be. As I ducked under the arbor leading to the patio, I nearly crashed headlong into Kevin Carlisle, the dentist from Kingston, Ontario, who'd checked in a few weeks ago.

"Oopsie!" I said, automatically stepping back to let him through. And then I remembered what lay splayed out behind me and quickly stepped in front of him again, blocking his path. I smiled a big toothy frozen smile and tried to think what to do. Was it better to be honest? More to the point, was it kinder? I wasn't sure Kevin's constitution was up to a shock of this size. There was no mention of any nervous ailment or heart condition in his medical file, but he was a pale sort of person, slightly shorter than I was, and narrow of eye and chest. He clasped a book to the latter, and I saw a Mississauga Library System sticker stuck to the spine.

"Are you just heading for the library?" I asked quickly before he could worm past me.

"Yes. I've finished my Margaret Atwood. Why?"

The library's parking lot adjoined my property, and it was quicker to cut through the yard than to walk around on the road. Guests always took the shortcut. Unfortunately, the flagstone path ran within a few feet of the vegetable garden. I grasped Kevin's free hand and linked it through my elbow.

"I'll have to ask you to postpone your trip," I said, trying to speak through clenched teeth. I hadn't been aware that I'd clenched them or that my hands were shaking somewhat. Kevin noticed at the same time I did. He recoiled, his hyperthyroidal eyes bugging out farther than usual.

"Why? Is something wrong?"

"Well, yes, rather. Could you come back into the house, please?"

He began to protest, but I towed him across the patio and back through the door. At the foot of the stairs, we met two more guests, who were dressed for tennis and carrying their racquets. Grant and Jason looked like a rabbit and a bear trying to pass as twins. Grant Calderwood was slim, a little less than six feet, with graying hair and moustache and a distinguished bearing even in white shorts and tennis shoes. Jason Baumgarten, on the other hand, was several inches above six feet and had sandy hair and a solid, square build like a wrestler. The racquet looked like a ping-pong paddle in his hands. His white shorts revealed powerful and astonishingly hairy legs. Musing that there were some things you didn't need to know about other people, I briskly linked arms with Grant and turned them all back toward the stairs, herding Jason ahead of us like a large sheep. With a man on each elbow, I had to resist the urge to start singing "Follow the Yellow Brick Road." I suppose the song popped into my head right then because I suddenly felt crazy enough to be in Oz. I don't know if Grant would qualify as a cowardly lion, but Kevin was certainly walking stiff enough to be the tin man.

Grant's silver eyebrows shot up to his hairline.

"What's all this, Mrs. Kilpatrick?" he asked as I bustled them right back up the stairs.

"I'm sorry, I'm going to have to ask you to go to your rooms and remain there for a while," I said, trying to sound as if this sort of thing happened frequently, like a fire drill.

"What's happened?" Kevin demanded, now sufficiently recovered to the point that he could be irritated.

"I'm afraid something has happened to Mr. Fortier," I told them. "I'm just going to call the police and Dr. Meacham, and then I'll come back and give you the details. If you would please wait in your rooms . . ."

"Is he all right?" Jason came to a dead stop. Being roughly the size of Mount Hood, he brought our procession to an abrupt halt. "Can I help? I know CPR if . . ."

I had a sudden vision of those meaty hands compressing my late guest's rib cage. His bones would crumple like a pop can under a boot.

"Mr. Fortier is unfortunately beyond the need for CPR, but thanks for offering," I said hastily. We'd reached the second-floor landing, and I let go of their arms. "Please stay in your rooms until further notice," I said shortly.

Kevin whirled around as soon as I released him, his mouth open to protest. I firmly turned my back on him and went back downstairs.

I bypassed the phone at the public front desk and used the one in my office instead. I had to dial the number twice because my fingers were shaking so much. There was an interminable minute while the line connected, and I found myself—whether out of habit or out of shock—humming a tune in my head. Don't they always say to sing a hymn to help yourself through a bad situation? The words currently going through my mind were, "In a world where sorrow ever will be known . . ." When I got to the chorus, I stopped, though, because it didn't seem appropriate to be scattering sunshine at a time like this. Finally, a tinny voice broke through, and with relief, I turned my attention back to the phone.

"9-1-1. What is the nature of your emergency?" said the voice.

"I want to report a body in my garden," I said, sitting on the edge of the desk. *Breathe in, breathe out. Stop the little whirly dots from spinning around in front of your eyes. That's better.*

There was the slightest of pauses.

"A body, ma'am?" said the voice suspiciously.

"Yes. Sprawled out in my green beans."

"Is the person injured, ma'am?"

"Deceased," I said. "Very much so. Can you send someone, please?"

There was another pause.

4

KRISTEN MCKENDRY

"Could I have your name, please, ma'am?"

"Erin Kilpatrick. The Whole-Life Wellness Center. 1610 Felicity Street, Mississauga." I wondered if she'd catch the irony of someone dying at a health center.

"Is there an apartment number?"

I clenched my teeth again. "No, it's a big, yellow brick building," I replied. "The gates are open. You can come right up the drive."

"Are you sure the person is deceased, ma'am? Perhaps there's—"

"Of course I'm sure," I snapped. "The man has no face left."

* * *

The officers who showed up at my door ten minutes later appeared to be as put out by the man's death as I was. They stood, hands on hips that bulged with paraphernalia, and scowled down at the figure in the dirt.

"What is this place again?" one asked for the third time. He'd introduced himself as Sergeant Layton. His partner, Constable Taylor, was taller and younger. Both had deep lines around their eyes that accentuated their annoyed expressions.

I pushed my bangs back from my forehead and let my breath out with a hiss between my teeth. "A wellness center. Sort of like a privately owned halfway house for people just coming out of detox. Alcohol mostly, but some recreational drugs. We help them regain their health, find their feet, and get resettled in the community."

"What's your position here, Mrs. Kilpatrick?"

"Owner and director."

"And this man was staying here?"

"Yes. His name is Michael Fortier. He spent the last six weeks in detox and came to us on Saturday. Usually, Dr. Meacham, who runs the detox center, brings our guests, but Mr. Fortier came by bus. It stops opposite our driveway," I added irrelevantly, as if he needed to know the intricacies of the Mississauga transit system.

We all contemplated Mr. Fortier for a while. He lay face up—or rather, what should have been his face was turned upward, his arms and legs sprawled out in unnerving stillness. Blood the color of crapaudine beets soaked his green golf shirt. He'd done little damage to my vegetables, though, other than the beans beneath him. An inquisitive fly settled on his shirt, and I fanned it away, chilled.

"The blood looks pretty dark," I remarked when the policemen remained silent. "His shirt looks almost dry. When do you think it happened?"

"We'll leave that to the coroner to say," Sergeant Layton said bleakly.

The distant wail of the ambulance came closer, and we exchanged glances. We all knew the ambulance was pointless, but it was, the sergeant informed me, standard procedure to summon one. He took off his hat and scrubbed his scalp through his thinning gray hair. He couldn't have been more than fifty, but his face was creased and worn and looked ten years older. He must have been melting in that uniform. It was cooler on the lawn under the maples, but here, where I'd turned the earth for my garden, there was no shade. I imagined what it would be like, wearing double-knit polyester and hung about with so many gadgets you could never let your arms hang straight down. Just the thought exhausted me.

"Let's go in where it's cooler," I suggested. "I'll show you which room was his."

Layton put his hat back on, looking more cheerful. We left the constable glumly standing guard over Mr. Fortier and went up the flagstone path to the back porch. As we walked, Layton pulled out his radio, which was clipped near his shoulder, and spoke into it, requesting his supervisor, a coroner, and a forensic identification services team, whatever that was. He signed off and gave me an apologetic shrug.

"The place will be crawling with people soon. I'll try to keep them out of your veggies."

I waved a hand. "It's all right. I wasn't having much luck with them anyway. My lettuce never even came up."

"That'll be the birds, I expect," he said, nodding. "They eat the seeds before they can even germinate. They got to my spinach last year, but this year I'm ahead of them. I put a bit of window screening over the ground until the seeds got a good start. That's what you want, a bit of window screening. The little mesh, you know?"

I nodded stupidly to show I understood what screening was.

"Lets the air, light, and water in but keeps the birds out," he said gravely. "That's what does the trick."

We went through the back door and walked to the front of the house to wait for the emergency services people to park and unload. Layton spoke with them briefly, directing them to his partner in the backyard. From down the block came the skirl of another siren, and a moment later a fire engine pulled into view. I wondered what my neighbors would think of the flashing lights and commotion. It occurred to me that I needed to call my lawyer the first chance I got.

The hymn in my head had shifted, and I paused to examine it. It had turned into "Master, the Tempest Is Raging." Equally uncomforting.

Layton turned back to me.

"Now, let's see what we can find out about this poor guy."

I liked him better for using the adjective. I dug behind the solid oak front desk for the guest book. Layton eyed it appreciatively.

"You have the patients sign?"

"We prefer to call them guests and treat them as such," I explained. "They sign in as if it were a hotel, to remind them that they're here voluntarily and that this will be a pleasant experience. At least, more pleasant than detox was. Signing a thick, old logbook feels comfortable and old-fashioned. It makes them feel pampered."

"And is that what you do here? Pamper them?"

I grimaced. "Hardly. We keep them on a pretty strict regimen that includes vigorous exercise, strict curfews, a carefully managed diet, daily therapy sessions, and close supervision. It may not sound nice, but we treat them very well. They leave in a lot better condition than when they came. We have one of the best programs in Canada."

Leaning over the open book, I held my blonde hair from swinging into my face with one hand and ran a finger down the column of writing.

"Here it is. Michael Fortier. Checked in at 3:40 on Saturday, June 10. I remember watching him get off the bus and walk up because it's not usual that a guest arrives by bus. As I said, Dr. Meacham usually brings them. But Mr. Fortier didn't wait for his ride. He left a note for Dr. Meacham saying he wanted to take this step on his own." I pulled out my heavy set of keys. "I put him in room 401, fourth floor, on the east side."

"How long was he scheduled to be here?"

"One month. Usually they come for a month or two for inpatient treatment, and then if they're doing okay, they check out and just return for outpatient counseling." I stopped, thinking how foolish and irrelevant that sounded. My unfortunate guest had already checked out—thoroughly.

"Where are your other patients—er—guests this morning?" Layton asked, pulling a notebook from his breast pocket as if just now remembering he should be taking notes.

Was he afraid they were dead too, strewn about the place like badly thrown newspapers? I sat at the desk and put my head in my hands, feeling drained.

"Some of them are on a nature walk at Riverwood Park with the activity director. They're stopping at a curry place for lunch on their way back." This was Bonnie's doing. I would have opted for Subway sandwiches myself to accommodate those with less adventurous tastes. But when on a field trip, Bonnie declared, the food was part of the recreation and therefore her domain. She also believed in the healing power of novelty. If guests were jolted out of their ordinary rut, she argued, they were less likely to go back to old habits when they returned home. I wasn't sure I held the same opinion of curry's reformational value.

"Just some of them went?"

"The others I sent to their rooms and told them to stay there until we get this figured out."

"Good move," he said, looking ready to pat me on the head. "I'll just go up and see his room now. Make sure no one goes out to the garden, please, while the paramedics are out there. More officers will be coming soon."

"Certainly."

His footsteps had scarcely faded before there was a commotion upstairs, and then Kevin Carlisle bounded down, face flushed and blond hair standing on end. In the short while I'd known him, I'd figured out that he was prone to hysterics. The smallest things set him off. A sparrow trapped in the dining room at breakfast had had Kevin practically hyperventilating by the time I shooed it out. A misplaced jacket and a suspicious knocking sound in the tree outside his room (which proved, upon investigation, to be a Downy Woodpecker) had sent him into panic. Why, just yesterday when Michael Fortier had accidentally walked in on him in the washroom, Kevin had caused such a scene that the two men had nearly come to blows.

This last thought made me pause, but I didn't have time to mull it over because Kevin was nearly on top of the desk, shouting into my face.

"I demand you tell us what is going on, Mrs. Kilpatrick. Was that a fire truck I just saw pull up? And a *policeman* going up the stairs?"

"Yes, it was," I said patiently. "And there are going to be a lot more of them in a moment, so if it upsets you, you should probably stay in your room this morning."

His voice rose to a squeak. "Just what exactly has happened to Mr. Fortier?"

"Someone has killed him," I said flatly, not inclined to coddle. "In the garden." When he continued to stare at me, eyes bugging and mouth open, I added, "They blew his face off."

Kevin Carlisle, Kingston dentist, made a gagging sound, rolled his eyes up into his head, and fell. On the way to the floor, he clouted his chin on the edge of the desk.

I stood, went around the desk, and poked him carefully with my foot. He didn't respond, but his skinny chest continued to rise and fall. I put my hands on my hips, considering whether I could lift him up to his room. I knew I could at least get him as far as the living room couch. I bent and took him under the armpits. He was sweaty, and the thought crossed my mind to let him lie where he was.

"I should charge you double," I hissed in his ear.

Chapter Two

"Allow me."

Jason Baumgarten appeared at my elbow, nudging me gently out of the way. I jerked a little in surprise, but I suppose it could be forgiven if my nerves were a little jangly. For being such a large man, he moved very quietly. I backed away and gratefully watched him pick up Kevin Carlisle and sling him over his shoulder.

"Where would you like him?"

"He's in room 403," I said, "but I don't expect you to haul him all that way."

"No problem," Jason said, giving me a nod before he went up the stairs. Kevin's dangling arms bounced lightly off Jason's back at each step. Sergeant Layton met them on his way down, sidestepping them with some alarm.

"Not another one!" he said, looking from me to Jason's disappearing hulk.

"Just a faint," I said. "That guest is a bit high-strung. He didn't take the news about Mr. Fortier very well."

The sergeant continued down the rest of the stairs and came to lean against the desk with arms folded. I felt he was settling down for a chin-wag and wondered if I should remind him he'd promised to stand guard over my veggies. Who knew what the others were doing out there with their clunky boots?

"Well, nothing in his room appeared out of the ordinary. I couldn't take a thorough look, but I've put tape across the doorway to keep people out. We won't be able to learn more until the coroner and crime scene people get here. Did the deceased seem at all depressed to you? Maybe upset over something?"

"Well, I mean, after six weeks of detox, he wouldn't be in the best of spirits, would he?" I pointed out. "But I guess now that I think about it, he wasn't as bad as most are when they first arrive. In fact, he was quite chatty and friendly with the other guests."

"So he didn't appear to you to be a likely candidate for suicide?"

I gaped at him. "You mean, do I think he shot himself?"

"Yes."

"If so, he's the first person I've ever heard of who was able to shoot himself in the back of the head and then walk to another location to lie down and die."

His eyebrows shot up. "You think he was shot somewhere else and then moved to your garden?"

Was he really this dense, or was he just trying to get information out of me? Even I could read the signs, and I didn't even watch that many cop shows.

"There was no gun around that I could see, and there was a lot of blood on the front of his shirt but not on the ground around him. He was lying on his back. The blood would have poured down to the ground if he were shot in the garden, not horizontally, to soak his shirt. He must have been shot while he was in an upright position, maybe sitting in a chair, and he'd finished bleeding by the time he was laid in my garden. And a shot like that—to blow off his face when the bullet exited—I would guess it was a rifle or shotgun of some sort. Not something you could aim at the back of your own head unless you had arms like a spider monkey."

He eyed me thoughtfully a moment then grinned. "You picked up on all that, eh?" He sounded proud, like a parent finding out at teacher conference that his child isn't a complete dunce after all.

"It seemed rather obvious." I smiled back to show I meant no insult.

"Not to most people, I'd bet."

"Well, it was a sight that will probably stay burned into my brain for some time to come," I said.

The front door opened, and my receptionist and file clerk, Laura, hurried in. Her short hair was flying, and her plump face was stretched wide with astonishment. "Erin, is everything okay? There are police all over the place." She caught sight of Layton's uniform and stopped dead.

"Mr. Fortier has had an accident," I told her. "The police are looking into it. If you don't mind, could you keep folks in their rooms until the therapists arrive?"

"You don't need me to watch the desk?" she asked.

"We won't worry about it this morning."

"Is—is Michael all right?"

"No," I said gently.

She stared at me a moment, her mouth open. Then she glanced at Layton again and, with a brisk nod, turned and went up the stairs two at a time.

"The part-time receptionist," I explained to Layton.

There was the sound of more cars arriving, and I envisioned my driveway in chaos. Not exactly the soothing country atmosphere we tried to provide our guests.

"Could you please tell me where you were last night and this morning?"

I came back to the front desk with a bang. "Me?" I squeaked.

He shrugged apologetically but remained with pen poised. "Last night and this morning," he repeated. "I don't know the time of death, you see, or rather, the time he was placed in situ, and . . ."

"Certainly. I understand." I own the place, after all. I'd found him. They'd want to know my alibi. I scrubbed my bangs out of my face, thinking. "Well, supper was over by about seven last night. I helped Rebecca clean up—she's the girl who cleans for me. I threw in a batch of laundry. I went over to my house and helped my daughter with a project she's sewing."

"Your house? You don't live here?"

"My daughter Jennie—she's thirteen—and I live in a cottage on the grounds. On the other side of the garage."

"Yes," he said, as if this somehow pleased him. He wrote furiously. "Please continue."

"After she went to bed at nine, I came back over to do the accounts for a while. I do that most nights. I watched a TV show at nine thirty."

"TV? Was that here or at your house?"

"Here. I have a small TV in my office. Sometimes I watch it here in the evenings when I don't want to disturb Jennie." Not to mention that half the electrical wires in our house aren't working at the moment.

"Go ahead, please. Which show was it?"

"Which show?" I asked stupidly. I wasn't sure how this would help his investigation.

"On the TV."

"*Hamish Macbeth.* It's a British show about a small-town policeman in Scotland."

"Ah. Like the police shows, do you?"

"Not particularly," I said, not liking the interest on his face. "It's really more of a drama than a police thing, anyway. But it was a rerun I'd already seen, so I turned it off at ten."

"Hmm. And then what did you do?"

"I said good-bye to two of the outpatients who were just leaving to go home. A handful of people were still up, playing cards with Kelly, the night nurse. I assumed the others were in their rooms."

"But you don't know that."

"No, not for certain. But none of them would have had a reason to go out late at night. Early to bed and early to rise is part of the program. They wouldn't go out alone, in any case." I heard myself babbling and stopped.

"Ah. Was Mr. Fortier one of those you saw, then?"

I frowned. "No, I don't think so."

"Did you actually see Mr. Fortier go to his room after supper?"

"No. I assumed he was there because he wasn't in any of the public rooms. Maybe one of the other guests can tell you."

"Mmm. So then what did you do?"

"I checked to make sure the doors were locked. Then I went across to my own cottage and went to bed. I was going to read for a while, but I was too tired and went right to sleep."

"You're sure the doors of this building were locked?"

"Yes."

"Can someone go out if the doors are locked?"

"Yes, they're only locked from the outside. No key required from the inside."

"Did you hear anything in the night? A car pulling up? A gunshot? Doors closing? Voices?" Layton asked.

"Nothing. Everything was quiet when I went to the cottage. And I slept like a log, I'm afraid."

"I see." He looked disappointed in me. "Let's move on to this morning."

I rubbed my cheeks vigorously, collecting my thoughts. "I was at work by six thirty. I helped Janet—she's the cook—get breakfast ready."

"How did she get in if it was locked up?"

"She has a key."

Layton wrote this down. "Do all of your staff members have keys?"

"Just Janet and I and the night nurse. The others have no reason to need one." I couldn't see how this was relevant. The body had been in my garden, not in my living room.

"Then what did you do?"

"I set the tables and did more laundry," I said. "By that time, it was about seven thirty and people were trickling down to breakfast."

"Ah. That could be an important point. Who came downstairs, and in what order?"

"First Jennie, my daughter, came over from the cottage, and Bonnie, the activity director, arrived just a few minutes later."

"She doesn't live on-site?"

"Most of the members of the staff don't. After hours, there's only Kelly Hardacre, our night nurse. She has her own room on the second floor. And, of course, I'm her backup."

"You're a nurse as well?"

"Social worker. But I wear a lot of hats around here—whatever's needed."

"We'll speak to Ms. Hardacre."

There was a bang outside, a car door slamming, and I saw more figures march past the window curtains on their way to the backyard. Sergeant Layton glanced up and then gave me an encouraging nod. "Who arrived next?"

I hesitated. Was I allowed to reveal patient names to the police? When he saw my expression, Sergeant Layton raised one eyebrow. I shrugged.

"I don't know what I can tell you," I said, spreading my hands. "Patient confidentiality and all that. Am I allowed to tell you their names?"

"I'm about to go interview them myself," the man pointed out. "It's not as if their names are going to be confidential for long."

"Still, until I speak to my lawyer, I don't think I should be the one to give you their information," I stammered.

"You want to speak to a lawyer?" His eyes narrowed.

"No, I mean, just about confidentiality issues. I don't know what I can or can't say to the police without opening myself up to a lawsuit," I explained. "Maybe you should collect that information yourself. I can tell you I didn't see Mr. Fortier come down. I didn't think much of it. He'd said last night that he wasn't planning to go on the nature walk this morning, so I figured he was having a lie-in."

He set down his pencil, stretched his tired hand, and picked up the pencil again.

"I thought you said early to bed and early to rise?"

I frowned. "I organize the program, and I offer it to them, but I can't force my guests to participate if they aren't so inclined," I said. "They're not here on court order."

"Sure. How is it exactly that they do end up here, Mrs. Kilpatrick? I mean, do they all go through detox first?"

"Yes. Dr. Callum Meacham operates a center near the hospital. When they're done with his program, ours is the intermediate step before they go home. They all choose to come on their own initiative when they realize they need help with their dependency. I admit, I've had some come back more than once."

He gave me a thoughtful look. I studied him right back, noting his tired eyes, the tension in his writing hand. *He could use a spot of care himself,* I thought. As if reading my mind, he coughed and straightened his shoulders. He consulted his notebook.

"And you found the body just after nine this morning?" he asked briskly.

"Yes. I was going to the garden to see if any vegetables were ready yet." I had a feeling I wouldn't be eating much out of my garden this season. Thirty bucks' worth of seeds down the drain.

He frowned and turned back a couple of pages.

"You haven't mentioned your husband." Layton's eyes slid up to me.

"He died several years ago." *Why did that never get any easier to say?* I brought my chin up and stared at him steadily, and he had the grace to look away. He also had the grace to refrain from murmuring something useless, like, "Sorry." I'd never understood why people said that when they wanted to show sympathy. Sorry for sticking my nose in? Sorry such a thing happened to you? But it wasn't their fault. I had to remind myself often that it wasn't anyone's fault, except, perhaps, the deceased's.

I was saved from mentally following that tangent by a loud bang on the door.

Chapter Three

Several large, blue-uniformed people entered my humble foyer, scuffling dust on the polished wood floor and taking up far more room than their dimensions would justify. There was a confusion of introductions and explanations as my guests were brought from upstairs to be interviewed, and I found myself repeating my story a number of times to various unfamiliar faces. At one point, Grant managed to pull me aside and put a hand on my arm.

"My dear girl, it must have been such a shock to find him. Are you all right?"

"I've recovered," I told him, charmed at being called a girl at my age. I patted him gently on the shoulder. "This will all be cleared up shortly. I'm so sorry this has interrupted your retreat."

"You ought to refund our money," Kevin said peevishly. He still looked pasty from his faint, and a purple bruise was forming on his chin where it had connected with the desk.

"She didn't plan to have a guest get himself shot just to inconvenience you," Grant said, frowning.

"My nerves are already at their breaking point," Kevin complained. "My doctor recommended complete relaxation. That was what I paid for."

"That isn't fair," Jason protested. "There's no guarantee . . ."

As Jason and Kevin began to argue in increasingly loud tones, Grant turned to me and said in an undertone, "I can see why dentists have such a high rate of suicide. Pity it didn't catch up with Mr. Carlisle."

"You might want to watch what you say when there's just been a murder," I whispered back, nodding toward the officers conferring not ten feet away.

Grant's moustache bristled in consternation. "You don't think they suspect one of us!" he said, lowering his voice further.

"Well, he was found in my garden," I pointed out. "I suppose they'll look pretty closely at me."

Jason overheard this last remark and turned from his argument with Kevin.

"You? No one could ever think you'd be capable of such a thing, Mrs. Kilpatrick."

"Well, thank you, Jason, but—"

"Didn't you have an argument with Mr. Fortier just yesterday?" Grant asked thoughtfully, looking at Kevin.

Kevin straightened with an indignant squeak. "Me? Are you implying I had anything to do with this?"

"Well, everyone else seemed to get along just fine with him," Grant pointed out.

"But Kevin argues with everybody," I added in all fairness.

"I won't deny Mr. Fortier and I exchanged words," Kevin declared, his pale face growing pink. "That pervert deliberately walked into the washroom when he knew I was in there. Not so much as an 'excuse me!'"

"Nobody's accusing you," I said.

"If this place had separate washrooms for each guest like a proper hotel, it wouldn't have been an issue."

"But it isn't a hotel. This used to be a convent back in the 1890s. When I renovated the house—" I began.

But Jason turned to me with a hunted look on his broad, homely face.

"No, they won't care about that," he whispered. "If they look closely at anyone, it'll be me."

We all blinked at him.

"Why would they? You didn't have anything against Mr. Fortier," Grant said. "Did you?"

"No, of course not. I'd never met him before this week. But it's just . . . I have a record, see," he said. As we continued to stare, he mumbled miserably, "Aggravated assault."

"Oh!" Grant and I exchanged looks. It was as if Smokey the Bear had just stood up in group and admitted to arson.

"Assault!" Kevin cried, as if he were undergoing one. "A record?"

Several heads turned toward us, and I gave Kevin a jab with my elbow.

"Quiet!"

"That does put a different light on it, doesn't it? But I'm sure you had nothing to do with this, whatever your past," Grant added kindly to Jason.

Jason spread his large hands, looking at me. "I was stupid. I served three years. I got out last summer and went right to the bottle. My parole officer thought I should enter detox, and I did. I've played it totally straight. When I leave here, I'm going into my own apartment. It's a big step for me."

Kevin snorted. "You didn't tell the police that when they took your name, I notice."

"I'm sure they already know," Jason said bleakly, glancing at the blue uniforms.

Kevin whirled to face me. "This is the kind of person you allow into your establishment, Mrs. Kilpatrick? Thugs and who knows what else?"

"One mistake four years ago doesn't have anything to do with Mr. Fortier kicking the bucket in my garden today," I said firmly. I stopped myself short of adding that a man who had until just recently downed a forty-ouncer of Scotch every day for breakfast hardly had the right to criticize anyone else.

There was another commotion out in the hall, and then the rest of my guests burst into the room, all talking at once. Jennie was with them, her eyes round and wide.

"There are policemen all over the yard!"

"There's an ambulance just pulling out!"

"Did you know that—"

"Whatever is going on, Mrs. Kilpatrick?"

"Did something happen?"

Bonnie O'Halloran, my activity director, pushed to the front, elbowing the others aside without effort. Bonnie was six-foot-two, with a head of electric red hair, the figure of a supermodel, and sun-bronzed skin that looked like it had the consistency of vinyl. I'd been best friends with her since high school, where she was voted Most Likely to Climb

Mount Everest. In addition to working part-time as my activity director, she'd been running her own gym in town. She had the stamina of a bulldog and the heart of a bear, and I'd seen her bite a leather dog leash in two (but that's another story for another day).

"Are you all right, Erin?" she demanded now, pushing her face into mine to examine my pupils.

"It's not me," I said ungrammatically. "Someone has shot Michael Fortier."

There was a collective intake of air, and then everyone started talking again.

"Who did it?"

"My word, is he dead?"

"Why would—"

"Cool!"

This latter remark came from Ed Polinsky. He and his father were both outpatients at the center. Ed's blue hair made a pretty contrast with Bonnie's red. Beneath the hair, his glasses, braces, earrings, nose ring, pierced eyebrow, and headphones made his head look completely encased in metal.

"No one panic. The police will figure all of this out soon, I'm sure," I said with false confidence. I put my arm around Jennie, who had remained worryingly quiet in the chaos. She gave me a faint smile.

"Everything will be fine. We'll handle it," I whispered to her, and she nodded. My own words shook me a little, eerily familiar. I had said the same thing three years ago, after her father died. But surely this wouldn't be anywhere near as difficult as that had been.

From the corner of my eye, I saw Eva Stortini put a hand to her forehead and sway a little. Jason reached out a meaty paw and caught her before she dropped. She and Kevin were two of a kind. Then again, her faint was probably due to her feather-light weight and avoidance of red meat. Jason lowered her limp figure to the rug with a soft chime of her earrings.

"Everybody give her breathing room," Bonnie ordered, dropping to her knees and preparing to resuscitate. Fortunately, Eva stirred and blinked before drastic measures were required.

"My therapist ordered complete avoidance of stress," Kevin whined. "This is going to set my progress back months."

"Oh, stow it. This isn't about you," Cathy Lewis, another guest, barked.

"Where'd they shoot him?" Ed asked, taking off his headphones and slinging them around his neck.

"In the garden."

"No, I mean—"

"In the head."

"Cool," he said again.

"It's not cool!" his father barked, scowling. "It's horrifying!"

"I didn't mean cool that he died," Ed protested, flushing an unbecoming red. "I just meant finally something exciting happened around this place."

His father looked ready to implode. He turned away from his son. "Do the police know who did it?"

"Not yet," I said.

"Was he the intended victim?" Kevin burst in. "Are any of us safe?"

I couldn't guarantee *he* was safe from any of *us*, but I tried to smile and look confident. "Of course. Why wouldn't we be?"

"There's a crazed killer roaming around out there."

"Or in here," Max Polinsky added, looking suspiciously around the room.

One of the other guests, David Metcalfe, reared back. "Are you saying you think one of *us* did it?"

"Someone did," Grant said reasonably.

David raked his fingers through his usually impeccably combed brown hair, making it stand on end. He was a small-time politician in Windsor, forty-ish and good looking. He took an inordinate amount of pride in his perfect hair, which was usually so coiffed and dark that it looked false. *He must really be upset*, I thought, *to spoil his "do."*

"Well, we have an alibi, at least," he cried. "We were on the nature hike in Riverwood. All of us except those three." He pointed at Grant, Jason, and Kevin.

"The police haven't determined the time of death," Grant reminded him. "It could have been done before you left. Or in the middle of the night."

"But why would someone—" Max started.

"I certainly didn't—" Cathy Lewis began.

I gave Bonnie the eye, and she nodded briskly. Putting her fingers to her mouth, she let out a piercing whistle. My guests froze. The officers snapped to attention like sheepdogs responding to a shepherd's signal. Cathy gave a squeal of alarm and ducked behind me.

I saw Layton start to make his way toward us from across the room, and I turned to my huddled group and tried to look each of them in the eye.

"Everyone calm down," I ordered. "The police haven't told us anything yet. There's no point in accusing anyone or challenging alibis yet. Fainting isn't very helpful either," I added to Eva and Kevin. The latter scowled.

"Right. All of you who just arrived, we will want to speak with each of you individually," Layton said, sounding tired. "Those of you we have interviewed already, it would be a great help if you would go to your rooms and stay there for now."

"Are we on house arrest? You can't detain us," Kevin began, but another glare from Bonnie stopped him.

"I think it's best if we cooperate," I said. "After all, no one has anything to hide."

Cathy opened her mouth then clamped it shut again. Bonnie herded everyone out. As I went to leave the room, Layton stopped me.

"I'd like to ask you a few more questions too, if I may."

"What more can I possibly tell you? I've been answering questions for the past hour and a half."

"If you please?"

I knew it wasn't a request. I sighed. "Certainly." I nodded at Jennie, who'd hung back, watching solemnly. "Honey, go find Rebecca and hang out with her until I come, okay?"

She went wordlessly. That alone told me she was shaken.

Layton watched her go then glanced at me. The other officers were clomping through the house, invading my quiet, orderly rooms and pounding up and down the stairs in their big boots to Mr. Fortier's room on the fourth floor. I heard more car doors slam outside. The hymn in my head segued into "Like Ten Thousand Legions Marching."

Layton gave a little cough. "Is there a quieter place . . . ?"

"Why don't we go over to my cottage?" I suggested. "Though I'm not sure it will be any quieter."

"Let's try it."

I led him out the front door and dodged the various police cars strewn in the driveway. The fire engine and ambulance had apparently gone. The air had heated up since this morning, and I could smell the hot asphalt of the driveway. Down at the end of the drive, where the big wrought-iron gates stood permanently open, I could see a crowd of neighbors gathered. I would have some explaining to do after this was over.

Chapter Four

My cottage was on the other side of the yard, beyond the garage, with its own smaller driveway connecting to the larger one. The renovators' pickup trucks were out front, along with a pile of broken drywall, a few empty plastic buckets, and a bunch of other rubble. The cottage had once been the groundskeeper's home, back in the days when this had been a convent. It was solely for my and Jennie's use now, and I'd filled the living room with squashy chairs, mismatched cushions, and family photos in dollar-store frames. Home-sewn, bright yellow curtains and a faded red rug from Goodwill tied it all together. It wasn't as nicely turned out or tidy as the public sitting rooms in the center, but it was friendlier. It was also, unfortunately, the only finished room in the cottage so far. When he saw it, Sergeant Layton nodded.

"Thanks, this will be good." He waved me into an armchair and dropped onto the loveseat opposite. With a sigh, he stretched his legs out in front of him.

Another officer had followed us into the cottage. I didn't recognize this one. He must have come in the latest wave. He was probably in his late thirties. His long, lanky form was dressed in civilian clothes, not a uniform, but he had the same no-nonsense haircut and world-weary eyes, though his were a becoming hazel instead of bloodshot blue. I dragged my attention back to Layton, who had pulled out his little notebook again with a look of loathing.

"We now have the names of your guests," he said, eyeing me pointedly as he thumbed back through the pages. "No need for you to give us any confidential information. And we know your general whereabouts last night and this morning. But Detective Harris and I did have some more things to ask you."

The lean detective took the armchair beside mine and nodded politely.

"All right," I said. "And then I need to focus on helping get lunch for my guests. What do you want to know?"

"First, how many do you have on staff?" Layton asked. "Not just the ones who are here right now but in total."

"Nine. A recreational therapist who acts as activity director. A mother-daughter team who cook and clean the rooms. There's the night nurse. Part time, we have a psychotherapist, an occupational therapist, a registered psychiatric nurse, and a receptionist."

"That's eight," Harris observed, and his voice was lower than the older cop's, a warm, rich baritone.

"That's all—oh, no, I forgot Greg Ng. He's fairly new. Plus, Dr. Meacham is our on-call psychiatrist. He's the one who runs the detox, but he's not technically on staff."

I had a sudden, deep need to phone Callum. He was more friend than colleague to me. He had a gentle and compassionate way about him, and I knew if anyone could soothe my jangled nerves, it was Callum Meacham. He had worked that charm on me more than a few times, helping me through the adjustment after Robert's death and through establishing this business three years ago.

"What does this Greg Ng do?" Layton asked.

"He's our groundskeeper, and he helps with the riding program. He takes care of the horses," I said.

Layton froze, staring at me. "Horses?"

"We manage a therapeutic riding center on the grounds," I explained. "We have ten horses. Our last fellow left in the spring, and I just hired Greg. He's a veterinary science student at the university." He was still a bit of an unknown quantity, Greg was, and I sensed he was more comfortable with the horses than with people, but he seemed to be working out well enough.

"How much property do you have here, Mrs. Kilpatrick? Is there room for horses?"

"Yes," I said, trying not to smile at his surprise. "We have ten acres, most of it pasture." I couldn't help wondering how good a policeman he was if he hadn't even noticed the stable and paddocks behind the garden. I sighed then reddened, hoping he hadn't heard it. "I'd be happy to show you around," I added.

"Later, thank you. Of those nine staff, who is not currently on the grounds?" Layton jerked a thumb in the general direction of the crowd we'd just left.

"Um, let's see. Bonnie, Greg, Janet, Rebecca, and Laura are here. So you're missing Kelly Hardacre, the night nurse, Ethan Holmes and Theresa Bixby, the therapists, and Sam Milton, the psychiatric nurse."

"Male?" Layton paused in his writing.

"Yes. It happens," I said with a smile.

"Bonnie is the . . . ?"

"Activity director." For someone who wrote constantly, he didn't seem to retain much of the information I gave him. I fought to control my impatience.

"Ah yes. And Laura is the receptionist?"

"Yes." I had never liked the title *receptionist*, frankly. It made it sound as if Laura's only duties were to smile and greet people and offer them seats. Truth be told, Laura was the grease that kept the whole show running. She handled admissions and discharges, dealt with payroll and accounts receivable, and deftly handled the impossible task of juggling all our schedules, not only of the staff and patients but of the volunteers as well. She was a true find, efficient . . . but a bit eccentric. For example, she filed patient files alphabetically, not under their names but by their failing of choice. Michael Fortier had been, I believed, filed under "Scotch and Soda."

I looked at Layton and thought Laura would have filed him under "Guinness." I added aloud, "I should tell you, Sergeant, none of the staff were here late last night except Kelly. She works from nine thirty at night to six in the morning. She's gone before breakfast."

"Could you provide me with a work schedule for your employees?"

"Certainly," I said. "And a list of the workers here at the cottage. They were here by eight o'clock this morning." As if to back up what I was saying, there was a muffled thump and a grating sound from the kitchen. Both officers tensed and looked over their shoulders.

"You have other staff here?" Layton asked.

"No. I'm having renovations done," I explained. "I focused on the main house first to get it ready for business, and I'm just now getting to the renovations on this cottage. They're working on the wiring today." As they had been for the past week, sad to say. At sixty-eight dollars an hour. According to Vinnie, my contractor, the aluminum wiring in the cottage made building a space shuttle from scratch look easy.

Sergeant Layton closed his notebook. "Yes, I'll need a list of them, too, and anyone else on the premises. Now, if you could clarify for us, some of your guests don't actually live on the grounds? You mentioned that you also have outpatients."

"Yes, currently there are ten inpatients and about twenty-five outpatients that just come here for therapy. And there are volunteers from the Ontario Therapeutic Riding Association coming and going all the time to help with the riding program. I couldn't even tell you how many of them we have, but I could tell you the regulars."

Layton gave an audible sigh. "Were any of the outpatients here last night or this morning? I think you said two were here late last night."

I smiled. "Ed and Max Polinsky. They were here until about ten last night and came early this morning to participate in the Riverwood excursion. The rest that you've met this morning are all inpatients."

Layton thumbed through his notes, muttering, "Polinsky, Polinsky."

"Blue Hair and his father," Detective Harris supplied.

"Ah yes. And to your knowledge, there was no one else on the grounds last night or this morning except you and your daughter, the guests, the night nurse, these Polinskys, and then the staff and renovators who arrived around breakfast time?"

"Well, obviously someone else must have been here at some point," I said. "Someone killed Mr. Fortier. You don't think one of our people did it, do you?"

"That's the question, Mrs. Kilpatrick."

"Ridiculous," I responded. "All of my employees are very carefully screened. And none of the renovations crew likely knew Mr. Fortier."

"Be that as it may," he replied, "as you pointed out, *someone* killed him. There were no other outside visitors here last night?"

"No, not that I know of." It seemed to me there was already an adequately long list of people to interview.

"Did Mr. Fortier receive any mail or phone calls while he was here?"

"Not to my knowledge, but you'd have to ask Laura. She handles the mail."

"The receptionist?"

"Yes." I gritted my teeth.

Layton consulted the notebook. "One of your inpatients, Jason Baumgarten. What do you know about him?"

"I imagine you guys can tell me more about him than I can tell you," I said drily.

Layton squirmed. "Answer the question, please, ma'am. What is your general impression of him?"

"He's got the friendly personality of a spaniel. He likes cold cereal for breakfast, he's an enthusiastic but lousy tennis player, he snores loud enough that I can hear him downstairs, and he could probably bench press three hundred pounds. He's due to go home tomorrow, actually." I hesitated then added, "I like him. I can't imagine how he could have ever committed assault on anyone. I've seen more vicious marshmallows."

"He told you about that, did he?" Layton looked deflated, as if I'd spoiled the surprise.

"Yes."

I glanced at Harris, who had hardly spoken during this interview, but he was gazing out the window at a white pine tree and looked like he'd lost interest. I wondered if he had taken note of the fact that no one could see the backyard or vegetable garden from this house.

"You keep good track of your guests," Layton replied, scribbling.

"I have to," I said, shrugging.

"I guess most of your guests had severe substance abuse problems in order to end up here?"

"No comment," I said flatly.

"But all of them come here by way of detox?"

"Yes. That's in our information brochure. Anyone can access that."

He sighed. "Eva Stortini."

I hadn't expected him to ask about Eva. Was she also a person of interest to the police? Or were they going to go through the entire list of guests? I couldn't imagine what crime she could possibly have in her past. Skinny-dipping in a public pool?

I looked up, smiling, to see Detective Harris staring at me with one dark eyebrow quirked. I quickly got my face under control. I ran my fingers through my bangs and sighed. "Eva's a leftover flower child, with long drapey dresses and crystals. A real earth mother type, you know? She wanders around the garden looking for ley lines or something. We're planning for her to go home this Saturday."

"How do you know when a person's ready to go home? How do you know Eva won't just go right back on the bottle once she leaves here?" Harris asked.

"Our mandate is to help them find alternative ways of thinking and coping. In Eva's case, her problem wasn't alcohol. She preferred . . . other substances. We've focused on associating staying clean with the interest she already had in living a natural, organic, and healthy lifestyle."

"I imagine the 'other substances' *were* organic in the first place," Harris said wryly and leaned back in his chair. I tried not to laugh. Layton, meanwhile, was still struggling over the spelling of *ley lines*.

"Did Mr. Fortier get along with the other guests? No signs of stress or tension?"

The banging and scraping in the kitchen was getting louder. I raised my voice a little.

"Well, the people who come here are going through a significant life change," I pointed out. "So there's definitely tension. There's bound to be friction between people now and then."

Harris frowned. "I don't mean generally. Did Mr. Fortier ever argue with anyone in particular?"

There was no getting around it. "There was a little row the other day when he accidentally walked in on Kevin Carlisle in the washroom," I admitted. "The guests have to share a washroom on each floor. When I renovated, there just wasn't the ability to give each guest his or her own washroom. I'm sure he walked in on Kevin entirely by accident, but Kevin was upset about it. The whole house heard it."

"Uh huh. What was Mr. Fortier's reaction?" Layton asked.

"He was courteous and apologetic and didn't get into the fight until right at the end when he made some snarky remarks back." I grimaced. "He went to his room after that and left Kevin spluttering."

"Has Kevin Carlisle had altercations with any of the other guests?" Harris suddenly leaned forward on his elbows. I jumped a little; the motion reminded me of a snake striking.

"Well, yes, he's had arguments with just about everybody in the short while he's been here. I don't think anyone likes him much. Quite frankly, I'd have understood it better if Kevin had been the one who got it in the garden."

Layton began to chuckle then caught Harris's eye and turned the laugh into a cough.

"That outpatient . . . Blue Hair." Layton turned a page in his notebook. I didn't like the speculative look in his eye.

"Ed Polinsky," the detective supplied. His tone implied that *he* didn't have to consult notes. In fact, he wasn't taking any.

"What can you tell me about him?" Layton asked with a sigh.

I had a sort of soft spot for Ed. He was the polar opposite of his pompous stockbroker father, who, I sensed, didn't have a clue how to relate to his son.

"Not much," I said. "He and his father, Max, have been coming here for a while. Max signed them up together, I think as a sort of attempt at bonding." I couldn't help smiling. "Ed is everything his father's not. Hair like a gas flame, so many nose rings and earrings you can hardly see his face, and he wears clothes that are ten times too big for him. My daughter thinks he's cool, and I like the mischief in his eyes. The world hasn't broken his spirit yet, and I hope it never does. Smart, clever as a cat, and inclined to lie even when he doesn't need to. But I don't get the feeling he's into anything terrible. In fact, he probably has more moral sense than his father." I didn't feel it necessary to add that I'd already caught Ed smoking pot once behind the bicycle shed. Nor did I add that I felt Max Polinsky was a bit of a bully, since I had only impressions to go on and no tangible evidence. But something in the son's sparkling eyes dimmed a little when the father was around.

There was a terrible grating sound of wires being pulled through the kitchen wall, followed by the clang of some metal tool being dropped on the tile floor. I winced a little. The kitchen fell silent. Then the door between the kitchen and living room opened, and the rugged, suntanned face of my contractor peered in. Vinnie was a classic southern Italian, all dark good looks and testosterone. He wore a white sleeveless T-shirt that showed off his biceps to good advantage. He started to say something then caught sight of Layton's uniform. He promptly withdrew, closing the door softly. I didn't think either of the policemen had noticed. But when I glanced at Harris, I saw he had turned his head away and his lips were twitching. Oblivious, Layton studied his notes a minute and then put them away. Apparently, the interrogation wasn't going to include the other guests after all.

"Thank you, Mrs. Kilpatrick. We'll let you know if we have any more questions."

"I'm sure you will," I said and stood up. Harris bounded to his feet and extended a hand to shake mine in a strong, warm clasp.

"Actually, I do have a few more questions," he said, and I thought Layton look miffed. "This program. How close a tab do you keep on your guests? Do they have much time during which they're unsupervised?"

"Well, we do keep them scheduled fairly heavily," I told him. "The basic premise is that we're trying to break their mental association between their . . . problems and entertainment or leisure. We introduce them to new hobbies and interests and schedule a lot of activities to try to break them out of their routines and habitual associations. Admittedly, part of the goal is to keep them so busy they don't have time to think about why they came here in the first place. After they've been with us awhile, we send them out in groups without staff. They go out and experience a football game without beer, fine dining without wine. Then they come back and discuss their experiences in group and individual therapy. But we rarely send anyone out alone unless it's for a job interview or something like that. And here on the grounds, even if they have some free time to themselves, it's hard to find a place to be completely alone unless they stay in their rooms. There are always people about."

"Yes, I'd sort of gotten that impression." Harris nodded. "To your knowledge, did Mr. Fortier ever go out on his own while he was here?"

"You'd have to ask Laura. She schedules everyone's lives. Arranges taxis, things like that. But I'd be surprised if he'd gone anywhere alone. He'd only been here a few days, and we tend to keep the reins a little tighter until we see how they do with their program."

"I see," Harris said. "Thank you for your help. We'll be out of your hair as soon as we can."

Chapter Five

It was well after two by the time the police finished preliminary interviews and I was able to help get lunch on the table for my guests. Laura was busy at the front desk, fielding phone calls from nosy neighbors ostensibly calling to make sure we were all right but really just looking for the scoop. Jennie disappeared with her cell phone. And Hilda Turner came over to ask what the ambulance, fire engine, and all the police cars were about.

Hilda was my visiting teacher, though, so far, her visits had consisted of polite, close-lipped smiles, three minutes of small talk, and perfunctory five-minute lessons. Her posture and tone made it abundantly clear that she would rather be anywhere else than in my chaotic home, sitting on my sagging sofa, speaking to my slapdash self. It was also abundantly clear she was not pleased that I had brought drunks and addicts into her neighborhood in droves. We had lived across the street from each other for three years, saw each other in church each week, and knew just enough about each other to know we had absolutely zip in common. If we hadn't been thrown together by the visiting teaching roster, we wouldn't have said boo to each other.

When I told her about my unfortunate guest, she didn't express alarm at the thought of a killer loose in the neighborhood. Instead, she sucked her lips into a disapproving mew and informed me pointedly that all the fuss had ruined the birthday party she'd been trying to throw for her twelve-year-old grandniece. The stress of the last few hours bubbled up in me like boiling Irish stew, and I couldn't quite keep my temper in check. I told her crisply that if I'd only known, I'd have arranged the murder for a more convenient day, and then I closed the door.

As I carried trays of hastily made sandwiches and tossed salad from the kitchen to the dining room, my anger faded to fatigue. I felt as if I were swimming through pudding. My brain felt fuzzy. I couldn't keep from glancing out the window whenever I passed it. There were still plenty of blue uniforms in the backyard, prowling through my vegetables and across the lawn. I wondered whether Mr. Fortier was still lying in the beans where I'd found him or if he'd accompanied the departing ambulance. If he was still there, for decency's sake, I hoped they'd at least covered him up.

There were outpatients scheduled for this afternoon. I would have to phone and head them off. The only thing to do was to cancel all appointments. Even if my staff had been able to continue, stepping into a crime scene might not be the best therapy for someone who was already in a fragile state. I tried to think how to phrase it to sound reassuring. "We've had a bit of a problem. Nothing to worry about." Or, "There's just the slightest, teensiest chance that one of our other guests committed murder . . ."

I realized I hadn't yet had time to call my lawyer.

"Mrs. Kilpatrick?"

I jumped and focused my eyes on Grant Calderwood, who was looking at me with a concerned expression. Apparently, he had called my name more than once.

"Sorry," I said, setting down the water pitcher I was holding and wiping my hands on the towel that served as my apron. "Did you say something? I'm afraid my mind was somewhere else."

"Of course," Grant said. "It's only understandable you're distracted today. I just wanted to ask you if there was anything I could do. To help, I mean." He shrugged and spread his hands. "Not that there's anything useful I can think of, but I wanted to offer . . ."

"You're so kind," I told him. "Thank you. But I really can't think of anything." Actually, the only thing I could think of was that *someone* close by had killed Michael Fortier. How well did I know any of these people, really? Just the sketchy outlines in their files. I knew their habits and their brief histories. When it came right down to it, I didn't know much at all. Take Grant, for example. I knew he was a retired businessman with grown children he rarely saw. Who knew what else he had in his past? Then again, looking at Grant's kindly face, I couldn't imagine him doing anything more criminal than jaywalking.

"I assume the police have notified Mr. Fortier's family?" Grant asked.

"Well, I gave them the home phone number he put on his form, so I assume so."

My heart went out to the unknown Mrs. Fortier, if there was such a person. I knew only too well the awfulness of that unexpected phone call, the police falling out of nowhere, the bitter news that should have stopped the world from turning but cruelly didn't. My heart shrank at the memory. Swiftly, I swept up the pitcher and continued my rounds without saying anything further. I didn't trust my voice.

It had been three years since I'd gotten that horrible phone call, followed by the uniformed officers on my doorstep. My mother made it clear she thought three years was long enough and I should be "over it" by now. It wasn't healthy for my daughter, she would insinuate, for me to mourn for too long. Others—my neighbors, my friends, the well-meaning women at church—still clucked and consoled as if it had happened only last month, and my Irish Catholic in-laws thought I should still be in black. They thought it was callous of me to go on with my life and try to make a success of my business when my husband had been lost so tragically, so young.

But this business had to be a success, and there was no one else to do it but me. For my sake and for my daughter's, I had to put his death behind me and go on living. And that meant putting food on the table.

The thought of food brought up images of my vegetable garden again, the flattened plants, the trampled earth. Again and again, I went over what I'd seen, my brain churning, trying to make sense of it all. I was certain the damage done to the vegetables was minimal. There had been no struggle, at least not there. There was only the damage you would expect from a person walking in and walking out, leaving the body there behind the hedge where it wouldn't be seen from the house. There had been a slightly flattened area beside it, as if the body had been slid or rolled slightly into position. But I was sure the body hadn't been dragged all the way from the path. Therefore, someone had lifted it into place. That meant it was likely a male who had done it, as Mr. Fortier had weighed too much for any of the women to have moved him (except perhaps Bonnie). I remembered the ease with which Jason had lifted Kevin to his shoulder, and I felt sick.

The staff usually ate with the guests, and when I saw Laura drift in, I went over to intercept her.

"How are you holding up?" I asked, thinking that her habitual smile looked a little tense today. There was a little yellow SIGN HERE flag stuck to her elbow like a price tag, and I discreetly removed it without her noticing.

"All right. I should be asking you," she replied with a stiff laugh.

"Listen, I just wondered, and maybe the police have already asked you this, but did Mr. Fortier receive any phone calls or mail while he was here?"

"No, and I told the police so. It isn't unusual, since he'd only been here a few days."

"Thank you. And did he ever go out on his own alone while he was here?"

I fully expected her to say no. It was standard procedure to keep a close eye on patients when they first arrived. But to my surprise, Laura said, "Yes, yesterday, after the field trip. He told Bonnie that he had to stop at a bank and would come straight back after, and he seemed in a stable mood, so she let him take a taxi while the others came back in the van. Everyone else got back here at about one o'clock, but Mr. Fortier didn't come back until two fifteen."

I frowned. "It takes over an hour to do some banking?"

Laura shrugged. "I didn't smell any alcohol on him when he got back. He stopped and chatted with me at the front desk and seemed in a good mood. So I didn't press the issue. Maybe he just needed some fresh air. He was back in time for his therapy session. That was the only instance when he was out unsupervised."

Except, obviously, at some point late that night or early the next morning, I thought.

"Would you mind helping me make some phone calls? We need to reschedule all our appointments for the rest of today. Maybe tomorrow too, but let me check with Callum and see what he thinks."

We discussed what needed to be done, and then I thanked her and went back to work. When everyone had been served and fed and they were starting to leave the table, I took my own sandwich, wrapped it in a paper napkin, and went into my office to phone Elliott McDougall, my lawyer. He was not pleased with what had happened, nor was he pleased that it had taken me a few hours to call and tell him about it. He gave me a few stern words about liability, good business practice, and today's economy—most of which I tuned out from sheer exhaustion.

By the time he let me go, I was in serious need of quiet time. I decided I would most likely find it on the back patio. The porch swing there was my favorite place to sit in the evening, where I could look out over my domain and pretend I was the lazy owner of a massive estate run effortlessly by servants, rather than the exhausted manager of a ten-bed treatment center with a mortgage the size of the Coliseum. I sat and watched the uniforms moving quietly around my yard. Two of them had cameras and were crawling around my vegetable patch like *National Geographic* journalists trying to spot endangered species in the rainforest. I was ridiculously embarrassed that I had lately neglected my weeding, though Layton was probably the only one who would notice. The body appeared to have been removed.

The cloudless sky was so bright it hurt my eyes to look at it. Out in the paddock, one of the mares was cantering in circles, and I could see the glimmer of heat waves rising from the horse's back as she moved, dust rising from her feet. I thought of all the other things I needed to do—clean up the dining room, phone Callum, fold laundry, check to see how Jennie was—but I couldn't get myself to go inside and do any of them. Instead, I sat listening to the quiet murmur of voices in my garden and imagining myself far away.

A shadow fell across my face, and I jerked awake, startled to realize I'd fallen asleep with a crowd of policemen in my yard. I squinted up at a tan shirt beneath a tweed jacket. Dark hair, piercing eyes. Detective Harris.

"Sorry to disturb you, Mrs. Kilpatrick," he said. I tried to detect disdain or sarcasm in his voice but couldn't. He meant it, then. I ran my fingers through my bangs and pulled myself together.

"Erin, please."

He dipped his head in acknowledgment. "We'll be going now, but I'd ask that no one cross the tape."

I craned to look and saw yellow crime tape wrapped around the arbor leading to the veggie garden. It looked ridiculously festive, like the remnants of a flea market. I nodded. So much for picking any peas.

"We'll be back tomorrow. But in the meantime, if you need us for anything or if any of your guests remembers something more, please call." He handed me a white business card, and I pushed it into my jeans pocket as I struggled to rise from the swing. I was surprised to see the sun had dipped quite low in the sky while I'd slept. It must have been nearing five o'clock. Why hadn't Janet called me?

For the simple reason that Janet wasn't there. When I went into the kitchen to find her, Bonnie informed me that Janet had left at three, taking Rebecca with her.

"Are they coming back to do supper?"

"I have no idea."

"Well, didn't she say anything?"

"Not to me."

I poked through the steel industrial fridge. "There's nothing left out for supper. She was supposed to thaw the steaks. I guess she forgot in all the excitement." I slammed the fridge and bit my lip. I felt suddenly unable and unwilling to cope with a houseful of hungry guests. I looked hopefully at Bonnie, wondering if she would be willing to cook. Bonnie caught my look and tossed her red hair.

"Don't even think of it," she said shortly. "I'm your rec director and your friend, but I'm not your chef. Order pizza."

It was the most useful thing I'd heard all day. I went to the phone in my office and ordered from the local pizza joint—four large pepperoni pizzas and two large vegetarian pizzas, though the teenager who took the call couldn't tell me whether the toppings were organic. In extreme times, Eva would just have to cope with vegetables of unknown provenance.

Then I forced myself to phone Callum. His cheerful voice was a comforting bass hum on the other end of the line.

"Erin! Glad you called. I was just going to call to let you know I'll need to move Michael Fortier's one o'clock appointment tomorrow to two o'clock. I have a meeting at the hospital at eleven thirty, and you know how they can go on."

"Callum, listen to me. That's why I'm calling."

"What's up?" he asked. "You sound funny. Isn't Mr. Fortier settling in all right?"

I closed my eyes. Callum truly cared about his patients, and I knew the news was going to hit him hard.

"I don't know how to tell you this, Callum."

"What? Are you having problems with him?"

"No, it's something else. It's awful. Mr. Fortier . . . well, there's been a problem. He's passed away." I thought what a benign sound that had to it, a flimsy sort of phrase, as if he'd merely faded away like mist. It wasn't robust enough to capture the brutality of the scene I'd witnessed in the garden.

"*What?* My word, what happened?"

I briefly told him, trying not to dwell too much on the details. I could tell the news had shaken him badly.

"Why didn't you call me earlier, Erin? I can come right over."

"There's really no need, honestly. We're all fine, and the police have left, and we're all just going to make it an early night, I'm sure."

"Are you feeling all right? It must have been such a shock for you."

"It's been a long day. I'm so sorry to have had to tell you. I imagine the police will contact you sooner or later to find out more about him."

"Of course. Oh, it's a shame. Fortier wasn't—well, he wasn't the nicest of people, I guess I'd say, but he certainly didn't deserve that. I hardly know what to say. How are the other patients taking it?"

"Better than I'd expected. Kevin's a bit squirrelly, but then, when is he not?"

"Maybe you and Jennie should stay with me."

I straightened at his tone. "Why?"

"I want to make sure you're both safe."

"What do you mean?"

"Well, we don't know who was responsible, Erin. I imagine the police will be looking pretty closely at everyone in the house."

"Including me," I added.

"You? That's ridiculous."

"I live here. I own the place."

"You didn't even know the man. I mean, how could you have? It's not like you'd worked with him for weeks."

Like he had. "Maybe the police should look at *you*," I tried to joke. He didn't laugh.

"Think about it, anyway, Erin. I'd be happy to have you."

"Thanks, Callum, but I'm sure Jennie and I will be fine." I hoped I sounded more confident than I felt.

"Tomorrow I'll clear off my schedule for the afternoon and come over. An event like this could set back everyone's progress."

"Yes, all right. Callum, I'm also calling to ask your opinion. I had Laura phone the outpatients who were supposed to come in this afternoon and just tell them we had to reschedule. We didn't tell them why. It was so crazy here all afternoon; I figured it was best to just cancel them. There are more scheduled to come tomorrow morning, and if the police don't let us get back to business as usual by then, I'll have to cancel them too."

"Yes. I imagine it could be a few days before sessions can resume."

"But I was wondering what I should tell them all. I mean, they're bound to read the papers tomorrow morning . . ."

He hesitated then sighed. "I think they should hear the news from you."

"I thought so." My heart sank as I thought of all the awkward phone calls that would entail.

"We need to be honest with them. Having said that, I wouldn't give them too much detail," Callum added quickly. "Just the bare minimum—that there's been an unfortunate incident, one of the inpatients has died, and you have to temporarily postpone their sessions while the police look into the matter. Tell them we will straighten everything out shortly, and you can offer to send them here to my office if they need urgent care in the meantime."

"Thank you, Callum. I appreciate it."

"I hope the police don't disrupt the program for long, Erin. The sooner you get the patients back into their routine, the better."

"All right."

"You're sure you don't want me to come over?"

"No, we're fine, really," I told him. Truth be told, I was too tired to face him tonight.

"How is Jennie taking it?"

"Quietly," I said worriedly.

"Well, I'm sure it's hard for her. Give her some space and see if you can get her to talk to you later."

"I will. Thanks, Callum."

"Call me if you change your mind. I can be there in fifteen minutes."

We said our good-byes, and then I looked at the phone on its cradle and braced myself to start calling all the outpatients. Probably best to start with the ones who were slated to come first in the morning, as they were the most pressing. Right now I didn't know if the more appropriate hymn to hum would be "Put Your Shoulder to the Wheel" or "Ye Who are Called to Labor." Both seemed equally appropriate.

I dug through my desk and found the appointment schedule Laura updated for me each week. I felt my stomach sink when I saw who was due to arrive first thing tomorrow morning. The Lewis sisters.

More of them, that is. We already had two of them living here full time. The other four were due at ten o'clock for their biweekly session. Even though all six sisters were married and had different last names, they still called themselves collectively the Lewis sisters, as if they were some sort of performing troupe. Over the past four or five decades, generations of the Lewis family had kept the substance abuse treatment community afloat in Peel Region. And knowing their temperament, I was ready for horrified outcries and demands for their money back. Instead, the woman on the other end of the line sounded positively chipper.

"Cathy already called and told us all about it," Ida May said cheerfully. "A murder! How exciting! I wish I'd been there today."

I should have known Cathy would have been on the horn to her sisters the minute the police left off their interrogation.

"Then it doesn't upset you . . . ?" I asked hopefully, loosening my grip on the receiver.

"Of course not, honey. Lucky Cathy and Judy, to be there in the thick of things. How thrilling for them!"

I wasn't sure Cathy and Judy, the two inpatients, had been thrilled at being interrogated and then confined to the house while the police prowled outside.

"We'll still be there as planned, bright and early," she went on. "Theresa is still expecting us at ten?"

"Well, that is, you see, I don't know if the police will allow us to resume—"

"Sure they will. We'll be there at ten, same as always." The phone clicked decisively as she hung up.

I replaced the receiver and shook my head. The police didn't stand a chance against the inexorable advance of the Lewises. It would be easier to stop an avalanche with a teaspoon. Right, then. Had the session room upstairs been cleaned lately? I'd have to check myself. I didn't know if Rebecca was coming back.

Rooms. What was I to do about the room so abruptly vacated by Michael Fortier? What was I to do with his belongings? And would the police allow Kevin and Jason to check out as planned tomorrow morning? They had technically completed their programs and were ready to return home and go into outpatient treatment. I needed their rooms for other guests who were slated to arrive next week. Maybe I should have asked Callum about that too. I felt a headache coming on as I dug in my pocket for Detective Harris's card.

After several transfers, I finally heard his voice flow over the phone.

"Sorry to bother you," I said after identifying myself. "But I forgot to ask: Two of my guests are due to be discharged tomorrow morning. Is it all right if they are?"

"Which guests?" he asked.

"Jason Baumgarten and Kevin Carlisle." Jason being one of the people Layton had inquired about specifically.

There was a pause. I heard papers rustling.

"All right. We have their home addresses and phone numbers if we need to talk to them again."

"Of course."

"It should be fine, then. Thank you for thinking to ask."

But it wasn't to be that simple. At dinner, when I informed Kevin and Jason that they were free to leave as planned, they objected.

"I was thinking of extending my stay," Kevin informed me at the same time Jason blurted, "I don't want to go."

I hadn't anticipated this blip.

"But you are only booked until tomorrow morning," I said gently. "I know this has been upsetting for everyone, but I'm not sure that staying is the best thing for you under these circumstances."

"I can't leave you now, while all this is going on," Jason said stoutly, but his eyes strayed toward Eva Stortini.

"But aren't you expected . . . ? I mean, aren't you anxious to . . . ?"

"No. I'd like to stay another week if you have the space."

I looked doubtfully at Kevin. "I thought you'd be in a hurry to get out of here," I said.

He shrugged. "How would it look if a murder happens and I skedaddle out of here the next day?" he reasoned. "I should stay the weekend at the very least."

"The police can reach you at home if they need you. They said it was okay."

"But I would feel remiss if I left you alone at such a time," Kevin said.

I glanced around the room at the crowd of other guests. "I'm not exactly alone. Maybe you'd better discuss it with Dr. Meacham tomorrow."

But in the end, I couldn't budge either one of them. I made myself a mental note to ask Callum tomorrow if the new guests' arrival could be delayed just a bit.

Chapter Six

I didn't sleep very well that night. Twice I got up to make sure my doors were locked, even though I knew they were. I was late getting to bed anyway, what with trying to catch up on laundry and plan breakfast. (There was still no sign of Janet or Rebecca, and no one had answered when I'd phoned them.) Once I finally hit the pillow, my eyes wouldn't close. Even though I was not personally responsible for Michael Fortier's death, I still felt some responsibility for not keeping my guest safe—or at least animated and breathing. Well, no, I admitted that wasn't entirely it. Every time I tried to close my eyes, the image of his faceless head sprang up behind my eyelids and drove all sleep away. I lay staring at the ceiling until the gray mist of approaching dawn came through the window, and then I figured I may as well give up. I dressed and read my scriptures for a while over a buttered English muffin and felt my soul settle a little. When the sun rose, I let myself out into the quiet morning.

My footsteps seemed loud on the crunchy gravel as I walked from the cottage to the center. There was no sound, not even of birds. The horses were still in the stable. The center's windows were dark, and there were no cars in the parking lot except Kelly's. Usually, I loved this time of day, the stillness giving me a rare sense of isolation. Alone time was hard to come by around here. But this morning, it made the back of my neck creep, as if eyes were watching me from the shadows. I broke into a jog and took the porch steps three at a time.

I tiptoed around to set the dining tables for breakfast, fill the sugar bowls and juice pitchers, straighten napkins and silverware. I felt a ridiculous need for everything to be neat, tidy, organized, and under my control that morning. I was in the kitchen whipping up pancake batter—every light in the kitchen on—when Janet and Rebecca arrived. They said nothing, only slipped into their places and began to work without looking at me. I waited for a while, and when they still said nothing about their unexplained absence, I set down the mixing bowl and left the kitchen to them, giving Janet a light touch on the shoulder as I went. She ducked her head and gave me a quick glance. I was relieved that things were all right between us again.

Grant was the first one down to breakfast, dressed determinedly for tennis again, looking refreshingly ordinary. He scrutinized my face as he came to wish me good morning.

"Forgive me for saying so, but you look horrible this morning," he said kindly. "Didn't you sleep well? No, I imagine you didn't. You really can't let all this upset you, my dear."

I smiled and hoped that laugh lines would help disguise the bags under my eyes. "Trying for tennis again today? Since Jason is staying on, maybe he'll play you this morning."

"I was glad to hear he'll be lingering a bit longer," Grant confessed. "I mean, it doesn't hurt to have a big, able-bodied friend around at a time like this. I mean, when you aren't sure who you can trust . . ." His voice trailed away, and he looked aside as if ashamed of himself for suspecting any of his fellow patients. I found it slightly ironic and touching that he considered Jason—the size of a muscular moose and the only one in the house, so far as I knew, with an assault charge—as a protective friend. I hoped his trust was correctly placed.

As the others trickled into the dining room, no one seemed to know what to talk about. Should they refer to the events of yesterday? Should they ignore Michael's empty place at the table? Jennie was completely silent. David Metcalfe rustled his newspaper and attempted to start up small talk about the economy but failed to find any takers. Eva said something neutral about the weather, and Jason emphatically agreed with her as if it were vital that we all acknowledge the blue sky. Kevin complained that his closet door was stuck open. I promised to take a look at it. My budget was stretched just to pay the staff I had. It didn't extend to hiring a maintenance man.

As the food began to flow and the sun rose higher in the windows, I began to relax. Maybe today wouldn't be so bad. I kept my eyes averted from the yellow police tape dancing merrily in the breeze between the trees outside the window and asked Eva if she'd like more toast.

At eight o'clock, Rebecca came to tell me I was needed in the lobby. I found Detective Harris standing at the front desk. Instantly, I knew the day was not going to allow us to sail along as if nothing had happened. I tried to plaster a smile on my face.

"Good morning, Detective. What can I do for you?"

His beautiful hazel eyes slid to the door of the dining room, from which poured the murmuring of voices, the clinking of dishes, and the lovely smell of sizzling bacon. He jingled something metallic—coins? keys?— in his pants pockets.

"Have you had breakfast, Detective?" I asked and saw from his expression that I'd guessed correctly. "Would you like something? The kitchen is still serving."

"Thank you, that would be nice," he said. "If you don't mind."

"You shouldn't leave home without a good breakfast," I said, leading him toward the dining room.

"I haven't been home yet," he replied calmly.

I stopped. "You've been working all night?"

"I wanted to get the initial report typed up while it was still fresh in my mind," he said. "I've brought your statement for you to read and sign. Maybe you'd care to look it over while I'm eating."

I took the folder he handed me and went into the sitting room. I read, approved, and signed my statement, noting that he had recorded everything I'd said quite well. He must have looked at Layton's notes.

Underneath my statement, in the folder, were other papers. Another report, summarizing the case and the information collected thus far, along with what I assumed were the others' statements, waiting for their signatures. There was also an envelope marked "photos," which I quickly tucked aside without looking into. One look at Michael Fortier had been enough for me, thanks. I was reading the general report when Detective Harris came back from the dining room.

"Thank you for breakfast," he said, looking brighter than he had before, though still not smiling openly. I got the feeling he didn't do that often. "It was delicious."

"Anytime. I've signed my statement. You captured everything very nicely. But I'm not sure you meant for me to see all these," I said, tilting the folder toward him so he could see the stack of paper.

For a moment, I thought he was going to choke. He leaped forward, swept the folder out of my hand, and tucked it inside his jacket. He saw my expression and gave a sheepish grimace.

"Sorry. I guess the lack of sleep is catching up to me. I shouldn't have given you all that."

"I didn't think so," I said. "I didn't look at the others' statements, only the general report. From what I read, it was accurate, though, for what it's worth," I added.

"Thank you. Well, I'd best go find the others—"

"Except for one little detail," I said.

He stopped mid-step. If he'd been a German Shepherd, his ears would have perked up.

"It may not be important, but I did notice one thing that wasn't right," I said.

"What was it?"

"His watch. It says there that it was on Michael's right wrist. But I know for a fact he wore it on his left wrist. And I don't know of anyone who switches sides."

Detective Harris dropped onto the sofa beside me and rifled through the papers in the folder until he came to the report. I tapped the paper with my finger at the spot.

"When Fortier checked in, I had him sign in at the front desk," I told him. "All guests sign in when they arrive."

"Doesn't your receptionist do that sort of thing? Where was she?"

"Laura had a half day that day. She left at noon to go to her son's orthodontist appointment. I was at the front desk in her place."

"Right. Go on, please."

"He filled out the logbook—name, phone number, and date and time of arrival. He wrote with his right hand, and I remember him lifting his left wrist to check his watch before he wrote in the arrival time."

"You're sure about this?"

"Positive. What does it mean?"

"I don't know. Maybe nothing, maybe something."

"Then maybe whoever wrote this report just put it down wrong."

"I wrote the description of the body myself, and I'm always meticulous," he said.

I didn't doubt it. "Did Mr. Fortier purposely switch sides to try to tell us something?"

"That's a stretch. It implies he had time to think about it before he was killed. And what would it be meant to convey? Anyway, who notices such things?"

"I do," I pointed out. "Well, then, did someone else dress him and get it wrong?"

"I don't know."

"We certainly know he was wearing his shirt and pants when he was shot. Those weren't changed. There was blood everywhere." I tried not to remember it too closely. "So he was up and dressed, but someone added his watch for him."

"It could be one explanation," he said carefully.

"There was blood on the shoes too, wasn't there, didn't it say?" I squinted at the report sideways, and he turned it for me to read. "Yes, here. Blood distributed in a pattern to suggest he was sitting upright at the time of the fatal wound. So he was up and dressed but watchless, and then someone added the watch? Why would someone do that?"

"Unless for some reason he simply put his watch on the other hand that morning. It might mean nothing."

"No one does that, do they? You get used to wearing your watch on one side, and you leave it there."

"Who knows?" he said. "I had an aunt who used to wear her apron backward to remind herself of something she needed to do. Like take the roast out of the oven."

I scowled. "Don't most people just use a timer?"

"Probably. But Aunt Cherry turned her apron around. Maybe Fortier was doing the same thing."

"I don't know if it's important. But it should be easy enough to find out which wrist he usually wore it on. It should have some sort of mark. Like this." I pushed up my own watch to reveal the white area of skin underneath, a watch-shaped strip that contrasted with the rest of my tanned arm.

Musing, Harris pushed up his own watch and studied the lighter area beneath it.

"We'll have to wait for the coroner's report," he said slowly.

"I'll be interested to see what it says."

He hesitated, and I spread my hands. "You're not going to share it with me? You'd just leave me in suspense?"

He shot me a sideways glare. "All right, when I get it, I'll tell you because you spotted it. But you really have no right to any other infor—"

"Nonsense. He was my guest, and I found him in my garden. I feel proprietary about him."

"The coroner's report always takes a few weeks," Detective Harris said, gathering his papers together again and preparing to rise.

"That long? That's nuts."

"That's the nature of the job."

"Can't you hurry it along a little?" I asked.

Harris stood and tucked the folder away again. "Nobody hurries along the coroner. I'm afraid I'm not that influential."

"That," I said, "I highly doubt."

I let him set up in my second-floor sitting room and then fed the guests in to him one at a time, once again, to sign the statements they had given the day before. Kevin complained about the bother, but the others didn't seem to mind it much. In fact, if I didn't know better, I'd say that Grant Calderwood was rather enjoying all the excitement. He hadn't even remembered the fact that he'd missed tennis once again.

I walked down to pick up my mail in the box at the foot of the drive. The day was still cool, and the fresh air tasted like pure water. I gulped it into my lungs as I walked. The neighbors had not returned to gawk that morning, but a couple of stray journalists that Bonnie had scared away from the front door were still wandering around outside the open gate, looking bored. When they saw me approaching, their faces brightened and one of them picked up his microphone, but I grabbed my mail and firmly turned my back on him. I tried not to look like I was hurrying as I went back up the driveway, nonchalantly glancing through my mail. Nothing but bills and flyers. Not that I was expecting a letter from anyone in this day of e-mails and text messages, but it still would have been nice. I made a point of writing to my in-laws in Nova Scotia every month, giving them updates on Jennie and sending occasional photos. There really wasn't anything else to write to them about, but I felt it important for Jennie to keep in contact with her other grandparents. We hadn't seen them since the funeral, though we'd invited them to stay a few times. They had politely declined, citing their health and age. They'd invited us there once too. But there didn't seem to be any opportunity to go, with the center to run and everything.

I was helping Janet clean up after breakfast when I heard voices in the lobby. I went out and found four women at the front desk. I had forgotten all about the other Lewis sisters.

"Mrs. Kilpatrick!" one of them boomed, sailing over with hand outstretched to pump mine. "How are you holding up, sweetie?"

"Just fine, thank you, Ida May. I'll see if Theresa is—"

"I've told the girls all about the murder, and they quite agree we can't let it interfere with our progress."

"I certainly appreciate your—"

"There's nothing to be done about it now, anyway, right? There's nothing we can do for the poor fellow. So I said to them we should come anyway, and they said yes we should. We can't let a little thing like murder get in the way, so here we are."

I felt a bit breathless. I disentangled my hand from hers, collected the other two Lewis sisters to join them, and guided them all up the stairs to the room where their joint session was held—a room that was, unfortunately, next to the sitting room. They were a chatty, noisy group and were as difficult to herd as a bunch of cats; none of them seemed to be able to speak and walk at the same time. The sisters were nice enough, but they all had the irritating habit of wandering off in separate directions and—more irritatingly—referring to themselves and each other as girls. Every one of them had to be over fifty. They kept stopping suddenly to say something, halfway up the stairs or along the hallway, causing logjams behind them. There they would stand, with their various sisters eddying around them as if they were rocks in a stream, their voices cheerfully raised as they called to each other. At one point, I saw Detective Harris come to the door of the sitting room to glower down on us in disapproval. I tried to hurry them along as best I could and decided the sitting room had perhaps been the wrong place to put him. The Lewises were only bound to get noisier once they were in their therapy session.

"It must be such a trying time for you. We won't be the least bit of trouble. Will we, girls?" they kept assuring me. They all had the same pleasant smile on their similar plump faces. They must have been murder on their teachers, all practically identical and only a year or so apart in age. By this time, I was looking desperately around for Theresa Bixby, their therapist. Wasn't she here yet?

"Did Martha tell you our idea? We had the most wonderful idea," Cathy was saying now, clinging to my elbow as I tried to scrape her off at the door of the therapy room. "Once Judy and I get home, we sisters are all going to get together and go somewhere this fall, just to get away from the kids and the jobs and the recovery for a couple of weeks."

"Doesn't that sound terrific?" Martha crowed, grasping my other elbow. "Cathy thought of it, really, not me. I can't take any of the credit. It will be such fun!"

"Ah, but you were the one who decided where we would go," Cathy corrected her with a fond laugh. "Martha suggested it, really. We're going to leave the hubbies at home to mind the farms, and we're going to go—you'll never guess where! Go on, guess."

"New Orleans? Disneyland?" I wagered.

"Oh, now those are splendid ideas, aren't they, girls? Maybe we should make this an annual event and do Mardi Gras next year. What do you think?"

"Let's!" shouted another. "How clever, Cathy!"

I refrained from pointing out that Mardi Gras didn't seem exactly the place for six recovering alcoholics.

"Tell her where Martha suggested we go this year, dear," Ida May chimed in.

Cathy finally released my elbow to spread her arms wide in triumph. "We're rafting down the Colorado River!"

I bit my lip. They were all beaming eagerly, waiting for my ecstatic approval. I envisioned a large, gray, rubber raft filled with plump and slightly tipsy Lewis sisters, careening down the rapids, elbows linked and voices raised in song.

"How delightful," I said weakly.

Theresa finally appeared on the stairs, her jaw set determinedly. She was clasping her clipboard to the front of her blouse like a downed airline passenger gripping her seat cushion as a flotation device. She found the Lewis sisters an exhausting challenge in group therapy but refused to meet with them separately instead. After all, she had pointed out when I suggested it, it would be even more overwhelming to have them stretched out over six hours instead of the one-hour group session. She gave me a smile through gritted teeth and ushered them all into the room before closing the door behind them.

"Break a leg," I murmured as I headed back downstairs.

By this time, Bonnie was pacing the lobby, anxious to get the other inpatients away for their daily nature walk. I walked back up the stairs and poked my head into the sitting room.

Detective Harris was alone, sitting at the games table, shuffling through papers with his feet up on the needlework seat of my antique chair. At least he'd placed a sheaf of newspaper under his shoes. He looked up when I cleared my throat.

"Bonnie wants to know if you're done with the guests," I said apologetically. "We had some activities scheduled today, and I'd really like to get everyone back into their usual routine if that's okay. They're supposed to go out for a walk this morning and then go horseback riding this afternoon."

"What? Oh yes, yes, thank you. I've gotten everybody, I think. Where are they walking?"

"Rattray Marsh, I believe."

He lowered his feet. Gathering his things together, he stood and took his jacket from the chair back. I noted one button was missing. Probably not married. In the tweed, he struck me as looking more like a university professor type than a detective.

"Is that it?" I asked. "I mean, are we free to go about our usual business now? Can I fix up my vegetable garden yet?"

"You can resume your activities, but please keep everyone out of the garden for now. When they've finished with the scene, I'll let you know," he said, following me down the stairs to the front door. "I'm sorry for all the intrusion. I'll try to have them finish here by tomorrow."

I hadn't meant to imply that the police presence had been overly intrusive. Still, the idea of getting rid of the yellow police tape and getting things back to normal appealed to me.

"Can I go in Michael Fortier's room yet? What shall I do with his things?" I asked.

"The officers have removed everything they want," Harris told me. "The rest we will ship to his family as soon as they're located. In the meantime, I'll have someone box up what's left, and you can have the room back."

"Thank you. I have more patients coming next week, and I'm stretched for space. I'm thinking I really should have added on to the building and put in a few more therapy rooms."

"With sound barrier insulation," Harris said briefly and went out.

Chapter Seven

I felt in need of a bit of a restorative after the flustered morning. Things seemed quiet for the moment, so I stole the chance to go down to the cemetery. I usually went once a month or so, bearing flowers cut from the garden. I'd gone only a couple of weeks before, but I felt the need to go again. It wasn't so much to visit my husband's grave as to walk among the beautifully tended rows of stones, listen to the birds, have a quiet dialogue with God, and just breathe for a little while.

The cemetery was half a mile from our house, tucked behind a wooded area in an older part of town near the gardening center. The grounds crew had installed a perpetual fountain in the middle of a small pond, and the graves stretched in rows up a slight hillside above it, overlooking the water and a couple of willow trees. It was the most peaceful spot I could find within walking distance (since our own land was usually overrun with guests, volunteers, or staff), and this morning, it was a balm to my soul to walk through the grass and listen to the splashing of the fountain. Flowers dotted the plots here and there, fragrant memorials to my townspeople's loved ones, and someone had dangled wind chimes in the trees to add a soothing, cheerful sound.

Inevitably, as I always did, I ended up standing in front of Robert's stone. It was simple, merely his name and dates and the cursive inscription: "Loving father of Jennie." I had added that for my daughter's comfort, something to reassure her down the road when she learned—as she likely would—what sort of man her father had been. Whatever his faults, whatever his weaknesses, Robert had loved her, no question. As for the rest, the smooth marble gave no indication. I thought that was as it should be. I couldn't very well, after all, have carved a great scarlet *A* into his headstone. If at the last moment he had regretted his betrayal, if some sort of repentance was possible even at this late date, the slate (or rather, the marble) would be clean.

I'd known Robert since college; he, Bonnie, and I had been the inseparable three. He and Bonnie had been more adventurous than I, the quieter one of the group. If there was a rowdy student protest, they were in the thick of it while I watched nervously from the sidelines for outbreaks of unruliness. They were the ones dressed as life-size chess pieces, laughing their way through a live game on the quad while I stood by with a camera. They dragged me to costume balls and danced half the night while I lurched around self-consciously in my Southern belle hoopskirts and frequented the refreshment table. Quite frankly, when Robert asked to marry me instead of Bonnie, I couldn't tell you which of us was more surprised. Perhaps he'd realized that constant madcap adventure wasn't the way to live a life. Maybe he'd realized Bonnie's mothering instinct would never kick in, and he wanted children. He'd been overjoyed with Jennie's arrival and heartbroken when complications during her delivery meant I'd never have any more.

Bonnie had taken his choice to marry me in good grace. She'd merely bared her white teeth and said, "I'm after bigger game." I think Robert's decision to finally settle down and live in a more conventional, peaceful way had disappointed her. We'd never spoken about it. But she had remained my friend, more than ever after Robert's death. And now, here we were, she and I. Though I'd become more confident and outgoing over the years, after Robert's death I'd had to be braver and tougher than I'd ever imagined I could be.

I stood looking at the words cut into the granite and wondered if, perhaps, today wasn't a good day to come here after all.

I looked up and gazed over at the other stones and wished I'd brought a Kleenex. I saw a familiar helmet of shellacked gray hair. Hilda Turner was halfway across the cemetery, carrying a bunch of yellow-gold flowers that looked like marigolds. She didn't see me as she ducked down out of sight behind the stones, presumably to set the flowers down. I'd seen her here a few times before, but I didn't know whom she came to visit. She was in her mid-sixties, and to my knowledge, she'd never married or had a family. She didn't see me, which was just as well, considering the rude response I'd given her at the front door. As usual,

I had spoken before thinking. I would have to go apologize later, but now wasn't the time. I turned and headed home before we could bump into each other. I didn't feel like facing anyone, much less Hilda. For someone who considered herself eager to avoid the limelight, I'd still managed to have a sensational murder in my garden that brought the news cameras out in truckloads. Somewhere, Robert was laughing.

* * *

My walk hadn't settled me as much as I'd hoped. I returned to the house without much enthusiasm. One stubborn camera crew was still lurking at the gate, so I took a detour around Arthur Street and came in the back gate by way of the library parking lot. I kept my eyes averted from the bean patch as I passed.

I called a quick staff meeting in my office to discuss recent events and reinforce how it should all be handled with the guests. I divided the remaining phone calls among the therapists, passing along Callum's instructions about what to say. There were too many of us to fit comfortably in the room, with people either standing against the walls or sitting on chair arms, so I kept the discussion brief. I told them I was proud of the way they were handling everything so matter-of-factly.

Ethan Holmes and Sam Milton merely shrugged with a "What can you do?" sort of air. Sam was a habitually laid-back sort of person with an easy smile and admittedly lax work habits that made me wonder how he expected to finish his Ph.D. within five years. Having worked at psychiatric institutions for several years, he'd seen just about everything, and I didn't think a body in the garden would faze him all that much. Ethan, older and more experienced than any of us, had once been on the army's payroll, so I didn't think I needed to worry much about him either. After their brief hiatus, Janet and Rebecca seemed to have returned to their stalwart selves and had come to terms with the situation. Theresa— well, Theresa always looked a bit haggard, but perhaps more so today than usual. Then again, that could have been because of her session with the Lewises and not because of the murder. Bonnie, of course, acted as if bodies dropped around her every day. A suicide bomber strolling through the front door wouldn't disconcert her.

But Laura, the receptionist, surprised me. She was in her forties, and I knew she was married with lots of children, I think several of them male teenagers, who gave her a run for her money. She approached her job conscientiously and honestly cared about the well-being of our guests, and she always handled things so capably and with such a brisk air of confidence that I assumed nothing could shake her. But as I began to wrap up the staff meeting, Laura burst into tears.

"Sorry," she muttered, dabbing at her eyes with her sleeve. "He just seemed like such a nice person, you know? I mean, I hardly knew him—he wasn't here that long, but . . . it's just such a *waste*, you know?"

I thought of Michael Fortier's pleasant smile, his strong, friendly handshake, that beautiful face, and I had to agree with her. I saw Theresa reach a hand over to pat Laura on the arm.

"Dr. Meacham will be coming this afternoon," I said. "I know this is a stressful time for all of you. Please feel free to talk with him anytime if you feel you want to. He's happy to speak to any of you."

To be honest, I doubted any of them, except possibly Laura, would take advantage of the offer. I was halfway to the kitchen when I realized Greg Ng hadn't been at the meeting. When I asked, no one had thought to invite him. Granted, he was new and we weren't used to having him around yet, but that was no excuse. I was embarrassed I'd forgotten him. But somehow he did seem like a person other people tended to overlook. I pulled on my boots and went out to the barn to find him.

The barn stood to the east of the garage, separated by a sprawling and sort of neglected lawn spattered with dandelions. My neighbors sometimes complained about the condition of my lawns, especially Hilda, who was directly across the street, but I was determined not to use herbicides. After all, weren't we a wellness center dedicated to getting people *off* of chemical dependency? Did it make sense for me to then make my yard dependent on chemicals? So I left the dandelions, and once in a while, I'd stake one of the horses on the lawn to keep it mowed for me.

To the south of the lawn stood my cottage, with its own smaller flower and vegetable garden behind it for my and Jennie's personal use. I couldn't help glancing at it fondly as I went past. The convent itself had taken a lot of work and most of the insurance money to renovate, and the cottage had been left for last. (Putting my needs last tended to be a lifelong trend; why break with tradition now?) The wiring was the least of its problems. The roof and plumbing leaked, there was dry rot in some of the walls and carpenter ants in others, and the floor in the kitchen gave ominously if you stomped too heavily across it. More than likely, the big old-fashioned oven would someday end up plummeting into the basement. But it was my own, the first home I'd actually purchased all by myself. It was snug and quaint and homey, and I was ridiculously proud of it. For a moment, I felt incredibly strong and capable. I was Warrior Woman, providing shelter and food for my family with my own two hands, without assistance from husband or family. I blew a fond kiss at the cottage as I walked past and then realized Vinnie and one of the electricians were looking out the kitchen window at me. Vinnie grinned and lifted a hand to wave, and I could see his eyebrows wiggling up and down. Feeling idiotic, I turned back toward the barn and saw Greg standing there, staring at me.

"Uh, hi," I greeted him, feeling my ears grow warm. He'd seen the kiss-blowing too.

He dipped his head, and his sleek black hair fell over one eye.

"How is everything?" I asked, feeling stupid under his wary gaze. "I mean, are you liking it here all right?"

He nodded, and it occurred to me that in the month he'd worked for us, I'd heard him speak only a few words. I knew he knew English; he'd spoken in the interview. Hadn't he? Or had I done most of the talking? I leaned against our small, orange Kubota tractor we used to haul hay and tried to look like I'd just dropped by for a casual chat.

"Horses okay?" I asked. "Is there anything you need?"

A small shake of the head. He pushed his hands into the pockets of his dirty jeans.

"I'm sorry about all the commotion, with the murder and everything," I said, knowing I sounded like a hostess brightly apologizing for the behavior of an unruly party guest. "It isn't usually this crazy around here."

Another nod and a half shrug. A tentative smile.

"I just wanted to find out if you're all right," I plowed on. "I understand if all this is upsetting to you. I just told the other staff that our psychiatrist, Dr. Meacham, is coming this afternoon. You're welcome to talk to him if you'd like to. About it all, I mean."

A blank look, half hidden behind the hair. His expression clearly implied, *Of course I don't talk.*

"Just, if it's bothering you or . . . or anything." It was like talking to a blank wall. I cast around for something else to say and blurted before I could think, "You didn't see anyone come onto the grounds that night, did you? Anyone who didn't belong here?"

A shake of the head. And then he murmured in perfect English, "I went home at five."

"Ah. Mr. Fortier came down to ride the horses with the group that first afternoon he was with us, didn't he?"

A nod.

"Did he seem in good spirits to you or nervous or anything?"

"They're all nervous their first time on a horse."

"Oh. Well, yes, I guess so. Which horse did he ride?"

A look that clearly said, *Does it matter?* Probably not, but now that I'd asked the question, I was curious.

"Thundercloud."

"I guess the police have already asked you all this, anyway," I added.

"Only what time I came and went and if I'd seen anyone."

I didn't know what else to ask. I gave up, mumbled something friendly as a good-bye, and left. I crossed the lawn and glanced back when I reached the garage. Greg was gone. The barn door was just easing closed.

He'd spoken. That was something, anyway. It surprised me that he had given Michael Thundercloud to ride. All of our horses were pretty gentle (they had to be for the therapeutic riding program), but Thundercloud could be stubborn and a bit ornery at times. I wouldn't have chosen him for a first-time rider. Had Greg purposely given Michael that particular horse in the hope that he'd buck Michael off and injure or kill him? Scenarios filled my mind as I headed toward the house. Greg was a dissident pretending to be a student but was really in hiding from the secret police because of a shady past back in China. Michael had found out and threatened to expose him, so Greg had needed to get rid of him. Or Greg was a serial killer using my barn as home base from which to foray at night in search of his next random victim.

I sighed. Thundercloud was stubborn but not deadly, and I'd never known him to buck. I wouldn't have kept him if he had. And what would Greg Ng ever have against Michael Fortier, anyway? They wouldn't have moved in the same circles. It was unlikely they'd ever met before. *Sheesh, just because the kid doesn't talk much doesn't make him a killer,* I scolded myself as I went in the back door. He was just a shy veterinary student who preferred animals to humans. Though I sensed he might have had a troubled past of some sort, I had no proof of it. I was seeing spooks where there were none.

Lunch was running late, and we were almost done serving when I realized I hadn't seen Jennie since breakfast. Rebecca had no idea where she was. Jennie often kept to herself, but with a possible murderer about the house, I couldn't help it; I'd feel better knowing where my daughter was. I searched the house with no luck. None of the staff had seen her. Panic was starting to rise, and I hurried across to the cottage. It was still and empty. I was about to jog down to the stable to search for her, when I noticed her ratty tennis shoes were gone from the back closet. Around the center, with people coming and going, Jennie always dressed nicely and wore good shoes (with a little insistence from her mother), but if she had her ratty shoes on, it meant she had gone out. With relief, I thought I knew where she'd gone. Like her mother, Jennie sought solace out of doors. I went back over to the center.

"Janet, can you manage without me for a little while?" I asked, poking my head into the kitchen. Janet, stirring a gigantic pot of chili, nodded.

I headed along the pasture fence line toward the back of our property, which butted up against a small hill with a creek as the boundary line. The creek, wandering and curving around the hill like the ruffle along the bottom of a skirt, had a dead log lying across it where we liked to cross. Jennie sometimes looked for solitude among the hardwood trees on the hillside when her spirit was hurting, especially in the year after Robert's death, and I suspected this was where she'd gone now.

The day was growing warmer as I walked through the grass, the long weeds snagging at my shoes. It was going to be an unusually hot summer, and the strawberries were long gone from the wild patches under the hedges I passed. I climbed over the fence at the back of the pasture and entered the trees, finding my way unerringly to the log that crossed the stream. I didn't even slow my pace as I walked across it, arms out for balance. The amber water made pleasant clunky sounds as it tumbled over the rocks.

The trees grew thicker on this side of the water, the underbrush catching at my legs and scratching my hands. Animals had probably originally made the faint trail, and it took its time meandering through the trees without seeming to make much progress. I finally found Jennie sitting on a bed of last year's autumn leaves in a hollow beneath the low branches of a scrub maple. She watched me approach, just sitting cross-legged, her ratty shoes muddy and spent tears still smudging her cheeks. I hoped my anxiety and relief weren't too visible on my face, and I uttered a quick, silent prayer that I would know what to say to comfort her.

I crawled into the hollow on my hands and knees and sat beside her. For a little while, we listened to the birds in the trees and the distant, hollow sound of the flowing creek. A bee buzzed industriously in the center of a yellow flower I couldn't name. The city could have been a hundred miles away. I felt the tension slowly leave my neck and shoulders. Maybe I should start coming here instead of the cemetery. In a way, it was more restful. But this was her place, not mine.

"I didn't even really know him," Jennie said at last, sounding apologetic. "It's stupid to cry about it."

"No, it's not," I said. "He was a human being, and we should mourn him."

"Nobody deserves to be shot in a bed of Kentucky Wonder beans," she said, sounding angry.

"No, nobody does."

"I'm sorry I wasn't there to help out with lunch," she sniffled.

"It's okay, Jennie. It doesn't matter." I put a hand on her blue-jeaned knee. "You have a kind heart, sweetie. I would worry about you if all this didn't upset you."

She sniffled some more and then subsided. I hesitated then asked softly, "Does all this make you think about your dad?"

She shrugged and looked away into the sky, where two small birds were chasing away a crow.

"They must have a nest nearby," she observed, and I knew she wasn't going to talk about it.

"That's right. You can always tell a mother bird. All screechy and flying in a hundred directions at once."

This got me a tiny smile. I patted her knee again and creaked to my feet, crouching under the branches of the scrub maple.

"Take as long as you want to, honey. I'll head back now."

"It's okay. I'll come with you."

She wiped her face on her sleeve and followed me back through the brush to the creek. She crossed the log nimbly, and I stepped up to follow her. But the mud made my shoes slippery, and I was overly confident. I went three steps, flailed like one of those whirligig lawn ornaments, and fell into the creek. Jennie came running back at my yell.

The sight of me sitting in the creek cheered her right up. The freezing cold water swirled around me up to my armpits, and the rounded rocks on the bottom were distinctly uncomfortable on mine. It took her awhile to quit laughing long enough to help me out.

Chapter Eight

Wet and miserable, my soaked jeans binding my legs, I opted to cut to the right and emerge on Arthur Street, where the walking would be easier, rather than hike back through the horse pasture. We were slopping along the road toward home, my shoes squishing out water at every step and Jennie still laughing, when a car pulled up alongside us. It was a dark car I didn't recognize, but when the window rolled down, I saw Detective Harris behind the steering wheel. For a moment, he just stared at me, and I drew myself up with what dignity I could muster and stared back. Then a slight curl lifted his lip, and he said mildly, "Care for a ride home?"

"I'd better walk, thanks," I said. "I'd get your car all mucky."

"Doesn't matter. Climb in."

I didn't believe there was a man alive who didn't care if his car upholstery was ruined, but I wasn't going to argue. I slipped into the backseat, and Jennie, back to her bouncy, cheerful self, jumped into the front passenger seat. Harris pulled back into the light traffic and glanced at me in the rearview mirror as Jennie recounted my mishap with great embellishment.

"You make it sound as if I dove in and swam the English Channel," I muttered.

The car turned onto Felicity and pulled up to the foot of our driveway. Mercifully, there was no sign of the camera crew now.

"I'm going to let you out here," Harris told Jennie. Another glance in the mirror. "Your mom and I need to talk for a second."

"Can I at least change into something dry?" I asked as Jennie thanked him and scampered for the house—no doubt to recount the story of my near drowning to Rebecca and Janet. I'd never live this down.

Harris reached over the backseat, pulled a sweatshirt off the floor, and tossed it to me. I held it up. Gray, with blue letters spelling *YALE* on the front.

"You went to Yale?"

"My brother did. It's his shirt." Harris casually pulled the car away again and turned back north.

"Won't he mind if I get it wet?"

"He died three months ago. He won't mind."

I stopped, staring at him in the mirror, but his face was impassive granite, his eyes focused on the road.

"I'm sorry," I said feebly and pulled the shirt over my head. It was true; there really was *nothing* else to say.

He drove back up Arthur to the gravel parking lot on the west side of the hill. Pulling into a parking space, he cut the engine and swiveled around to look at me, one arm along the back of the seat.

"After we talked this morning, I went and called the medical examiner. He let me go take another look at the body."

I shivered. "And?"

He shook his head. "Fortier's left wrist was exactly the same as the rest of his arm. No marks or tan lines or imprints to indicate he ever wore his watch on the left. But the right wrist showed such indicators."

"So he always wore his watch on the right."

"Yes, it seems so."

I thought a moment then spread my hands. "What can I tell you? I know the man who signed my register had his watch on his left wrist. I don't have it backward. I can still picture him lifting it to look at it so he could note the time down in the book."

"The body in your garden wasn't the man who signed your register. To be certain, I had them compare his fingerprints to all the prints taken from Fortier's room. The victim's didn't match. And they don't bring up a match in our system."

"Wait. What are you saying?" I couldn't grasp it. "It wasn't Michael?"

"No."

I turned this around and around in my mind. I forced myself to picture the body in the garden again, the sprawling limbs, the torso, the head . . .

"I'm so sorry . . . I just assumed it was Michael. He had the same body type and clothes, and his hair—what there was left of it—was the right color . . ."

"An honest mistake."

"But then, who was he?"

"That's what we're trying to determine."

"But if it wasn't Michael Fortier, then where is Michael? He disappeared at the same time I found the body . . ."

Harris lifted one slim eyebrow. I saw where he was going and shook my head in protest, more than a little disturbed by this new information.

"You think Michael killed someone, dumped the body in my garden, and took off?" I said.

"Flight is a good indicator of guilt," he replied.

"It's hard to picture. Michael was a stranger to me, I know, but for the few days I knew him, he seemed very ordinary and cheerful to me. He seemed to get along with staff. He participated in the activities. He was chatty with the other guests. That is, other than the little argument with Kevin, and really, it was Kevin doing most of the shouting. Michael was trying to smooth it over."

"That doesn't mean he didn't have a bone to pick with someone else—outside of your center."

"It seems weird that he'd go to the hassle of dropping the body in my veggies, though, after killing him somewhere else. I mean, why leave the evidence right at your own doorstep?"

Harris shrugged and reached for the ignition. "We'll know the truth of it eventually."

"Do you always get your man?" I asked as he turned the car toward home.

He looked at me again in the rearview mirror, and I saw his hazel eyes flicker to the Yale lettering on my chest.

"Always," he said quietly.

* * *

It seemed only polite to invite him in for a late lunch. Most of my guests had finished eating and had headed out to the barn to go riding, but a few were still lingering at their tables, and Janet assured me she had plenty of chili and cornbread left over. She settled Harris in the dining room with his meal while I ran upstairs to change into clean clothes. When I came back down, carrying the damp sweatshirt, Harris was deep in conversation with Grant, David, and Sam. I got myself a bowl of chili and sat down with them.

"Jennie told us about your adventure in the creek," Grant commented with a smile as I joined them.

"The little gossip," I replied. "Such a trial to have a faithless daughter." I set the sweatshirt on the chair beside me and began to eat.

"No harm done," David said, shrugging, but he was having a hard time hiding his grin.

"Lucky the detective here came along in time to rescue you from certain pneumonia," Sam said brightly.

"Yes, well, I just needed to discuss some aspects of the case with Mrs. Kilpatrick," Detective Harris said.

"Any new developments?" Grant's voice was hopeful.

"How did Michael's family take the news? Poor people," David added sadly.

"They haven't been notified, actually," Harris said.

There was a pause.

"What do you mean?" Grant asked. "Why not? The poor guy has been dead for more than a day."

"We're just waiting for the results of the fingerprinting," Harris said, looking slightly uncomfortable. "It's standard procedure to confirm the identity of the victim before notifying the family. No sense upsetting the wrong people unnecessarily."

Thank goodness for procedure, I thought.

"What are you talking about?" Sam interrupted. "We know it was Michael."

"Are you saying it might not have been?" David asked, wide-eyed.

"Actually, we're pretty sure it wasn't," Harris said, glancing at me.

The others stared at him, thunderstruck, and I saw Grant rub his forehead vigorously, as if trying to force the information into his skull.

"Then who was it?" he demanded.

"The fingerprints aren't on file in our system, so it's taking a little longer than usual to identify him."

I looked up to see Kevin, dressed for riding and standing in the doorway, straining to hear our conversation. When he saw me notice him, he gave up all pretense of not listening and came over to join us.

"Did you say the body might not be Michael Fortier's?" he demanded.

"It looks like I might have been wrong in identifying him as Michael," I said miserably.

"Well, but who else would it be?" Grant asked. "Michael is missing, isn't he?"

"There might be another explanation for that," Harris said, reaching for another slice of cornbread from the platter. I passed him the butter.

"But you saw the body," Kevin said to me. "Couldn't you tell if it was Michael or not?"

"It was hard to tell." I squirmed. "I mean, who could identify a body without referring to his face? I doubt I could identify my own body without looking in a mirror."

Harris ducked his head but not before I saw his lips twitch again. He seemed determined not to let anyone see him smile.

"It seems so unfortunate," Kevin complained. "The poor fellow has been dead for this long, and his family doesn't even know. Your misidentification of him has hindered the investigation."

"All right," Grant said sternly. He put a consoling hand on my shoulder. "Fortier was missing from the house. This fellow resembled him in general. She assumed it was him. Anyone would have made that assumption. We all did, and we didn't even see the body."

"And as I said, we always confirm identification anyway." Harris glanced at me again, his eyebrows lowered. "Mrs. Kilpatrick hasn't hindered anything. She's been very useful."

"So how will you figure out who he is if his prints aren't on file?" Sam asked.

Harris set his fork down with a clink. "Right now we're checking the missing persons reports and liaising with other jurisdictions. We'll find out who he is eventually."

"But where did Michael go?" Sam persisted, troubled.

"That's the question," I said.

David shot Harris a disapproving look. "You think Fortier is the murderer, don't you? He conveniently disappeared the same time the body appeared."

"We don't know that he's guilty," I said. "Maybe there's another explanation. Maybe he stumbled across the murderer depositing the body of his victim in the garden, and the murderer abducted him to keep him quiet."

Grant gave me a kindly smile. "I don't want him to be guilty either," he said gently. "But it doesn't look good, does it?"

Harris pushed away his empty bowl and stood. "Thanks for lunch," he said. "Before I go, Mrs. Kilpatrick, could I speak to you in your office, please?"

I left my half-eaten meal and took him into the small room, remembering after we got in there that I'd hidden an overflowing laundry basket there with the idea of getting to it later. Harris didn't seem to notice it. He stopped in the doorway, and when I turned to face him, he was watching me closely.

"I want you to disregard what Kevin Carlisle said," Harris said firmly. "Anyone would have made the same assumption that the victim was Fortier. I assure you it didn't slow down the investigation."

"Do you really always confirm the identity of the body anyway? Or are you just trying to make me feel better?" I asked. "Because right now I'm feeling awful that I messed things up, that his family hasn't been notified yet because of me."

"I told you the truth," Harris said. "It was only a matter of time before we confirmed the body wasn't Fortier's. And it's our own problem to try to identify him now. Remember, you are the one who clued in to the watch. That may yet turn out to be significant."

"Detective, will you let us know when you find out who this man really was?"

"I will. But I'm sure it'll be all over the news anyway."

I dragged my fingers through my hair and let out a sigh. "Never assume. A lesson to us all."

"But Mrs. Kilpatrick—"

"Erin, please."

"Erin, I think for now, it'd be best for you to keep the whole thing about the watch to yourself. We don't know what it means yet, if anything. You're privy to more information than we usually give the public in an investigation like this. Evidence is best kept to a need-to-know basis for the sake of future prosecution. I'm sure you understand."

"Don't blab. Got it." So long as the future prosecution he referred to wasn't of *me*.

He spread his hands. "I know you already know that, but I had to reinforce it."

"Of course. I hope you figure all this out soon," I said. "And if you find Michael Fortier, you'll tell me too? Just so I know he's safe." When Harris hesitated, I explained, "I'm concerned that he's just disappeared. The body in my garden was wearing his clothes. He was dumped here where Fortier was staying. So the killer must have intended for us to mistake him for Fortier, don't you think? To lead us off the scent? Fortier could be in real trouble. The killer could have him somewhere right now—"

"You just don't want to consider that the killer was Fortier himself, do you?" Harris said, shaking his head.

No, I didn't. I was relieved to know the body in the garden wasn't his, but it saddened me to think my smiling, congenial guest was a killer. "If he was, he would know what wrist to put the watch on," I argued.

"Unless he just wasn't paying attention to details," Harris said. "Maybe he took off the man's watch and replaced it with his own without thinking about which wrist it was on."

My brain danced to catch up with his. "So Fortier checks in, kills someone else, puts the ringer in the garden to be discovered, and then disappears. Why? Was he faking his own death? Escaping a bad past? Assuming the other man's identity? It all rests on who the poor man was in the garden."

"We're working on that. Have some patience."

I let out a long breath and nodded. "Sorry. You're right." I turned away and, for want of anything else to do, lifted some bedding out of the laundry basket and started folding it. My mother had plenty of laundry songs, and she used to sing "Let Us All Press On" when she was ironing, but I didn't feel up to singing anything at the moment. I dropped the folded pillowcase onto my desk and reached for another, my actions automatic.

I didn't know Fortier, really. Who was I to argue that he wasn't the murderer? I would have to screen people more carefully from now on before booking their stays. Name? Address? Credit card number? Criminal record? Next of kin, just for larks?

Harris leaned into the doorjamb, with his hands in his pockets, and watched me fold pillowcases for a moment, seemingly in no hurry to go. When I pulled a sheet out of the basket, he stepped forward and caught two of the corners in his hands. Deftly, without speaking, we folded the sheet between us, stepping closer together as the fabric folded into smaller and smaller squares. He nipped the final fold from me, placed the sheet on my desk, and lifted another one from the basket.

"One thing," he mused aloud as we worked. "If you saw Fortier come here by bus, he didn't have a car, right? How could he have gotten away in the night, killed someone, and brought the body back here without access to a car?"

"Well, either he did have access to a car I didn't know about," I reasoned, "or else the fellow he killed was close by and easy to carry to the garden."

"Firstly, if he were close by, someone would have heard the shot, and no one did. Secondly, the victim was about a hundred and ninety pounds. Not easy to carry that much dead weight. Especially difficult to carry him without dripping a bloody trail all the way." He placed the second folded sheet neatly on top of the first.

"True. No long-distance carrying, then."

"We've interviewed your neighbors. Your cottage and several of the guests' rooms overlook the driveway—a driveway, which, by the way, takes a full thirty seconds to drive up if you're driving cautiously. But no one saw or heard him coming or going."

I went to the window. From the office, I could see only the courtyard and breezeway connecting the house to the garage. The line of trees behind the breezeway formed an effective green screen to hide the vegetable garden from view. I pictured the path beyond it, the arbor, and, farther on, the wooden gate. It occurred to me that in a place that had multiple people coming and going unpredictably, the killer had put the body in the only spot that wasn't visible from the house, my cottage, the road, or the barn.

"If he parked a car at the library—maybe even the victim's car—he would've only had to come through the gate and walk about fifteen feet to the vegetable patch. The hedge would have hidden him from the house pretty well. The fence would have hidden him from the library parking lot. The back entrance is the only logical way he could have come and gone without being seen."

Harris came to stand behind me, looking out the window over my shoulder. He stood so close I could smell the fabric softener on his shirt and the butter from his cornbread.

"How late is the library open?" His breath stirred my hair.

"Nine in the summer," I told him.

"But employees might have been there later?"

"Maybe. I've never paid attention."

He was a solid, capable bulk behind me. I wondered for a brief, insane moment what he'd do if I leaned back an inch and rested against that broad shirtfront, just for a moment . . .

He turned and headed for the door.

"I'll make sure we interviewed them. Someone may have seen a car parked in the lot or seen someone coming or going from your gate."

* * *

Callum—whom I referred to circumspectly as Dr. Meacham in front of the guests—arrived at two o'clock. He gave me a one-armed squeeze around the shoulders and did the same to Jennie then called the guests all together in the therapy room for a quick debrief. He had always been excellent at diffusing the stress of any situation. When everyone emerged from the room, they seemed a little more cheerful, and Callum was smiling. He came into the office, where I was going over bills.

"How are you, Erin?" he asked, plopping into the chair in front of my desk.

"Good, all things considered." A thought had occurred to me, and I wanted to talk to him about it. "Callum, the police are saying the victim might not be Michael Fortier after all."

I could see he hadn't heard this news. I was surprised Grant and the others hadn't told him. Maybe they'd assumed someone already had. Callum's jaw dropped, and he made a gurgling sort of sound in his throat before wheezing, "Are you sure? I thought you said—"

"We all thought it was Michael. But now they're saying the prints don't match and, well, they're not sure who he is."

"But then, Michael is missing," Callum said, wiping a hand across his upper lip.

"Well, yes. The police seem to have some theories about that too. Did Michael seem the murdering type to you while he was in detox?"

He reared back, eyes wide. "Heavens no! I wouldn't think so at all. Is that what the police think?"

"That's one idea. He might have killed this person, dropped him in the garden to make us think it was Michael, and then skedaddled. A new identity, maybe, leaving his old life behind."

Callum thought about this a moment, hands clasped between his knees, slowly shaking his head. His blond hair, worn a bit long, flopped boyishly over his eyes as he studied the floor. Callum was the age that Robert would have been now if he'd lived. Robert's hair had been starting to thin, a fact that irked him to no end, but Callum's was thick and feathered.

"I suppose anything is possible, but it would surprise me if so. I mean, he wasn't the most friendly of people, but who is while they're going through detox?"

"True. Though I found him quite friendly while he was here," I told him. "I kind of liked him, actually."

"I wouldn't call him my favorite patient," Callum confided. "He could be a bit impatient and aggressive. Verbally abusive toward other people. And frankly, he had quite the ego, didn't you think?"

"Well, no. He was confident and self-assured, maybe, but he seemed nice enough to me. But as you say, by the time I got him, detox was over."

We mused over it a while, and then Callum gathered his briefcase and rose to go.

"Did Jennie want to talk to me at all?" he asked.

"I don't think so this time, but maybe down the road. Thanks for coming, Callum."

"No worries. Try to get some sleep," he said gently, leaning over the desk to kiss my cheek. He went out, and I sat a moment longer, fingering my MasterCard bill and puzzling over the description he'd given of Michael Fortier. It didn't sound like the man I'd briefly known at all.

Chapter Nine

That evening after supper was cleared away, the guests went into the sitting room to do various activities. Grant and Jason played chess, with Grant giving gentle and not-so-subtle hints to Jason when he went to make a wrong move. Eva sat close by, watching intently and making encouraging noises when Jason captured one of Grant's pieces, though I doubted Eva had the slightest idea herself how to play. From time to time, I saw Jason give Eva shy, grateful smiles.

The other guests ostensibly watched TV or read the paper, but after a while, I realized they were all sneaking quick peeks at each other from behind their newspapers and TV guides. Whenever they caught each other's eyes, they would quickly avert their gazes and pretend great interest in their activities. The tension in the room was palpable, other than the congenial bubble surrounding the chessboard. I didn't have to guess what was on their minds. For all they knew, they were sharing a quiet evening with a murderer. I preferred to assume the guilty party was an outsider, not one of our little family; but if I were honest, I would admit this was a viewpoint based on hope, not probability. I glanced from face to face. Did they suspect each other for valid reasons unknown to me? Or was theirs just a generalized fear based on the concern that where murder had happened once, murder could happen again? In spite of the obvious mistrust, I noted that none of them went to their own rooms. It seemed there was safety in numbers, even if one of those numbered was the killer.

After a few minutes, I slipped downstairs, went out the back door, and ventured into the yard. The air was cool against my hot face. I hadn't gone to the garden after dark since finding what's-his-name, but now I made myself walk down the path to the vegetable patch. I didn't touch anything or step on the scene but stood looking at it for a long while and fighting to reclaim my garden from the image of that faceless body. I knew I had to exorcise that vision from this place if I were ever going to be able to remain living here.

The shadows were thicker under the trees than I'd ever been aware of before. The moon gave little light, though there was some light from the lamps in the library parking lot across the fence. My own shadow startled me as it moved across an open patch. I could hear Hilda Turner across the street, bellowing for her dog Dribbles to come in. "Poochie, Poochie, wanna nice cookie from Mommeee?" (Why was it that otherwise perfectly sane adults resorted to brain-melting baby talk around sensible animals? If Dribbles knew what was good for him, he'd make a dash for freedom while he had the chance.) There was the sound of a car going up Arthur. One of the horses whickered in the stable. Then silence.

I moved closer under a maple tree so as to submerge my disconcerting shadow. A slight breeze rustled the hedge. I could hear my own heartbeat in my ears. It was all too easy to imagine someone opening the gate; silently coming up the path with his terrible burden across his shoulders, a black bulk against the night; and coming into the yard, staggering under the weight like the silhouette of Quasimodo. Laying the body down, the arms flopping on the ground, with a muffled sound like a wet bag of laundry hitting the earth. While everyone lay ignorantly sleeping behind the windows right above . . .

Enough exorcising for one night, I decided, and fled back into the house.

* * *

Saturday morning, I awoke to the unmistakable patter of rain against the window. I crawled out of bed and peered out into the gloom. The rain looked like the streamers you see tied to fans in a department store, flapping and flowing from the overflowing troughs on the eaves. Bonnie's planned expedition to a local bird sanctuary was going to have to be postponed, though knowing Bonnie, she'd insist everyone don Macs and galoshes and go anyway. I pictured a houseful of bored and irritable guests lounging around with nothing to do but nurse suspicions of each other. I felt distinctly reluctant to go over to the center and begin my day, and I lingered longer than I should have in the shower and took my time reading my scriptures. When I finally came downstairs, I found a pool of water on the floor beneath the kitchen window and streaks on the wall below the sill. Groaning, I stepped closer. The wood frame around the window was bulging, swollen, and damp, and the frame itself was starting to split. Just terrific.

I wrote a note to Vinnie and his crew and left it stuck to the window with tape so they'd find it. If they even bothered to come in this kind of weather, that is. They didn't seem the sort to put themselves out. I wondered how much damage had been done inside the wall and what it was going to cost me. There was no sign of Jennie, and I went back up to her room. She didn't answer my knock, and when I poked my head in, all I could see was a lump in the bed and one bare foot dangling.

"Rise and shine," I called out. "Time to get up."

Her foot twitched.

"Come on, sweetie," I prodded and started singing "Up, Awake, Ye Defenders of Zion." I'm an enthusiastic but admittedly untalented alto. There was a moan from under the covers.

"Curse Grandma for ever insisting you learn the whole hymnbook," she muttered.

"Breakfast."

"Why can't morning come in the afternoon?" she whined, and finally her head emerged from under the blankets. Her gold hair was hopelessly tangled and hung over her face.

I agreed with her. I would have liked to have stayed in bed myself and pretended the day didn't exist. But piles of things awaited my attention. I pulled on rubber boots and went outside. The pile of broken drywall on the front lawn was slowly disintegrating in the rain like melting meringue. There was no sign of Vinnie's truck. The driveway was more mud than gravel as I slogged over to the center. Sourly, I began to hum "I Have Work Enough to Do." Who said all hymns were encouraging, anyway?

The kitchen was warm, and the smells brightened my spirits somewhat. Janet was slinging pancakes at the stove, and Detective Harris was seated at the kitchen table, sipping orange juice and reading the *Toronto Star*. An empty plate, sticky with syrup, stood at his elbow. I looked at the clock above the doorway. Seven fifteen.

"Don't tell me you worked all night again," I said by way of greeting.

He turned an idle page. I saw he was looking at the careers section.

"Sleep is highly overrated," he replied briefly. He set his empty glass down and frowned at it.

I poured him another and plunked it beside his elbow. I knew I was surly and out of sorts and resented the fact that he looked bright and fresh.

"Are you always on the job this early?"

He shot me a look, as if questioning my ability to tell time. I thought he would say something like, "This isn't early; the day's half over." But instead he quirked one eyebrow and said mildly, "Who says I'm on the job?"

"Aren't you?"

"No. It's Saturday."

For the first time, I noticed he wore a blue T-shirt rather than the jacket and tie. I forked two more of Janet's pancakes onto his plate and pushed the jug of syrup closer. He thanked me and indicated the chair next to him with his head. I dropped into the chair opposite him instead so I could watch his face.

"So you don't work on Saturdays?"

"Generally not. Do you?"

I waved a hand around, vaguely taking in the kitchen, the house, the whole rain-soaked acreage. "I'm always working." I was still puzzled. "Was there something in particular you wanted?"

"Are you going to eat?" he replied.

"Later. I have things to do. Eva Stortini is leaving this morning."

"We got a match on the fingerprints belonging to the man in the garden."

I sat up straighter. "Oh good. They were on file after all?"

"Not in our system, but he had a DUI in New York last March. They had his prints on file there." Harris finished his pancakes in two bites and returned to his newspaper.

"So you were you able to identify him?"

"Yes."

"Well, who was he?"

Harris turned another page of the paper and studied it. "Michael Fortier."

I stared at him until he finally put the paper down and looked at me.

"Say that again," I directed.

Harris's lips tightened, and I couldn't tell if it was a smile or a grimace. "The man whose body you found was Michael Fortier, age forty-three, CEO of Clearwater Holdings in Toronto."

"But I thought we had decided it wasn't because of the watch thing and the fingerprints not matching." I knew it was early, but I was usually quicker at grasping concepts than this. I'd forgotten about Janet behind me, and Harris's hooded eyes flicked to her briefly. Janet picked up on the look and moved farther away, rummaging in the fridge and making noise as she got dishes out of cupboards. Harris leaned closer and lowered his voice slightly.

"The only facts we knew were that the man who checked into your establishment wore his watch on one side and the body in your garden wore his watch on the other side. And the victim's prints didn't match the ones belonging to your guest. Now we have confirmed that the victim's fingerprints belong to a Michael Fortier of Toronto. My partner is notifying the family now."

My mind skittered away from the thought of the unsuspecting family going to answer the door. "Are you saying there are two Michael Fortiers?" I asked, befuddled.

At the stove, Janet forgot she wasn't listening and gave a sound suspiciously like a snort. "Maybe they had a disagreement about who got to use the name."

Harris impatiently blew his breath out through his nose. "No. I think it's safe to say the real Michael Fortier ended up in your garden, and the man who stayed here as your guest was only impersonating him. Did you ask to see a driver's license or anything?"

"No, the thought never occurred to me. I take it for granted that people are who they say they are."

"Another lesson learned." Harris sighed and pushed away his empty plate.

"Was Fortier—the real one, I mean—the person who attended Dr. Meacham's detox center? Or was that an impostor too?"

"We're checking into that, trying to trace his movements in the last few days. As soon as Dr. Meacham's center is open this morning, we'll look at the medical record in his possession and have him come down to identify the body. Hopefully he'll be able to tell if the victim was his patient or not."

I cringed at this reminder of my own blunder. "So we have no idea who my guest was. If he was only pretending to be Fortier, well, he could be anybody!" I said.

"Well, not just *anybody*," Harris said. "He had to be someone who had a reason to impersonate Fortier."

"So how do you figure out who he was?"

"I don't know yet," Harris said. "But I will." He retrieved a hooded sweatshirt from the back of his chair and pushed his arms into it. "Thanks for breakfast."

It wasn't until he'd gone that I remembered that, once again, I'd forgotten to give him back his brother's Yale shirt.

* * *

People began to wake up and trickle down to breakfast. Several of the outpatients arrived early, and I took their wet coats and ushered them into the sitting room to wait for their sessions. Laura arrived at the front desk in time to arbitrate a dispute between (according to her filing system) Rum and Coke and Dry Martini (addressed to their faces as Dennis Lastowski and Julie Einstoss). The latter claimed the former had stolen her parking space, and they loudly refused to sit in the same room with each other. A handful of the Lewis sisters arrived, cheerful despite the weather and asking how my renovations were going (the thought of which succeeded in thoroughly depressing me). I promised again to take a look at Kevin's stuck closet door (I'd have to remember to write it down this time, I told myself, even while knowing full well I wouldn't). I gave Bonnie the money for a new volleyball net, wrote out a grocery list on a paper napkin, and made a note to remind Janet that Grant Calderwood's birthday was next Friday and we should have a cake for him. But through it all, my mind was far away, and by the time we'd gotten everyone through the meal and either shuffled off to counseling sessions or organized into activity groups, I was nearly stamping with impatience to have them all gone. At last, they departed, Bonnie taking one hale and never-say-die group to the bird sanctuary after all and the leftovers taking themselves into town to roam the mall at Square One. I had only to see Eva through the checkout process and drive her to her apartment, and I was free for the rest of the morning.

But things never work out the way you want them to. By the time the dust had settled and the various groups had departed, I discovered that

Eva Stortini had gone off to Square One with Jason's group, apparently forgetting that she was due to leave today. I thought about getting angry about it and then decided it was a gift in disguise. There was no hurry to get to her apartment, after all, and my morning was now completely free.

And then the Polinskys walked in.

"Good morning," I greeted them. "Were you hoping to go on the bird sanctuary trip this morning? I'm afraid they've already left."

Max Polinsky blustered up to the desk, his ordinarily red face an even deeper plum color. Whatever was bothering him, he had let it work him into a lather.

"I came to inform you that we won't be coming back for treatment anymore," he said in a loud voice. "I came to pay you whatever is outstanding up to yesterday, and then that's the end of it."

I looked from his furious scowl to the embarrassed look on Ed's face as he hovered behind his father.

I said calmly, "I'm sorry to hear it. What is this about, Mr. Polinsky?"

"I don't feel this is a safe environment for my son. Quite frankly, I question the usefulness of any therapy given in such a place."

"Oh!" This startled me. "I'm—"

"For all I know, the therapist we've been seeing is a murderer. How can I trust you or your employees?"

"Now, wait a minute," I protested. "Nothing has been—"

"I'm not here to discuss it. I'm just here to pay my bill."

"Aw, Dad, it's not like she planned for the guy to drop dead," Ed groaned.

I tried again. "I know the murder is upsetting, but—"

"Please just tell me what I owe you, and I'll be going," Max replied, looking harassed.

"We can't go *now*, Dad. It's just starting to get interesting," Ed protested. "Something exciting finally happens and you want to *quit?*"

Max turned to glare at his son.

"Ed, I've told you twenty times, someone's unfortunate death is not entertainment. I'm appalled at your attitude."

"You're appalled at everything," Ed whined.

Oh dear, the bonding hadn't gone well after all. I went into my office and printed out the Polinskys' last invoice.

When I returned to the lobby, Max was in full voice. "This all comes from playing too many war games on that stupid Xbox of yours!"

I watched Ed's face transform into something roughly the color of a tomato.

"Leave the Xbox out of this," he said. "It has nothing to do with it, and you know it."

I placed the invoice on the desk in front of Max and reached for a credit card receipt. I held a pen out, but he didn't appear to notice it.

"If you spent more time doing other things, healthier things—" Max bellowed at his son.

"What, like wading through the rain to look at a bird sanctuary that's probably five feet under water?" Ed replied. I thought he had a point.

"I've made my decision," Max said flatly. "We're not coming here anymore."

I saw the anger in Ed's face and was frankly surprised that he didn't want to quit his treatment with us. He'd never seemed that responsive to the therapy we'd provided and had participated reluctantly and sometimes in full protest. And yet, here he was, not wanting to quit. I wasn't sure I understood it.

"Perhaps you'd like me to recommend another place where you could attend—" I began, but Max whirled to face me.

"I won't take advice from you!"

I recoiled, surprised. Max was an assertive and unpleasant person at the best of times, but he'd never been openly hostile. From the corner of my eye, I saw Jennie peer out from the kitchen, her eyes round and frightened at the sound of shouting. The thought of her being alarmed made me angry, ruining my determination to avoid conflict.

"Mr. Polinsky, I don't know what has set you off, but I will thank you to lower your voice and deal with me in a more professional manner," I said tightly. "If you are withdrawing from the program because of the murder in the backyard, I want to assure you that it has nothing whatsoever to do with the Whole-Life Wellness Center or its employees. It was an unfortunate freak event."

"I wouldn't say the death of a patient isn't connected to the center."

"He wasn't a patient," I said.

"Michael Fo—"

"It wasn't Michael Fortier. That is, Michael wasn't who you thought. The man who died is a complete stranger to me. Why he was in our garden, I have no idea, except that it was a conveniently sheltered spot not visible from the road. I don't appreciate you casting suspicion on our facility or the people in it." It occurred to me belatedly that perhaps I wasn't meant to spread the word of the victim's true identity. Then again, Harris hadn't specifically told me not to. I also had no proof that no one at the center was involved, but I decided to ignore that little fact.

"See, Dad? I don't think we should quit just because of what happened," Ed said.

"I have to get back to work. I don't have time to argue with you," Max said dismissively. His tone implied his daily allotment of parental feeling had been used up along with his time. He turned and took the pen from me and hovered over the page, looking for the appropriate amount to fill in on the credit card receipt. I pointed helpfully.

"Oh, like the entire stock market will crash through the floor if you take a morning off," Ed snapped. "You're the one who dragged me here in the first place, remember? You're the one who said we should get treatment. I didn't ask you to. I didn't want to come."

"Exactly. So I would think you'd be totally happy with withdrawing now," Max replied, waving the pen around.

I started sending messages by mental telepathy. *Sign the receipt. Just sign and pay up and go.*

"You want me to show an interest in something other than war games," Ed countered. "So okay, I'm interested in what's going on here, and I want to stick around and see what happens." I saw his eyes stray to Jennie down the hall. She immediately popped back into the kitchen.

"You picked a fine time to decide to be interested in anything," Max grumbled, signing the paper at last. "It's ghoulish, that's what it is. Maybe you'd learn some human feelings for once if you stopped wasting your time with games and smoking weed and started interacting with real people once in a while."

Ah, the truth was out about the weed. I glanced at Ed, feeling his misery, watching the shameful blush reach his ears. He thrust his chin out in false bravado, but even he could see the game was up.

"I don't smoke anymore—" he began to deny, but his father whirled around to face him.

"Don't say it, Ed. Don't even try to deny you were smoking marijuana the other night. I saw you coming in from the library parking lot, and when you passed me in the hall, you reeked of it."

Ed ground his teeth and shot me an embarrassed glance. Max ripped off his copy of the receipt and held the other copy out to me. I ignored it.

"Ed," I said quietly, "what night was that?"

"What night?"

"When you were smoking in the library parking lot behind the house."

He looked ready to protest again, but then the fight went out of him and his shoulders slumped. He knew I'd already found him smoking once behind the shed, and he didn't want me to bring that up.

"Dunno," he said sullenly. "It was the same day as that stupid trip to the waterfall. We stayed here for dinner, and Dad got to talking with some of the others, and I was bored waiting around, so I went outside."

Wednesday night. I had found the body Thursday morning. I had forgotten that the Polinskys had lingered late at the center that night. I leaned across the desk and looked him in the eye.

"What time were you out in the parking lot?"

"Dunno. It was dark."

"It was just before we left," Max told me, frowning. "Why?"

They had left around ten o'clock, just as I'd made my rounds to lock up. I felt a rising excitement. "Think, Ed. This might be important. Did you see any cars parked in the library parking lot that night?"

He shrugged his skinny shoulders, and his nose chain jingled like wind chimes. "Might have been."

"Try to remember exactly."

He frowned, looking funnily like his father. I waited, and Max, glancing in puzzlement from one of us to the other, waited too. Finally, Ed nodded, jingling the chain again.

"There was just one, parked kind of far from the library, closer to your back gate. A Chevrolet Cavalier, four doors, either dark blue or black. I couldn't tell. It had one of those ski rack things on top. Nobody was in it."

"And you're sure it was a Cavalier?"

"I remember reading the logo thing on the back and wishing Dad'd let me get my license." He stopped and glanced at his father.

Max scowled. "We're not going into that again. You were drinking under age at that party, and I'm not letting you so much as look at driving lessons until you prove to me you're clean." He held out the receipt again, snapping it at me.

I shook my head. "I'm sorry, Mr. Polinsky, but I think your son needs to talk to Detective Harris. He might have witnessed something they need to know." I reached for the phone.

Chapter Ten

So much for Harris not working today. But his voice hadn't sounded regretful. After Max and Ed were sent on their way to meet him at the police station, I went into my office and closed the door. After thinking and chewing my lower lip for a while, I picked up the phone again. The phone number written in the guest register rang and rang and didn't answer. But then, if he hadn't really been Fortier, he wouldn't have written Fortier's real number, would he? Taking the thick Toronto phone book, I sat at my desk and did a quick check. There was a column of Fortiers listed, but only four of them with the first initial *M*. None of them were the number written in the register. I dialed the first one. On the second ring, a chipper female voice answered, "Melissa Fortier!"

"Is this the home of Michael Fortier, please?" I asked.

"Sorry, wrong number," the bouncy voice said, as if delighted to deliver the news, and hung up.

The second number had been disconnected.

The third number was answered by another female voice, this one sounding much more subdued.

"Fortier residence."

"Hello, could you tell me please if this is the residence of Michael Fortier?"

There was a pause, and then the voice said, "Yes, but I'm sorry, he isn't here."

"Michael Fortier, the CEO of Clearwater Holdings?" I wanted to be sure.

"Yes, but . . ."

"I'm sorry, is this his wife?"

The voice on the other end broke. "Yes, but I'm afraid Michael is—is dead."

Bingo.

* * *

She really was very nice about it. She agreed to see me at eleven o'clock that morning and told me the address and how to find the place. I figured if I left right away, I could get there in time. It wasn't really sticking my nose in. It was just going to be a courtesy call, really.

I poked my head in the kitchen and told Janet I was going out.

"Will you be all right without me? It's only Jennie and Greg Ng for lunch. The others won't be back 'til after."

Janet waved me away. "I'm fine. Go take a little break, Erin."

I wasn't sure visiting the wife of a murdered man qualified as a break, but I didn't argue. I told Jennie I was going out, but she was busy on the computer and hardly noticed. I slopped through the mud to my car and headed for the freeway.

* * *

It had stopped raining by the time I arrived. The Fortiers lived in a ritzy part of Toronto, not quite in Rosedale but close enough to be significant. The house was old brick with stone and had a deep bow window in front. The walkway to the front door was narrow, and the gardens on each side of it were lovely—professionally landscaped, a refined riot of color and texture. The driveway in front of the double garage was overshadowed by a large, drippy golden chain tree and was empty of vehicles. The place shrieked money. I felt very aware of my faded jeans and rubber boots as I parked my car and went to the front door.

Andrea Fortier was not what I would have pictured. She was older than I'd anticipated, for one thing, probably closer to fifty than her husband had been, and she wore a very nice, very expensive sweater and skirt the color of butternut squash. Canadians don't wear shoes in the house, but Andrea had on slim mottled house moccasins that reminded me of overripe banana skins. Her makeup was perfect, pearl earrings exquisite, and graying hair stylishly done, but her eyes gave her away. They were red and bleak from crying, the only flaw in her image. I was reminded forcefully that, while I'd had time to get used to the idea of Michael Fortier's death, it was shockingly new to her.

She waved away the thanks and apology I offered, showed me where to stash my boots, and ushered me into an antique-filled living room roughly the size of a corporate boardroom. I could smell beeswax and roses. I waited until she'd sat in a delicate Queen Anne chair before lowering myself to the edge of the slippery-looking sofa. Now that I was here, I wasn't sure quite what to say. I knew Harris would have plenty to say if he knew I was here.

"The police just called first thing this morning," Andrea Fortier said, and her voice sounded as it had on the phone: subdued, controlled, with the slightest of tremors in it. "I—I couldn't believe it, really. But they said they were sure; they checked his fingerprints. They aren't releasing his body yet. I wanted to go down and see him, but they said it would be better to wait until I had someone with me."

How true that was. In a morgue or in a bean patch, I couldn't bear the thought of her seeing what I had seen.

"I'm so sorry," I said, feeling again the inadequacy of the words. But it was true—there was nothing else to say. "Are you alone here? I mean, is there anyone you can call to be with you right now? Family?"

The smallest shake of her head, as if she were afraid that if she shook it vigorously, it would fly right off.

"Michael didn't have any living relatives," she said. "And I only have two sisters. One is in the Dominican on holiday, and the other lives in Kingston. She's on her way, but it will take her time to get here." She reached over and pulled a tissue from a wooden decorative box on the coffee table, but she wadded it up in her fist and didn't use it. Perhaps afraid of smudging the makeup.

"Thank you for seeing me this soon," I said, deciding I'd better get my errand over with and go. "As I told you on the phone, it was my garden Mic—er, Mr. Fortier was found in."

"Yes, and I've been trying to imagine ever since I spoke to you what on earth he could have been doing way out in Mississauga. I have no idea how he could have ended up clear out there." As if Mississauga were in the Outer Hebrides rather than a forty-minute drive away. Something in her tone implied that someone from her end of town wouldn't have been caught *dead* in my end of town. But he had been, and she was puzzled by it.

"Oh, I'm sorry. I thought I mentioned it. I operate the Whole-Life Wellness Center," I explained.

"Yes, you did mention that," she said. "Is that name supposed to mean something to me?"

"It's a treatment center people attend after going through detox."

"I see." She still looked puzzled.

"I had a guest staying at my center who called himself Michael Fortier," I explained. "Wednesday night or Thursday morning, my guest disappeared and your husband was put in my garden. At first I thought the—er—person I found was my guest. But then we figured out he was not the same person who checked into my center. And then we discovered that the . . . gentleman was indeed your husband, and the man who'd been staying at the center was an impostor." I wondered what Harris would say to my including myself in the actions of the police, as if I were one of them. Talk about impostors. What was I doing here?

She nodded a little more naturally this time. "Yes, the police officer tried to explain that to me, but I'm not sure I caught all of it. They thought the victim was Michael, then they thought it wasn't, and then they thought it was again. That's why it took so long to notify me."

"The police are sure now," I added, in case she was hoping they'd change their minds again and call the whole thing a mistake.

"But you're saying someone checked into your center using Michael's name?"

"Yes. And someone went through two months of detox before that, also calling himself Michael Fortier." I hesitated then added carefully, "I don't know if the person who attended detox was your husband or the impostor. The police are checking into that."

"My husband? In treatment? Certainly not."

"Of course," I said quickly. "I mean, you'd know if he'd been away for the past two months, after all."

She looked a little startled at this. "Well, yes, he has been," she said. "But Michael was on a series of business trips, first to Ottawa, then to Thunder Bay, and the last two weeks he's been in Sault Ste. Marie. He certainly wasn't at any detox center!"

"I see."

"I'm sorry." Now she did dab at her eyes with the mangled tissue. "I shouldn't snap at you. It's just so hard to believe he's been dead since Thursday and I didn't know."

"I understand."

Andrea Fortier rubbed her hands together as if trying to warm them over a meager fire. "So who *was* the man who called himself Michael? The one who stayed in your center?"

"That, we don't know," I said. "I was wondering, maybe, if I described him to you, you might have an idea who he was. I mean, he must have been someone who knew your husband."

"Why do you say that?"

I shrugged. "Because the police suspect he might have been the one who killed your husband. He disappeared very conveniently right before your husband was found. And, well, people don't usually go around impersonating and then killing people they don't even know."

She turned a sort of mushroom color when I mentioned killing, but she pulled herself together and nodded again, vigorously this time.

"Tell me what you remember about him," she directed. "I'll see if he sounds familiar."

Atta girl, Andrea. I frowned up at the crown molding, picturing him again in my mind. "Six feet tall. Dark hair cut quite short in a businessman's cut. Brown eyes. Very handsome, really. About a hundred and ninety pounds. Built like a tennis player. I thought he looked about forty at the most, certainly not any older. He was right-handed and wore his watch on the left wrist. A local accent, probably from Ontario. Deep voice like a baritone, maybe, but not a bass. Charming, articulate, a drop-dead smile, and he showed interest in everyone he talked to. You know, the type who really looks at you when you're talking, instead of just half-attentive like most people. He arrived by bus." That was all I could think of. As I described him, I realized he didn't really fit the profile of the usual person in my center. Looking back on it, he didn't strike me as a recovering alcoholic. The firm handshake, the confident, charming smile . . . Why hadn't I noticed that before? Most of my guests arrived looking tired, a bit shame-faced, maybe even grim, but determined, like earthquake survivors.

Andrea Fortier had been watching me intently as I spoke, and now she frowned, thinking. "Well, the physical description certainly sounds a lot like my Michael," she said at last. "Except for some key things. Michael was left-handed and wore his watch on his right wrist." *Aha.* "And he was originally from New Brunswick. He had quite a pronounced accent. I don't notice it much any more—I didn't," she corrected herself, looking slightly flustered. "But people meeting him for the first time would always ask him if he was from down east. He couldn't hide it. And . . ." She looked away at the window for a moment, as if debating with herself about whether to speak, and then she looked at me again and gave an apologetic smile that didn't reach her eyes. "I wouldn't have described him as charming."

"No?" I asked gently.

"No," she said, firmer now. "Michael was always in a hurry. He hardly listened to anyone. He rarely smiled, certainly not drop-dead smiles." Her own small smile was painful. "He was a very busy man with a lot of responsibility. He sometimes gave the impression of being too busy to notice other people."

I wondered how often he'd forgotten to notice her.

"I see," I said. "Do you know any of your husband's acquaintances who might fit the description I gave you?"

"I can't think of anyone. Most of his friends and business colleagues are older men, going gray, certainly not built like tennis players."

"You understand why I felt I needed to ask."

"Yes, of course. The police couldn't have given me a first-hand description the way you have. It was worth a try. But I'm sorry, it doesn't ring any bells."

"Did your husband have any enemies you know of?"

She gave this serious thought before shaking her head. "He was involved in a lot of business dealings. The stock market. The trade board. Once, he ran for city council, but he didn't win. He was a founding partner of Clearwater. Michael was ambitious, and I suppose he might have stepped on a few toes here and there, especially during the campaign, but not enough to make enemies of *that* sort. I mean, people might avoid him at the office water cooler or forget to invite him to parties but certainly not murder him. Clearwater is an environmental protection group, and not everyone likes 'tree huggers,' as they call them, but any disagreements would have been dealt with in court, not directly with him personally."

"Was he involved in any court battles at the moment?"

Andrea thought a moment. She was a careful woman, at any rate, not prone to speaking without thinking first.

"No, I think the last problem they had was eventually dropped or settled out of court. A mining company wanted to buy the rights to some protected parkland. It would have disturbed important wetlands. Michael had an environmental study done. He told me they'd found a solution to that particular fight."

"He didn't say what that solution was? Or mention the name of the mining company?"

"I'm afraid I don't remember, but if the police want the records from his office, I'm sure they could get them. But you see, things like that came up all the time. There was one fellow, Philip somebody-or-other, who represented a development company—anyway, he and Michael were embroiled in arguments all the time. It was just part of the business. But I wouldn't call him an enemy. I'm sorry, but I really don't see how anything he did at work would be connected to this . . ." She shrugged, at a loss for adequate words to describe the situation, since "unfortunate event" just didn't cut it.

"I'm sure you're right," I said. "I just wanted to cover all the bases."

She hesitated again then looked away, out the window, her expression bleak. "I don't think Michael got to know people well enough to make enemies, really. You have to know someone pretty well in order to hate them, don't you?"

I was getting a clearer picture of the real Michael Fortier, and it wasn't a happy one. It also sounded more like Callum's impression of him than the charming stranger who'd stayed in my center. Could the real Fortier have gone to detox and the switch was only made last Saturday when the impostor had taken his place? Or had it been the impostor all along? I wondered how difficult it was for a person to fake the medical symptoms of alcohol withdrawal. Surely Callum would have clued in that it was a sham. But faking the done-with-detox-and-now-just-recuperating-at-the-center wouldn't have been so difficult. If I were going to pretend to be Fortier, I would have chosen the switch from detox to wellness center as the time to make my move. Could the real Fortier have gone to detox without telling his wife, hiding behind a series of faked business trips? Why would he have done such a thing?

Had he planned, perhaps, to return home a changed man and surprise her with his reformation? The idea was heart wrenching.

I looked around the perfectly appointed room, trying to think of what else to ask, trying to glean any personal information I could out of the furnishings. There was very little about the room that was personal: a small landscape painting above the fireplace, a couple of candles and potted plants, a shelf of books that looked as if they'd never been opened, and some silver-framed photos on the polished black surface of the upright Kawai piano. I stood and went over to look at them. One was of Andrea standing beside a dark-haired man in a brown suit. The two figures were close but not touching, as if each were unaware of the other, both looking steadily into the camera. I studied the picture for a moment—his handsome, pleasant face, the stiffness of his stance. Fortier. I felt I knew him; I *had* sort of met him in a way. But it was the face of a stranger. I felt a wave of sorrow and turned swiftly to the other photos. A Pekingese wearing a red bow and looking remarkably sanguine about the whole thing. A picture of Andrea alone, wearing a red jacket and a broad smile, a formal professional portrait.

The last photo was of a slender teenage girl with pale skin and white-blonde hair hanging limply on each side of her face. She could have been pretty if it weren't for the heavy black makeup that emphasized her paleness. My heart gave a lurch. Had Fortier had a child? Jennie's face swam into my view—the struggle she'd had after her father's sudden death—and I felt a sudden desire to weep. Instead, I swallowed and kept my voice steady as I asked quietly, "Your daughter?"

Andrea had come to stand beside me. She touched the silver frame lightly with her finger.

"No, unfortunately we didn't have children. That's my niece, Candace, taken several years ago. My sister's daughter. Candace is studying art at Ryerson. She's a very talented oil painter."

"Ah." I was ashamed of my relief. A niece wouldn't be as devastated as a daughter . . . though I supposed that was probably not an accurate assumption. Maybe she'd been very close to her uncle. Perhaps she hadn't even been told yet.

Briskly, I rerouted the conversation. "Can I ask when your husband left for his first business trip to Ottawa?"

We returned to our chairs, and Andrea told me the date. It was the same day Fortier—or someone pretending to be Fortier—had checked into Callum's detox center.

"And you're telling me you haven't seen your husband in the weeks since then?"

"Seen him? Or had contact with him?" she asked in her careful way.

"What do you mean?"

"Well, I haven't *seen* him since he left for Ottawa. But he phoned or e-mailed now and then."

"He didn't come home between business trips?"

"No, but that's not unusual. He was always flying all over Ontario for work. But the last *contact* I had with him was Tuesday. It was my birthday, and he sent me a message on my Blackberry, wishing me a happy birthday and saying he wished he could be here. He sent a virtual bouquet." Her voice gave a hiccup of emotion, and she cleared her throat, bringing it under control.

"Virtual flowers? Well, that's . . . nice," I said. "He didn't phone, though?"

"No, but I'm used to that. Michael is a busy man. He missed a lot of my birthdays." She swallowed and shot me a rather angry look, as if daring me to take that as a slur against her husband. She added pointedly, "And I'm a real estate agent, so I'm on the road a lot too. We keep in touch by e-mail a great deal of the time." She winced, as if suddenly remembering the present tense no longer applied.

I decided the red jacket portrait on the piano was probably the real estate agent photo that she used in her ads. It had that sort of formal friendliness to it, an expression that said, "I'm here to help you."

"So as far as you knew, your husband was on these business trips." I wondered how long it would be before she clued in to the fact that this woman who'd come on a condolence call was firing questions at her like the Spanish Inquisition.

"Yes. Why would I doubt that?"

"The stay at my center was to end in about three weeks," I said. "May I ask when your husband was due to come home?"

She pressed her lips tightly together for a moment before replying. "In three weeks, he said." She looked away.

"He was found in the garden of the wellness center," I went on carefully. "Not in Sault Ste. Marie."

She had nothing to say to that. She wadded up the shreds of her Kleenex, tossed them onto the table, and took another.

"I'm sorry to pursue this, but I know your husband was arrested for drunk driving last March."

Her head came up sharply. "You know about that?"

"Yes. I'm sorry, I do. So maybe your husband did have a drinking problem."

She eyed me for a moment. After a short struggle with loyalty, her shoulders slumped, and she gave a short, jerky nod. "Sometimes he went too far," she conceded. "He was under stress at work, you know. Juggling so many things. I didn't blame him, but I'd asked him a few times to get help. He always said he didn't need it. And now you're thinking maybe he *did* get help without letting me know?"

"Maybe the reason he didn't want to tell you was that he was afraid it wouldn't be successful and he didn't want to get your hopes up. Maybe he was a little ashamed to admit he had a problem. Or," I added brightly, "maybe he just wanted to surprise you."

She gave an unladylike snort. "More likely, he figured it wasn't any of my business."

I felt unutterably sad. I bit my lip, not knowing quite what to say to her. There was nothing to make it better.

"It's all conjecture at this point," I finally said. "I imagine the police will find out soon enough whether it was your husband in detox or not."

"Mrs. Kilpatrick . . ." she asked slowly.

"Yes?"

She hesitated then looked at me with eyes gone very sad. "Why would someone impersonate my husband? This fellow who was passing himself off as Michael . . ."

"Yes?"

"Was he trying to steal his identity? I've read about that in the newspaper."

"I don't know. I expect the police will be looking into that," I said.

She shook her head slowly, looking down at her banana-skin slippers. "Frankly," she said quietly, "I can't imagine why anyone would *want* his identity."

I nodded. "I know what you mean. If someone wanted my identity, I'd tell them, 'You want my mortgage, my teenager, my parent-teacher conferences, my ratty hair and clunky car? Go for it! I'll go be someone else!'"

She gave a sharp laugh and then clapped a hand over her mouth. I smiled and stood to go.

"Thank you for your time, Mrs. Fortier. Again, I'm really sorry about all of this."

"Andrea, please." She crossed her arms, gripping her upper arms with her hands as if she were cold. "I'm sorry. I didn't even offer you coffee or anything."

"Not a worry. Thank you. I never drink it, anyway."

She shook my hand and walked me to the door, but I hated to just leave her there alone and comfortless. "What will you do now?" I couldn't help asking.

"I'm supposed to call the funeral home and make arrangements," she said, sounding suddenly very unsure of herself, like a child who had been sent to the grocery store by her mother and couldn't quite remember the list of what she was supposed to buy.

I felt the urge to pack her up and take her home with me. Instead, I laid a comforting hand on her arm. "Is there anything I can do for you? Do you want me to stay with you until your sister comes?"

Another tiny shake of her head. "Thank you, no. I'm—well, I'm not all right, but I can't think of anything anyone can do for me. But thank you for asking. It—it feels good to be asked."

I dug paper and a pencil from my purse and scribbled my phone number.

"Keep this, and give me a shout if you need anything," I said. "I mean it. Anything at all."

"But why?" she asked bluntly. "You know, just because he was found in your yard doesn't mean you're responsible for watching out for me."

"That has nothing to do with it," I told her. Knowing full well that it did.

Chapter Eleven

When I got home, I tried to busy myself with mundane, daily chores to take my mind off of everything, but it didn't work very well. The hymn entrenched in my mind had turned to "Come, Ye Disconsolate," which of itself might have had a comforting message, if only I could have gotten past all the anguishing and languishing. I felt depressed and sorry for the woman I'd just met. The guests had returned to the center, and they and my staff tiptoed around me, I guess picking up on my vibes. I was in no mood for socializing, and fortunately, no one tried to strike up a conversation. Even the twittering flock of Lewis sisters steered clear and just gave me sad, knowing glances. When the phone rang at three o'clock, I knew it would be Harris. It was.

"Fancy finding you at home," he said right off. I didn't like the nastiness in his tone.

"What do you mean?"

"Well, imagine my surprise when, after I finished interviewing the Polinskys, I went to see Michael Fortier's wife and learned that the nice woman whose garden he'd been found in had been at her house this morning."

"I felt I owed her a condolence call at least."

"And you figured as long as you were there, you might as well ask a bunch of questions while you were at it."

"I suppose I asked a few," I said evasively.

"Mrs. Kilpatrick—"

"Erin. You can't show up for breakfast at seven in the morning and still expect to call me Mrs. Kilpatrick."

"Erin." He sounded ready to strangle me. "How did you get her phone number? Have you been prying through my files again?"

"Why, have you been leaving them lying around again?" I retorted. He made a spluttering sound, and I relented.

"I looked her up in the phone book," I told him. "That's not restricted for police use, last I checked."

"You can't go around interrogating people as though you're on the case," Harris said.

"I didn't. I paid an innocent social call," I protested. "Is it my fault she wanted to spill her heart out to someone, and I was the only friendly shoulder around?"

"Don't give me that," he snapped. "What did you find out?"

"First, tell me what you've found out," I countered.

I expected him to say something rude and hang up. Instead, he astonished me by saying bluntly, "Coroner agrees the guy was killed elsewhere and dumped in your garden late Wednesday night. He'd been dead about two hours before he was moved."

"How can they tell?"

"The coroner tends to know these kinds of things," he said in a patronizing tone. "It has to do with rigor and the way the blood settles. It leaves a distinctive—"

"Forget I asked. Did Callum—er, Dr. Meacham—confirm that the body in the morgue is the same man who attended his center?"

"Dr. Meacham wasn't available to go down to the morgue until tomorrow. He had a court case today. But we'll see if the body matches the medical record in the detox center's possession; that's more certain than visual identification anyway. After all, you weren't able to tell just by looking," Harris pointed out.

"I wasn't acquainted with his body the way his medical doctor would be," I replied.

"I should hope not. So tell me what Mrs. Fortier told you, in case it was different from what she told me."

"Why would it be?" I asked.

"A great detective such as yourself should realize that when someone is killed, most of the time, the spouse is involved," Harris said.

"All right, all right, lay off. I said I was sorry," I said, even though I'd done no such thing. "I described the fake Fortier to her as well as I could. All she told me was that he fit the general physical description of her husband, but she couldn't think who the impostor might have been. No one she knew."

"Uh huh."

"That's not to say it wasn't someone her husband knew," I pointed out. "Or at least someone who knew him. You don't impersonate people you don't know."

"Agreed. And?"

"She also told me she wasn't aware of any plan for him to go into detox. She'd never heard of the Whole-Life Wellness Center. As far as she knew, he'd been on a series of business trips for the last two months. The last time she heard from him was Tuesday."

"That's what she told me too," Harris conceded. "He e-mailed her for her birthday, and she picked it up on her Blackberry."

"Yes. They often communicated that way," I said, glossing over the fact that Andrea Fortier had been a lonely, neglected woman (my interpretation, after all. I mean, who was to say she didn't *like* being left alone?). "He didn't come home between trips, which sounded like the ordinary routine. If it turns out he *was* in detox, we can assume the trips this time were a front to cover his going into treatment."

"A crummy secret to keep from your wife," Harris remarked acidly.

"An addict can have all kinds of reasons for not letting people know about it," I said gently.

Harris was silent a moment. "What sort of guy e-mails for his wife's birthday, anyway?" he finally said irritably. "Why didn't he call her in person?"

"Maybe he knew she was out working and didn't want to interrupt her."

"That's lousy. The last thing she has to remember him by is an e-mail."

I shrugged. "Better than a text message."

"True."

* * *

Late that afternoon, I went out to collect my mail (rain soaked) and saw an ambulance parked in front of Hilda Turner's house across the street. The lights were spinning, but the siren was silent, and as I watched, two attendants came out of the house with Hilda on a gurney. They lowered her carefully down the steps and wheeled her to the back of the ambulance. I hurried down the driveway and across the road as they began to load her.

"I'm a neighbor," I told one of the paramedics. "Is Hilda okay?"

"It's her heart," one of them said briefly. "She called us."

Hilda, her face half hidden by a plastic oxygen mask, swiveled her eyes up at me at the sound of my voice. Her helmet hair was flawless as always, and her blue eyes were alert, but I thought her face was a pasty gray. I bent over the bed.

"Is there something I can do, Hilda? Do you have any family I should call?"

She shook her head and then rolled her eyes toward her house. As they lifted her into the ambulance, she gave a mumbling sound and looked again from me to the house.

"I'll take care of Dribbles," I assured her. "Is the house unlocked? I'll take care of him until you come back."

Her eyes closed briefly, and I read the thanks and relief in her face. The attendants pushed me gently out of the way, climbed in beside Hilda, and closed the door. The ambulance pulled away, and after it had reached the main road, I heard the siren start up like a hysterical woman screaming. I hated that sound; it always made me want to scream along with it.

I went up Hilda's steps and into the house. I'd never been inside her home. It was like stepping into the American Wild West. A spotted cowhide rug stretched before an impossibly tartan couch. The living room was paneled in knotty pine. A rocking chair, apparently made from driftwood, stood next to an iron woodstove, whose unused top was festooned with dried flowers. An autographed, commercial photo of John Denver stood on a table, overshadowed by a lamp made from an antique butter churn. I smelled candles and tuna fish.

Fascinated, I moved farther into the house, forgetting for a moment the errand I was supposed to be on. I never would have imagined Hilda living with this sort of décor. I had pictured her more as a Martha Stewart sort of woman, with carefully appointed furnishings and pastel colors straight out of a magazine. The song in my head couldn't help itself; despite my efforts to control my thoughts, it turned into "Battle Hymn of the Republic."

As I tiptoed from living room to dining room, I realized that there were sweet sayings all over Hilda's house. Painted plaques and framed embroidery on the walls declared that families were forever and Jesus loved me. Painted rock paperweights informed me that God was the rock of my salvation. A large wooden sign above one doorway told me I should return with honor. Another told me to look forward with steadfast faith. Everywhere I looked, hope sprung eternal, roads rose up to meet me, and the wind was at my back. I've always liked the idea of posting cheerful thoughts or encouraging messages where I could see them, a sort of self-motivation, but this was over the top. But maybe they weren't all just for her own benefit. I saw a few duplicate items and wondered if, perhaps, Hilda had *made* all of these things. Did she sell them? It occurred to me that I didn't really know her at all. It seemed wrong, somehow, that I didn't even know this basic thing about my neighbor.

One wall held an especially elaborate cross-stitched sampler, done in a nineteenth-century style but obviously recently worked. I paused to examine the skillful stitching and saw Hilda's name carefully embroidered at the bottom. It must have taken her weeks or months to stitch. I tried to picture her sitting in the driftwood rocker, sewing by the light of the churn lamp. I felt a twinge of regret for opportunities lost. She had been just across the street but a world away. Maybe our personalities, given time, would mesh after all. I wondered if she'd ever watched us from this side of the road as we'd ridden our horses and wished she could join us. Surely a woman with Wild West decor would like horseback riding. When she was home and feeling better, I'd invite her.

I found the kitchen (golden harvest appliances, rickrack on the plaid cafe curtains, and more sayings on the walls) and discovered Dribbles huddled under the table. He was a poodle mix of some sort, the color of wheat, with wet, pinkish stains beneath his sad eyes. I found his kibble and water bowls, located his leash, and coaxed him out from under the table. He came wagging his tail and slinking with his belly to the ground, living up to his name all the way. I mopped up after him with paper towels, turned off Hilda's lights, found a spare door key hanging on a hook made from an elk antler, and locked up as I left.

Dribbles seemed overjoyed to be going to my house. He bounded into the cottage with a whiney bark, and Jennie came running down the stairs to see what the noise was. She dropped to her knees beside Dribbles and put her arms around his neck.

"A dog!" she cried. "Really?"

"Not ours," I said quickly. "We're babysitting him for Sister Turner across the street. She's in the hospital."

"Aw." The sound was my first indication that Jennie had ever even considered wanting a dog. Maybe this was what she needed to distract her from recent events. I handed her the leash, dishes, and bag of dog food.

"He's your responsibility for now," I told her. "I don't know how long we'll have him, but I'm sure you'll do a great job dog sitting."

"Cool! You bet I will!"

"Do you know what to do?"

She shot me an exasperated look. "Yes, Mom. He's a dog, isn't he?"

She gathered Dribbles and his belongings and nearly skipped to the kitchen.

I washed my hands of Dribbles germs and phoned the Relief Society president to let her know Hilda was in the hospital. There was no answer, so I left a message on her machine. Then I walked over to the center. Jason was just coming down the stairs, moving at a good clip, and one look at his face told me something was wrong. He was very red, and if I didn't know better, I'd have said he was crying. He swept past me and out the door like an avalanche, without even acknowledging me. A moment later, Eva clattered down the stairs after him in her floppy sandals, looking distressed.

"Have you seen Jason? Did he come down here?" she asked, grabbing me by the arm.

"Yes, just a second ago. He went outside at a run. What's the matter?"

Eva dabbed at her eyes with the back of her wrist. She was one of those lucky people who looked pretty even when she was in tears.

"I had no idea he'd take it so hard," she wailed. "He'll never forgive me."

"Why? What's going on?" I glanced at the wall clock. At this time of day, the therapists on staff were gone, but Eva didn't seem to mind using me as a substitute.

"I told him about Michael. I honestly didn't think he'd get so upset. I mean, it was a little thing, really. It didn't *mean* anything."

"What didn't? What about Michael? You mean Michael Fortier? I mean, the guy who we—"

"Yes," Eva sniffled. "Wednesday, when we were on the trip to the waterfall, Michael and I were walking a little behind the others. Jason was up ahead on the trail. And Michael—" She stopped to sniffle, and I searched out a tissue from the box on the front desk, biting my tongue to keep from prompting her. Eva thanked me, blew her nose daintily, and resumed in a calmer voice.

"Michael pulled me off the trail, said to let the others go on ahead of us. He wanted to rest. So we stood a moment and looked over the valley, and it was really very nice. And then Michael said he'd enjoyed getting to meet me, and he kissed me. He was so sweet. It was just a friendly smooch. I—I enjoyed it, but it didn't mean anything."

"I see."

"I didn't know Jason would be so upset about it, or I wouldn't have even told him. We were just reminiscing about Michael, you see, upstairs just now. And David said he thought he'd seemed like a good fellow. And Grant said he didn't think he could be the murderer. And I said I didn't think so either because he seemed very kind to me, and I told them about the kiss. And Jason got all upset over it." She stopped, looking puzzled.

"Give him some time to calm down," I advised. "Then you can talk to him later and everything will be fine, I'm sure."

"Do you think so? I hope so," Eva said frankly. "I don't want to hurt his feelings."

"I know you don't," I said. "Just give him some time."

I knew I would need some time to think about this new development myself.

I worked in my office for a while and then went back to the cottage to start supper for Jennie and me. I liked having meals together sometimes, just the two of us, away from the crowd at the center. But when I opened the door, noise hit me like a fist: dog barking, Jennie calling out, hammering, the whine of a table saw. I put my hands over my ears and went into the kitchen—or rather, what was left of my kitchen. It was bedlam. When I'd left this morning, the only sign of the renovations had been the small holes the workers had punched in the walls that allowed them to feed the new wiring through. But now, in no time flat, the place had been totally demolished. The sink and counter had been removed, the cupboards pulled away from the walls, chairs piled on top of the table, and a fine white dust covered everything. There was a blank gap where the leaky window had been.

Vinnie and two other guys were huddled over an electrical outlet. Vinnie looked up and saw me, and I saw his eyes spark with something more than a friendly greeting. I'd been avoiding him since the kiss-blowing incident, but I could see he hadn't forgotten it. He grinned, his teeth very white against his olive face.

"What is all this?" I demanded, spreading my hands to indicate the destruction. "What have you done to my kitchen?"

"No worries," he replied. "Everything's under control. We just had to feed new wires up from the basement."

"And you had to take out my sink to do it?" I squeaked.

"Naturally, we had to get behind the cupboards," Vinnie explained in a tone that implied I was a silly female for not knowing this. "It was that or drill holes through the backs of your cupboards to get at the walls, eh?"

"You couldn't have consulted me first? You couldn't have warned me?"

Vinnie shrugged and stepped closer. My tirade didn't seem to faze him. I didn't like the interest in his eye. He wore a sleeveless blue sweatshirt, and I found myself musing that I'd never seen such a hairy individual. I took a polite step backward, nodding, the house-owner capitulating to the greater knowledge of the contractor.

"Yes, well, I'm sure you'll get everything back to the way it was when you're done, right?" I said.

"It's all under control, *cara*," he replied evasively and reached out a hand toward my shoulder. I turned and fled.

Jennie and Dribbles were now hiding in her bedroom, curled up together on the bed, looking at a magazine. When I came in, Dribbles jumped to the floor and ran at me, barking.

"It's me," I told him. "I'm the one who rescued you, remember?"

"All the noise has made him jumpy," Jennie said. "Vinnie and his crew showed up right after you left."

After not making an appearance all day, they had to come at suppertime? I let my breath out slowly, tamping down my frustration. Jennie tossed her magazine aside and sat up, swinging her feet to the floor. I was about to scold her for wearing tennis shoes in the house but then remembered the broken drywall and bits of snipped wire all over the floor of the kitchen. Maybe it was better to keep the shoes on for a while.

"Mom, is it true Ed Polinsky's dad made him drop out of therapy?"

"Mr. Polinsky has decided they won't be coming anymore. That's right," I said, sitting on the edge of the bed beside her.

"That's stupid."

I studied her face, trying to figure out what I was reading there. "You liked him, didn't you? Ed, I mean."

"Well, I know you sure didn't mean his dad," Jennie said, laughing. I noticed she didn't answer my question directly, but she didn't need to. I sighed.

"Maybe you'll see Ed around town," I suggested vaguely, not sure whether I hoped for this or not. In a town the size of Mississauga, it wasn't likely anyway.

"Nah. He wouldn't want to hang around with someone my age," Jennie pointed out. "He's lots older than I am. He's in high school."

Ordinarily, I'd have agreed with her, but I remembered the look on Ed's face when he'd seen Jennie looking out from the kitchen while Max Polinsky argued with me at the front desk. Maybe that explained why Ed was reluctant to stop coming to the center. I glanced at Jennie's sober expression and reminded myself that she was thirteen.

"You aren't really old enough to be hanging around with anybody anyway," I felt obliged to remind her.

"Fortuna is dating a boy who goes to Clarkson, and she's my age."

"Maybe Fortuna's parents don't love her as much as I love you," I replied. After all, I nearly added, they named the poor girl Fortuna.

"Lots of girls date when they're thirteen or fourteen," Jennie said stubbornly.

I grabbed a handful of my hair and yanked on it. What had happened to the sweet little girl who had no interests beyond horseback riding and mint chocolate chip ice cream? "Are we really having this discussion, Jennie? Are you really telling me you want me to give you permission to date Ed Polinsky? Because it isn't going to happen."

Jennie's eyebrows came together, and her lips pouted out in the signal I'd come to know so well. We were about to have a tantrum.

"You just don't like him because he dyes his hair and pierces his nose!" she declared.

"I like Ed. I really do," I said flatly. "He's probably my favorite outpatient, even if I'm not supposed to have favorites. I don't mind if you keep in touch with him. You can even invite him over sometimes to ride when the therapeutic riding group is here because I know he's going to miss that. But it would be a—a conflict of interest for the daughter of the center's owner to date a patient."

"Ex-patient," she retorted.

"Same thing in the eyes of the law," I said glibly. I figured taking a little liberty with the truth was okay given the circumstances. I should have known my intelligent child wouldn't fall for it.

"What are you talking about, Mom?" she demanded.

"I mean it wouldn't be ethical. Besides, you aren't dating anyone until you're sixteen. And when you do start to date—"

"I know, LDS boys." She fell over onto her pillow.

"You've known that all of your life, Jennie, and it isn't going to change now. But you can still have Ed over to ride when the volunteers are here. That's my compromise."

Jennie hesitated, torn between looking for a good fight and rejoicing in the idea of horseback riding with Ed. While she was debating her response, I stood and went to the door.

"Since we apparently don't have a kitchen at the moment, I guess we'll eat at the center tonight. It might be a good idea to keep Dribbles in here or bring him over to the center with us," I told her. "This place is kind of dangerous right now."

I went out. Vinnie was waiting in the living room. *Dangerous in more than one way*, I thought grimly. I wasn't sure how to explain to him that I'd been blowing kisses at the house, not at him. The Italian male ego might not take kindly to the idea. He also might—justifiably— think I was insane.

"Erin, *mia cara*," he said, straightening and beginning to approach.

"I'm sorry, I have to get back to work now," I said briskly. "Whatever it is, just leave me a note on the counter or . . . or somewhere," I added, remembering I had no counter. I breezed past him and out the door, leaving him looking after me forlornly.

Chapter Twelve

When the phone rang late that night, I was surprised to hear Harris on the other end of the line. I had been just about to go to bed, and I felt unreasonably embarrassed to have him catch me in my pajamas. I sat on the edge of my bed and pulled the comforter up around my shoulders.

"Are we starting to make this a regular thing?" I teased and then thought how stupid I sounded. Luckily, he chose to ignore me.

"I'm confused," he said without preamble. "Help me think this through."

"What is it?"

"This afternoon, Hawkins, my partner, went to Fortier's office to look through his papers and things. The secretary gave him access to his calendar on Outlook. Mr. Fortier was booked for business meetings for the past several weeks, to Ottawa, Thunder Bay, all of it just as his wife said. He even bought train tickets."

I thought about this. "Maybe that had been the original plan. But then he decided to go into detox, didn't make the change in his calendar, and had already bought the tickets."

"The secretary denied knowing anything about detox."

"So? So did his wife. You think his secretary knows more about his life than his own wife?" I asked.

"Of course," Harris said, sounding surprised.

"It can be very demoralizing for a person to admit they need help for substance addictions," I said. "I'm not surprised Fortier tried to hide it. He wouldn't be the first. I'm just surprised he managed to keep everyone in the dark for so long."

Harris made a skeptical sound. "And I, on the other hand, don't think he could have kept them in the dark. I think it's possible he really was on those trips as planned. As far as the secretary knew, Fortier went. He never cancelled the train tickets, which he would have if he'd decided to go into detox. He would have tried to get his money back."

"Maybe. Maybe not, if he was trying to keep his cover. Had anyone seen him since he left for Ottawa?"

"No, he didn't come back into the office between trips. He just went straight from one meeting to the other. Apparently, that's ordinary behavior; others in the office do that too. Unless there's something urgent they need to do personally, they don't come into the office all the time. But Fortier kept in touch regularly by phone and by e-mail. Just like with his wife."

"So really, there's no saying where he was. Because he could have e-mailed or phoned from anywhere, right?"

"True."

"But if Fortier *was* off on business trips, who was in Dr. Meacham's detox all those weeks?" I asked.

"The ringer."

"I don't buy it," I said. "Why would someone impersonate Fortier and go to detox for him?"

"Maybe Fortier knew he needed to go but didn't want to. His drinking was out of control. He had a DUI. Maybe he paid someone to pretend he was Fortier and go through the program in his place."

"But it's not as if the program were mandatory. He wasn't there on court order."

"Then maybe it was to get Wifey off his back."

"Doesn't fly, Detective," I said. "Wifey didn't even know he was in detox, remember?"

"So she says."

"Why would she lie?"

"If she could make everyone think she really believed her husband was in Sault Ste. Marie, she'd be innocent when he was found dead in Mississauga."

"I don't follow you," I said. "Are you really thinking Andrea Fortier killed her husband?"

"I imagine a lonely, neglected woman might find a reason to do it."

Drat. He'd picked up on that lonely and neglected part too. But I had a strong aversion to the thought of Andrea being the murderer. Murderess? Did anyone use the feminine form of nouns anymore? I was still smarting from the curt remark I'd gotten the last time I'd been in a restaurant and asked for the waitress. What else was I supposed to call her, for Pete's sake? A wait *person*?

While I'd been musing, Harris had gone on. "So Fortier pays someone to take his place so he can go on with life as normal. Spare himself the trouble of detox."

"Detox by proxy? Are you listening to yourself?"

"Well—"

"And then Andrea somehow finds out about it and flies into a rage, drives eight hours up to Sault Ste. Marie, kills her husband, throws him in the back seat, and then drives down to Mississauga—making the trip in just two hours, mind you—to dump him?" I said scornfully. "She made sure he went to my program dead or alive?"

There was a pause.

"You're right, that's stupid," Harris said. "Then how about this? He plans to go into detox himself. He doesn't tell his secretary because he's embarrassed. He tells Andrea Fortier, though. Andrea, the neglected wife, has been putting up with him for years and decides she's had enough. She goes out to Mississauga and kills him and pretends she knows nothing about detox or the wellness center to distance herself from the scene. She says as far as she knows, he's in Sault Ste. Marie. The naïve secretary can back up her story."

"Naïve? A minute ago, you said secretaries know everything."

Harris made a mumbling sort of sound.

"Then who is the fake Fortier? How does he fit in?" I demanded.

"I don't know yet. Maybe Andrea hired him to cover for her husband . . ."

"You're just grasping at straws," I said. "The only answer is that Andrea can't have been involved. I think the real Fortier went to detox but hid the fact in his calendar and didn't tell anybody. I don't think the ringer stepped in until the switch from detox to my place. It's the only logical time to make such a switch. And Callum will be able to confirm that when he goes to the morgue tomorrow."

"All right, say we concede the switch happened between detox and your place. Did Fortier hire the man to take his place at the wellness center? And Andrea found out about it, got mad at him for not following through, and—"

"You're still determined to pin it on her, aren't you?" I said.

"And you're determined not to," he countered.

"If she says she didn't know he was in Mississauga, I believe her."

"Which is why you're not the detective," Harris replied with a sniff. "Either Fortier hired the guy or Andrea did."

"Why would she hire someone to impersonate her husband?"

"To cover the murder. No one would know for days that he was dead."

"But he wasn't dead for days," I protested. "According to the coroner, he didn't die until Wednesday night or Thursday morning. If the switch happened Saturday, when the fake Fortier came here, we don't know where the real Fortier was for the four days prior to his death."

"Okay, I don't know what happened," Harris said tightly. "But obviously something went wrong, the body was left in the yard, and the fake Fortier flew the coop. Andrea Fortier hides behind the story that she thought her husband was up north."

"If you were going to hire someone to impersonate your husband, it seems like you'd give him better instructions about how to act to be more convincing. For example, 'Don't be charming' or 'Don't snog the other patients.'"

"Don't what?" Harris yipped.

"Apparently, the fake Fortier kissed Eva Stortini on a field trip. But the real Fortier doesn't sound like the kind of guy who would have a friendly, casual fling."

"I agree. If anything, he was too busy to have an affair." Harris sounded sad.

"So I don't think Andrea hired the fake."

"Or the fake was a bad actor."

I shook my head. "I will concede that Fortier might have hired the guy himself, though. I don't know why, unless he was just planning to cut his recovery program short and wanted out. But if so, he could have just walked away at anytime. No one was keeping him in treatment against his will."

"True. But maybe he was up to something elsewhere and didn't want anyone to know where he really was."

"Like what? He wasn't an arms dealer, for pity's sake. He was a boring CEO. And it also doesn't explain the murder."

"I guess it does seem a bit far-fetched that he'd be faking his presence in two places at once—the business trips *and* the wellness center," Harris agreed.

I thought a moment. "When was the last message the secretary got from Fortier?"

"Tuesday afternoon, I think. Saying he was enjoying Sault Ste. Marie." There was a smirk in his voice. "Which takes us back to my original idea that Fortier really was at the business meetings."

"Okay, say he was," I said, following his earlier tack. "Wouldn't it be easy enough to confirm it? Check the hotel he stayed in? See if he ever boarded the trains? Check with the people he should have been meeting with to see if he ever showed up?"

There was a pause, and then Harris said impatiently, "I'm just about to do that, if I can ever get off the phone."

"Who called who?" I demanded ungrammatically.

Harris snarled a good-bye and hung up. I went to bed, humming.

It didn't occur to me until the next morning that it was weird that Harris had called me at all. He had a detective constable for a partner. Why would he bounce his ideas off me?

* * *

Dribbles settled into the routine of the center as if he'd always lived there. I phoned the hospital and learned that Hilda Turner had been placed in the ICU. Her prognosis was guarded. As I watched Jennie run around the front lawn with her foster pet, I wondered if we were about to inherit the dog. I admitted I wasn't overly close to Hilda, but I was still shaken at the thought of her dying. I regretted speaking to her so flippantly on Thursday.

Dribbles wasn't the only one quietly settling in. Eva, who was supposed to have checked out on Saturday, made no mention of leaving, and I didn't approach her about it. With future guests' arrivals temporarily suspended, I supposed we had enough room to get by if Eva wanted to linger longer. From her fragile look, it was probably a good idea to let her stay for a while anyway. She seemed especially sensitive to the tensions in the house and jumped at every little noise. She wouldn't venture into the garden at all. More than once, I caught her casting worried, sad little glances at Jason when he wasn't looking. For his part, Jason was casting his own sorrowful glances at Eva when her gaze was turned away. I didn't interfere. Sooner or later, their timing was sure to synchronize.

I had to admit I missed Ed Polinsky. I missed his mischievous glance and cocky attitude. I hoped he would be all right. Jennie and I hadn't talked about the matter again, by careful, unspoken agreement, but Ed seemed to hover between us, nonetheless.

Sunday was peaceful. Vinnie's crew mercifully didn't work on Sundays, so the cottage was blissfully quiet, even if I couldn't get into my poor, desecrated kitchen and tracked white gypsum dust everywhere I walked. I prayed it wouldn't rain again while I had nothing but a plastic garbage bag taped over the missing window. It wasn't the most secure solution with a murderer on the loose. If someone were determined to kill Jennie and me in our beds, they wouldn't hesitate to punch through a plastic bag. Then again, if someone were determined to kill us, they probably would have by now. There had been ample opportunity.

Somehow this didn't reassure me.

At church, a few of the older women flocked around me, wanting an update on Hilda's condition. I was sorry I couldn't tell them more. It felt like a confession; I lived across the street from her, but I hardly knew her. I didn't even know if she had family around, though she had a grandniece, I remembered, so there must be *somebody*. Sister Watson, the Relief Society president, told me she'd sent flowers to the hospital, though she hadn't been allowed to visit. This also gave me a twinge of guilt. I hadn't thought of doing anything like that. Then again, I was caring for the woman's dog.

We were about to get into our car afterward when the bishop hurried over. He always looked as if he were walking uphill against a stiff wind, his tie flying, his graying hair mussed, shoulders hunched.

"Sister Kilpatrick, I was hoping to catch you," he said, leaning against the car as if it had taken all his strength to cross the parking lot. I wondered what damage my dusty car was doing to his nice black suit. And I wondered if he'd heard of my failure as Hilda's neighbor and was coming to take me to task for it. But Bishop Sand's face was kindly and his voice gentle as he said, "I owe you an apology."

"You? I mean, what for?" I blinked.

"I heard about all the trouble at your place on Thursday, but I haven't had a chance to come over all week. I read in the newspaper a man had been killed."

"Oh! That," I said, waving a hand.

"I'm so sorry I didn't come sooner to see you. I should have at least phoned. Is there anything you need? Can we do anything for you?"

I was astonished. I had been fretting over my own care of Hilda, seeing after the needs of my patients and staff, worrying about Jennie. My own needs hadn't even been part of the equation. My mind went blank.

"I'm all right," I mumbled, embarrassed.

Bishop Sand bent over and peered directly into my eyes. "Are you really?"

For a moment, all I could do was return his stare. I felt a sudden desire to throw myself at his feet and sob out my exhaustion, my worry . . . and my fear. Someone in my life was a murderer, and I didn't know who. This horrible, awful thing had invaded my home, and I didn't know why. I was afraid of my own backyard. I didn't know what all this would do to my business. I had trusted the impostor and accepted him at face value. What did that say about my own instincts? Could I trust them anymore? I was badly shaken, more than I had realized. I desperately wanted someone in my life to assure me that everything would be okay, that I would make it through this.

But I didn't throw myself at his feet. I told him that everything was all right and I didn't need anything but thanked him for asking. He shouldn't feel bad at all about not coming over. We were fine. And then I practically pushed Jennie into the car, jumped behind the wheel, and drove away, leaving him standing there, watching me go with a concerned look on his kind face.

I *was* fine, really. I was handling everything one day at a time, better than I'd ever expected of myself. If I could just stop the visions that invaded my thoughts during the day . . . and the night . . .

When Jennie and I returned from church, everything was quiet at the center. The Lewis sisters had gone to explore the town and had hauled most of the other guests with them. The rest were out for tennis or riding or walking the paths around the grounds (casually avoiding the garden). Jennie went off with Dribbles, engrossed in the dog. Most of the staff members, including Janet, were off, and lunch was a simple collection of cold cuts, breads, and salad that didn't need a lot of my attention. Having the rest of the day pretty much to myself, I finished a novel I was reading and then put on the Yale sweatshirt and took myself off for a brisk walk.

And somehow ended up at the cemetery again.

There were a few people visiting it, loaded with the obligatory bouquets. The garden center next door was strategically placed and no doubt did a brisk business in cut flowers. I walked the long way around, purposely avoiding Robert's stone (two visits in one week surely bordered on pathetic), and found myself in the section of the grounds where Hilda Turner often came. Curious, I poked around among the graves until I saw a bunch of red-gold marigolds planted neatly in front of a stone. I went over to read the inscription.

Matthew Bailey, 12 June 2002—5 September 2004. Forever in our hearts.

That was odd. I had been expecting Hilda to be visiting a brother or distant relative, not a child. I knew she had none of her own, especially not one this young and recent. Perhaps it was a nephew or something, a relative of the birthday girl. I looked around, getting my bearings, certain this was the place I'd seen her visit.

There were more marigolds on the next grave down the row.

Catherine Jackson, 1 May 2001—14 July 2003. Never forgotten.

I frowned. There were more planted marigolds at each grave all down the row. And others farther on in the next row up. Puzzled, I walked along, reading each inscription. Each stone belonged to a child, the oldest of which had died at the age of fifteen. Some dated from the past decade, some more recent, and the oldest dated back to just 1980. I counted eleven children with marigolds planted in front of their stones. None of them had the same last names, and one of them read simply, "Danny" with no last name at all and only a death date, no birth date.

I walked back home slowly, mulling it all over. Who were these children? What were they to Hilda Turner? Did she simply have a soft spot for children? But they had all been placed in the same general location in the cemetery, and none seemed to have other family around them. For a brief moment, I entertained the idea that my neighbor had had eleven children out of wedlock, all of whom had mysteriously died. But that was impossible. Hilda was sixty-five at least, and besides, some of the children had been born impossibly close together. It was all very odd.

I was still thinking about it on Monday morning when Kevin presented himself at the front desk with his suitcase. Laura hadn't arrived yet, so I stepped over to help him.

"I figure it's safe to check out now," he said in a low voice. "I mean, it won't look so suspicious now, will it?"

"It wouldn't have been suspicious if you'd checked out when you were originally supposed to on Friday," I told him gently. "After all, that's what you had arranged weeks ago. But anyway, I'm sure it's okay if you go now."

"The police couldn't possibly suspect me anyway," he said, pulling out his wallet. "I mean, if they're going to be suspicious of anyone, it should be that big thug on the third floor, huh?"

"You mean Jason?" I asked icily.

Kevin shrugged elaborately. "No doubt the police will catch the culprit soon," he said.

"How are you getting home?" I asked him. The plan was for him to return home to Kingston, but as far as I knew, he had no car. Callum had brought him here, like the others.

"I'm taking a taxi to Union Station and catching the train," Kevin said, and then his eyes slid aside in slight embarrassment. "Theresa helped me book it."

I couldn't help softening a little at the anxious look on his face. I put a hand on his arm.

"You'll be all right," I told him. "Just remember the things you've learned here. You're a stronger person now." This I doubted, but I had to think of something encouraging to say. I added more practically, "Keep in close touch with your therapist back home."

"I will. Thank you. In spite of—everything, I think this stay has been helpful."

"I'm glad to hear it."

He paid and signed out and carried his suitcase to the door, where he turned back to me with a concerned look. "You'll be okay without me here, won't you, Mrs. Kilpatrick?"

"We'll try to manage somehow," I assured him. He gave a brisk nod and went out.

Chapter Thirteen

I was doing a small celebratory dance in my office when the doorbell rang. I was closest, so I answered it. Andrea Fortier stood on the front steps.

She looked better, her eyes not red or puffy, her clothing even neater—if that were possible. She wore a smart black skirt and turquoise top with black sling-back heels.

"Mrs. Kilpatrick? I am so sorry for dropping in like this. I should have called first, but you know, I wasn't sure I'd have the courage to do it unless I just got in the car and came."

"Not at all! Please come in. How are you?"

"Better, thank you."

I ushered her into the sitting room, and she looked around with quick, darting eyes before taking a seat on the sofa. For a moment, the real estate agent shone through.

"This is a beautiful house," she said. "Is all this trim original?"

"No, but I've tried to restore it as close to the original as possible," I said. "The house was built in 1890 as a convent, but someone redid it decades ago with no regard at all to the period of the house. It needed a lot of work."

"You've done a lovely job. How long have you been working on it?"

"I bought it three years ago . . . after my husband died," I added.

Andrea looked pensively at me for a moment, and then she nodded, as if accepting this proffered bond between us. She tucked her purse into a corner of the couch and smoothed her skirt with her palms. "I knew I felt a connection when you came to the house on Saturday. I thought I'd tell you, the funeral is going to be on Thursday. Ten o'clock at Rose Park Anglican. Not that I expect you to come. I really don't. It's fine if you'd rather not, but in case you *wanted* to know . . ."

"I'll be there," I assured her. "Thank you for telling me."

"Oh good." She looked relieved. "I wanted to tell you, I—I don't know if 'enjoyed' is too strong a word in the circumstances, but . . . I did. I enjoyed talking to you, Mrs. Kilpatrick. It was what I needed at just the right time. It was so kind of you to show your concern and to let me talk."

I smiled, remembering the interrogation session somewhat differently. But if she thought it had been genuinely helpful to her, all the better.

"Did your sister arrive all right?" I asked.

"Oh yes, and my other sister will be flying in tonight. My niece Candace is staying with me now too. So I'm all right, really." She sounded as if she were trying to convince herself.

"Was there something else you wanted to talk to me about?" I guessed when she hesitated.

"Well, sort of," she said reluctantly. Her eyes darted around the room again, taking in the polished wood floor, the heavy green drapes, the wrought-iron andirons on the fireplace. "The police told me this morning that it has been confirmed; Michael *was* at the detox center for the past two months."

"Ah." Callum must have been able to identify him then, or else the medical records at the center had verified it. I supposed it was unreasonable for me to feel miffed that Harris hadn't called to tell me.

"It's been bothering me to no end," Andrea went on. "For almost two months, I thought Michael was on those business trips. I still can't believe he wasn't. I mean, he phoned and he e-mailed, and I never once guessed he was lying about where he was. Why would he feel he had to lie?" She darted a bright glance at me. "I would have been supportive."

"We can't know what he was thinking," I said gently. "But I'd like to believe he never meant to hurt you."

"But is it wrong for me to want the proof? I mean, I shouldn't doubt my own husband, but I don't feel like I should doubt the police either."

"It's natural to want to feel loyal," I said.

"And, well, if he lied about this, did he lie all the other times he was away on 'business trips' too?" she went on. "How do I know that all the other traveling he did was for work and not—not to hide something else?"

"Do you think he might have been doing something that he didn't want you to know about?" I asked slowly.

I was thinking something more along the line of shady business dealings, but Andrea's eyes widened, and she said, "Like what, an affair? I'm not just being loyal when I say I highly doubt it. Michael was nothing if not faithful. And he certainly wouldn't have had—well, I mean, he hardly had any interest in other women." When she saw my face, she added, "I mean, you know, being so busy and all." She clamped her jaws shut then, as if knowing she'd said way too much.

I thought about the fake Michael Fortier kissing Eva on the path to the waterfall. Was the fake Fortier trying to behave the way he thought the real Fortier would have acted? Or had he acted only as himself in that instance? Or was it all an attempt to burn his presence on that date into Eva's memory?

"Not an affair, then. What about business dealings? Do you think he had anything to hide there?" I asked.

"No, I really don't. And I don't think it's just wishful thinking. Michael was an honest man. That's why this is bothering me so much." She pressed her lips tightly together then added, "I hate myself for even asking these questions."

"I think as his wife, you can trust your own instincts," I said carefully. "There's no need to think he lied every time just because he may have deceived you once."

"Thank you. I feel better just having confessed my doubts," she said.

Why was it people kept unburdening themselves on me? Did I have a face that said, *I have no life of my own. Feel free to park yours here*? I gave her an encouraging smile. "I don't think you need to worry too much about it, then. Just focus on taking care of yourself right now. Remember him as you knew him. You'll get through this." When she looked at me, I added quietly, "I speak from experience. Just focus on each day. Remember to breathe. You'll be all right in time."

"Thank you," she said. She hesitated again, her gaze going to the window, and I knew what it was she had really come for.

"Mrs. Fortier, do you want to see the garden?"

She looked at me, her face suffusing with pink, and the tears welled in her eyes.

"I know it's awful of me to ask, but could I? I need to see where—where he was."

"Of course," I said gently. I stood and helped her up, keeping a light touch on her arm. "Come out this way."

We walked down the hall to the back door and out into the garden, where the sun was already making the yard uncomfortably warm. Andrea said nothing as we went down the path and turned into the vegetable garden. The yellow tape was gone, and the marks of heavy shoes had mostly faded, but you could still see the crushed area in the muddy bean patch where the activity had centered. I was grateful there was no blood visible. We stood awhile, arm in arm, and I could feel Andrea trembling slightly as she looked down at the ground. Then I saw her lift her head and look around the yard, taking in the shade of the trees, the crisp scent rising from my mint patch, the breeze moving gently through the flowers, the distant neighing of a horse. She took a deep breath and let out a great sigh, as if setting down a burden at the end of a long journey. When she turned to me, the tears were gone, though her eyes were still very bright. She pinched her lips together again, smudging the lipstick, and then said, "Thanks. I needed that. I feel steadier."

"No worries," I said simply, and we turned back toward the house. I asked if she'd like to stay and maybe have something to eat, but Andrea shook her head and said she had to be going.

"I've intruded on your morning enough already. Thank you for everything. I'll see you on Thursday?"

"I'll be there," I said.

* * *

On Tuesday it rained—go figure. I kept switching towels placed below the missing kitchen window to catch the water. The plastic bag turned out to be woefully inadequate. There had been no appreciable change in the condition of my poor kitchen. Vinnie and his men had not made an appearance at all, and as I knelt there wringing out wet towels and muttering darkly, I felt I was kneeling beside a wounded friend. Would I ever have my lovely little kitchen back again? I felt as if my home had been violated. I itched to be able to cook a nice meal for just Jennie and me, by ourselves. I should never have hired that leering Vinnie and his irresponsible crew. In the prolonged contest between project and pocketbook, I suspected I knew which would win. Maybe my in-laws had been right; maybe this *had* been a harebrained idea all along. I felt sorry for myself as I slogged through the drizzle to the center.

My guests, after their initial disappointment that the horseback riding excursion would have to be postponed, settled in for a relaxing day of board games, TV, and billiards in the lounge on the second floor. Grant was happy enough, winning game after game of Chinese checkers against all challengers. (I had to consciously quell the tune "We Meet Again Around the Board" in my mind. Really, having a hymn constantly in one's head could be downright annoying.) Jason and Eva seemed content to sit on the window seat and watch the rain with their shoulders lightly touching. Apparently, all was well again between them. But the Lewis sisters, who wanted to get out and about, were irritable.

"I was looking forward to touring Rattray Marsh," Cathy whined when she wandered down to my office around eleven o'clock. "I'm so interested in ecology and the environment, aren't you? The Marsh is one of the last undisturbed wetlands in this area. Now I can't see it until another day."

It did seem unfair that wetlands would be off limits when it was wet outside. I nodded absently, sorting through some paperwork, only half listening. I had some bills looming that needed my attention. Running a place this size was expensive, and since insurance companies tended not to cover our fees, we didn't always have a steady stream of clients. Things ran a bit tight from time to time. There was quite a gap coming up in August. I was tempted to tell Callum to hold off sending anyone else and just shut down for a couple of weeks. I could give everyone a much-needed break and take Jennie to visit my folks in Peterborough. But no patients meant no income, and that could never be good.

"I wanted to see a Great Blue Heron. I've never seen one in real life." Cathy sighed. "Martha and Alice saw one once, but I missed it. I hoped to see one today."

"I'm sorry to disappoint you," I said. "But I doubt you'd see one in the marsh either. It isn't as undisturbed as you think. In fact, I've heard the frogs and fish are dying, so the birds are moving away."

She stared at me as if I'd slapped her. "That's so terrible," she said. "I thought it was a protected area. Is it so polluted, then?"

"I don't think it has to do with pollution. I read something about it being because they sprayed all the mosquitoes last year during the West Nile Virus scare. It killed them all, and that took a vital link out of the food chain. So no West Nile, but no food for the frogs and fish."

Cathy finished the thought. "So they started to die off, and, of course, frogs and fish are what the birds ate. So they had to move on to find food elsewhere. Like dominoes." Cathy sighed. "It's so sad. I hadn't heard about it happening here. People really don't look at the ramifications of their actions before they act, do they? It's like the Redcreek Forest problem. Nobody studies the issue from every angle before they go off half-cocked. If it weren't for Clearwater, the developers would have killed off the whole thing without a care."

I looked up from my papers, my attention fully caught now. "What was that? Did you mention Clearwater?"

"Yes. I was saying that if it weren't for them and other organizations like them, the developers would have ruined the world by now. They're driven by greed, that's all. No concern for the world or what they're leaving behind for future generations to clean up. Like Redcreek, as an example."

"What's Redcreek?" I asked. "I'm afraid I'm not up on the issues like you are."

"Oh, my dear, it was a narrow escape, I can tell you," she said, leaning breathlessly toward my desk with a gleam in her eye, as if about to recount the daring tales of a nobler age. "Redcreek Forest is a tract of land about two hours from here, down near London. It's not just your usual hardwood forest. They call it a Carolinian forest—eastern deciduous—and there's hardly any of it left in Ontario anymore. Eighty percent of all of Canada's Carolinian forest has been destroyed already. There are endangered species of trees there, tender ones that don't usually grow this far north, like the tulip tree or the pawpaw. Have you ever seen one of those? No? It's simply splendid, let me tell you. Black flowers that stink to high heaven. Anyway, this forest is very valuable from botanists' and environmentalists' points of view."

"I see," I said. "And it was threatened in some way?"

"A couple of years ago. It was privately owned for generations, but the last owner decided to sell it. Some idiot developer wanted to rip it all out and build a complex of condominiums, within commuting distance of London. Well, with the university there and everything, they would have made a killing selling units to people who wanted investment properties to rent out to students. But think of the loss it would have been to our province! It's a habitat for nuthatches, and there are some particularly fine chestnuts that—well, anyway, you see the point. The owner didn't care about all that. He only wanted the money. He was asking an exorbitant amount. Ridiculous, really. I mean, no private buyer could ever afford it. But a developer could."

"I see. Yes, that's very unfortunate."

"Some environmentalists raised a cry, though none of them could afford to do anything about it. The land was going to go to the highest bidder. But then Clearwater heard about it and said they wouldn't stand by and let one of the last remaining Carolinian forests be destroyed. They raised the funds and bought the land themselves. Bet the developers never thought someone would be able to outbid them!" Cathy gave a laugh of triumph. "It stopped them dead in their tracks."

And the CEO of Clearwater was now dead in *his* tracks. I set aside my folder of bills and leaned forward on my elbows. Without meaning to, my voice dropped to a conspiratorial whisper.

"How do you know about all this, Cathy?"

"Oh, it's been in the paper off and on," she said. "Not the bigger papers, probably, but the local ones in London. That's where Ida May and I used to live, so it's dreadfully important to us. I wouldn't want to see condos going in anyway, even if it didn't mean destroying the forest."

"You must be very glad that it's safe, then," I said. "Tell me, how much do you know about Clearwater? I don't know much about it myself."

"Well, mind you, I only know what I've read in the paper," she said. "They're an environmental group. Land that is designated as provincial parkland or protected wetlands or what-have-you isn't always as protected as you might think. Government lands and provincial parks are sometimes still subject to development, mining, or logging in spite of their designation. Some corporations have found loopholes and persuasive arguments that have given them the right to exploit the land's resources."

"That doesn't seem right," I said. "If it's protected, it should be protected forever, from everything."

"Exactly what I think," Cathy said. "But you'd be surprised what companies can get away with. Several years ago, some people who felt the same way you and I do, who didn't like how things were going, got together to lobby and fight to have these loopholes closed. They wanted the protection of the land strengthened to prevent exploitation. When that wasn't entirely successful, a few of them pooled together and began to purchase vast tracts of property so it would be in private hands, not the government's. And they put up strict rules about what the land could be used for. They founded Clearwater Holdings to have stewardship over the property and make sure the restrictions are enforced."

"And now they fight people who want to obtain the mining rights or whatever on the land?"

"Yes. They're buying up land right and left and, at the same time, lobbying to have laws changed to expand the definition of 'protected.' They encourage landowners to have conservation easements put on their land. There's a fundraiser every September. It's always a bit too pricey for me to attend, at a hundred dollars or more a plate, but if you're interested, I can get you the details."

"Thanks, but that's too pricey for me too," I confided. "It's very interesting, anyway, Cathy. And now if you'll excuse me, I really have to get some work done here."

She left to go back dispiritedly to her Chinese checkers games with Grant, and I mused over what she had told me. A company that thwarted the ambitions of high-power developers could certainly make some enemies. Perhaps they weren't enemies of Clearwater alone. Did any of it go deeper than that—to a personal level?

Chapter Fourteen

Thursday morning I went to the funeral. After some debate, Jennie decided to go with me. She hadn't gone to a funeral since her father's, and I wasn't sure how she would handle it. She didn't ever even go to the cemetery very willingly. Dressed in her best pale blue, looking oddly grown up in nylons and pumps, her long hair pulled into a French knot, she hovered at my elbow, not speaking. But when we joined the line of mourners shuffling past the family to give condolences, she didn't hesitate to shake Andrea Fortier's hand. Andrea was looking fragile, very pale and neat in a gray suit, but she smiled back at Jennie and thanked us for coming.

Jennie looked the woman in the eye—they were almost the same height—and said, "I'm so sorry for your loss" with a soft but confident voice.

I gave Jennie's hand a squeeze to show I was proud of her as we made our way into the sanctuary and found a seat.

The smell of the heap of white lilies at the front was cloying. I suppose that served a purpose back in the days before embalming, but the scent always turned my stomach. I had banned lilies from Robert's funeral and had given him white tulips and heather instead.

The service began, and when the organ started to play, Jennie closed her eyes and tilted her head back, as if basking in the warmth of the summer sun. The light was dim in the church, but my daughter's face was radiant, with an inner glow that made me feel she was silently conversing with angels. I slipped my hand from hers so as not to intrude. After awhile, Jennie's eyes opened and she looked at me with a sweet smile.

"It's okay," she whispered to me, even though I'd said nothing. And then she settled back in the pew to listen to the unfamiliar Anglican service.

A few minutes into it, there was a stir in the aisle, and Detective Harris slipped onto the bench beside me, late. He nodded a greeting and folded his arms across his chest, straining the black suit coat he wore over a white shirt. The soft light from the leaded windows settled on his dark head like a benediction. His hair was slightly mussed, and my fingers itched to smooth it. I turned my eyes toward the priest and swallowed hard.

It's a weird thing to attend the funeral of someone you don't know. People whose relation to the deceased you can only guess at talk about events and people you haven't heard of. Subtle references bring quiet chuckles from the initiated in the audience, while you sit there blankly, not part of the joke. The tears and platitudes take on an air of unreality, even falseness, because you can only watch them dispassionately since you don't share the feelings. But even though I hadn't known Fortier and hardly knew his wife, this funeral affected me deeply. Perhaps it was because he'd been part of my world, however briefly. Perhaps it was the sight of the shiny mahogany coffin, discreetly closed to veil what I had already seen and continued to see in my nightmares. Perhaps it was, after all, because I—like Jennie—hadn't been to a funeral since my husband's. But I found myself swallowing back emotions and scowling so I wouldn't cry. I'm sure the priest later sought out Andrea to ask who that woman was, frowning so fiercely at him from the eighth row like the wrath of God incarnate.

When at last the music announced the end of it all and everyone stood as the family went out, I jumped to my feet and surreptitiously wiped at my eyes with the backs of my hands. Jennie noticed and put her arm around my waist, leaning slightly against me. Fortunately, Harris had turned toward the aisle to watch the family go past and didn't see me making a wretched fool of myself.

Andrea was openly weeping as she followed the priest at the head of the procession. Beside her walked two blonde women with similar faces and sad eyes, whom I took to be her sisters. There was also a tall, thin blonde girl who looked about twenty and wore a short black dress. But the dress wasn't a typical mourning outfit suitable for church. As she drew closer, I saw it had spider-web lace inserted in panels in the long sleeves, which were so long they reached the tips of her fingers, and her shoes had clunky soles four inches thick. There was a waifish look about her, and her black eyeliner was smudged below her eyes, giving her the look of a Charlie Chaplin film orphan. It was the face from the photo on the piano but older and somehow harder. Candace, the art-student niece. As she drew even with me, I looked into her eyes and was startled by the glow I saw there. I couldn't identify it immediately. Grief? Certainly, but it was also something more than that.

Assorted other people followed, young and old, male and female, blurring into a homogenous stream. I fished in my purse for a tissue and then thought better of it, thinking it seemed too cliché. As the rest of the congregation began to follow the group out, Harris glanced down at me.

"Are you going to the cemetery?"

I felt Jennie stiffen beside me. I pulled myself together and tried to look impassive. "I don't think so. We need to get home."

He nodded, and when we reached the doors of the church, he fell in step with me as we turned toward the parking lot. I'd managed to snag a parking spot not far from the road, and Harris, since he'd been late, had parked farther away. When we drew up beside my car, he stopped with us.

"Well?" he asked. Now that the formalities were over, he'd unbuttoned the too-small suit coat, and his discreet gray and white tie fluttered in the breeze.

"Well, what?"

"What were your impressions?"

"Why?"

He shrugged nonchalantly, but his eyes were intent on mine. "You're observant when it comes to people. I've seen that in you. I'm curious to know what you thought."

"I thought the priest was a little impersonal, and the anecdotes in the eulogy were a bit forced. I kind of got the impression that the members of the audience were friends of Andrea's, not her husband's."

"And the grieving widow? How did she seem to you?"

"Grieving," I said.

"Not put on?"

"If it was, she's the best actress I've ever seen. I think she's lost weight this week."

Beside me, Jennie nodded. Harris glanced at her then ducked his head and stared grimly down at his shoes.

"Nothing else jump out at you?"

"No, should it have?" I asked.

"I guess not. Nothing jumped out at me either." He gave me a polite nod. "I'll see you later," he said and moved off.

We watched him go, and then Jennie observed, "He never smiles, does he?"

"Not that I've seen, though he's come close once or twice."

Jennie was quiet most of the way home, and then she said flatly, "He suspects Mrs. Fortier, doesn't he? They always suspect the wife or husband."

"It often turns out to be the case," I agreed.

"I don't think she could have done it."

"Well, honey, I know she seems very nice, and I'd like to think she's innocent," I agreed. "But you don't know if—"

"She's too small."

"What?"

Jennie shrugged. "She's too small to have carried him into the garden. He was already dead when he was put there, wasn't he? That's what you said. So how could someone that little carry a grown man by herself? She's my size. She'd have to have had help."

It was a point.

"You can tell Detective Harris that the next time you see him," I told her, smiling.

We were almost home before I was finally able to put a label on the emotion I'd seen in Candace's black-rimmed eyes that glimmered behind her sorrow.

It was anger.

* * *

A glutton for punishment, I called the hospital when I got home and found out Hilda Turner had shown little improvement. The nurse began to tell me something else then stopped and asked, "Are you her next of kin?"

The horrible words that never boded well.

"No, I'm not," I said.

"Then I'm afraid I really can't tell you any more than that," the nurse said sadly.

"Let me just ask you this. I'm watching Hilda's dog for her. We have about a week's worth of food left. What do you think?"

"I think you should buy another bag," the nurse said.

"That's what I thought," I said. "Thank you."

* * *

"I can't believe it! It's just what we were talking about the other day!" Cathy Lewis didn't bother knocking as she came into my office. She tossed the newspaper onto my desk and jabbed a chubby finger at it.

I had been sneaking a pre-supper Cadbury Fruit & Nut bar. The funeral that morning had really drained me. I tucked the chocolate out of sight under a stack of papers and read the headlines she was poking. "Development Gets the Go-Ahead." "Project will Put Town on the Map."

"London's already on the map," I said, blinking in confusion at the banner on the top of the page. It was a local London, Ontario, paper with today's date.

"It's the Redcreek Forest," Cathy wailed. "It's been sold out from under our feet."

"What are you talking about?"

"What I was telling you the other day. Danbury Homes, the ones who wanted to build those big, awful condos outside of London, they've bought the forest after all, and they're going to tear it down and go ahead with their plans."

"How could they buy the last remaining piece of Carolinian forest in the area?" I asked, trying to speed-read the article. But it appeared they had. After a fight of two years, Clearwater Holdings, the owners of the land in question, had changed their minds and sold the property to Danbury Homes for an undisclosed amount of money that was probably in the millions. Environmentalists were outraged at the announcement. Words like "betrayal of the public trust," "unfaithful stewards," and "money-hungry turncoats" were bandied about. Apparently, the negotiations had been kept hush-hush until the deal was final. According to the paper, Philip Lockerby, president of Danbury Homes, made the announcement just yesterday, to the surprise of all and the delight of the economists.

"I'm just horrified," Cathy cried. "I'm going to get to the bottom of this. I don't want the forest to come down and those huge, terrible buildings to go up. It's a shame, that's what it is. That land should be protected. People shouldn't be allowed to buy it under the guise of preserving it and then turn around and sell it."

I didn't think they *were* allowed. I smoothed the paper with my hand, thinking hard. Had Clearwater Holdings really approved the sale of the land after putting up such a fight to get it only two years ago? How could they raise funds from trusting fellow supporters of the environment and then turn around and sell out to the developers? It would be raising money under false pretenses. That would constitute fraud.

Looking at Cathy's livid face, her eyes popping with anger, it occurred to me that a rabid environmentalist (such as Cathy?) might conceivably resort to murder to stop such a deal from going through. Or rather, a rabid environmentalist (definitely such as Cathy) might have learned of it too late to stop it and murdered Michael in a fit of rage. Being at the center, she certainly had had opportunity, and now it looked like she also had motive. Was this show of temper in my office merely to make me think she'd only just now learned of the land sale? Or had she really learned of it, say, last Wednesday night?

But it didn't explain the impostor. Where did the fake Fortier fit into it all? If Cathy had really found out about the land sale on Wednesday, wouldn't she have murdered the guy we all *thought* was Fortier? Had she ever, in her involvement in environmental causes, met the real Fortier and immediately known the fake one was a ringer when she met him here at the center? If so, wouldn't she have exposed him? It would have been more understandable if Cathy had been the one murdered, not Michael, to keep her from exposing the impostor. Then again . . . My mind leaped ahead as it occurred to me that Cathy might have been the one to hire the impostor to hide the murder of the real Fortier. But that would only have covered it up for a few days until the body was found. Still, a few days were enough for her to make good her escape after committing the murder . . . except she hadn't escaped. She and her five sisters were still very much here. And it didn't explain why she would have dropped the body on—so to speak—her own doorstep.

After Cathy stamped out of my office, I closed my door and looked up her file. (It took me awhile to find it. Laura had stashed it under

Tequila.) The file was surprisingly thick. I spread it out on the desk and skimmed through. It revealed a typical Lewis childhood: minor poverty, alcoholic parents, never finished high school. Cathy had been in and out of therapy most of her adult life and in rehab twice, each time unsuccessful. There had been a brief dabbling in recreational drugs in her twenties. She was on, it turned out, her third marriage. A total of four children, all now in their twenties. And there was a criminal record: one conviction for petty theft and—this was interesting. One conviction for assault with a weapon. I was looking at Cathy Lewis with new eyes.

I put away the file and sat a moment, thinking. Then I called the Fortier home. After a moment, a young woman answered, and when I asked for Andrea, I was told she was lying down.

"I'm sorry to bother her, but it's kind of important," I said, squashing my guilt. Andrea would want to know about this.

The girl cupped her hand over the receiver in that futile way people have and yelled, "Aunt Andrea! It's for you!" If Andrea had indeed been resting, she was now going into fibrillation.

It was a full two minutes later that Andrea's voice said, "Hello?"

"I take it that was your niece," I said conversationally. "This is Erin Kilpatrick."

"Oh, hello, Mrs. Kilpatrick," she said, sounding positively cheerful. "Yes, that was Candace."

"Erin, please."

"Erin," she agreed. "It's been so nice having her here the last few days. She's always so busy at school that I hardly ever see her. I would have introduced you to my family at the funeral, but there wasn't really time."

"Oh, not to worry. I hope you don't mind my calling. It's terrible timing, I know. But I had a couple of quick questions."

"All right."

"Your husband was Chief Executive Officer and, I think you said, a founding partner of Clearwater Holdings?"

"Yes."

"He was a strong advocate for the environment, then?"

"Yes, always. Michael had degrees in conservation biology and ecology. He cared more about his various nature causes than he did about most people, frankly. He and three colleagues founded Clearwater years ago."

"Was he free to act on his own accord, or did he have to clear everything with his partners first? Decisions about land, I mean."

"Well, he didn't have to account for every little thing he did every day," she said, sounding confused. "His partners are all older than he is—was—and are slowing down a bit, so over the last couple of years, he took on more of a leading role. He dealt with most of the day-to-day responsibilities, the fundraising and staffing and land registry and whatnot. But for any big decisions, he would consult with the other partners, and they would decide together. Especially when it came to allocating money to buy property. Why are you asking?"

"Are you aware of something called Redcreek Forest near London?"

"Of course. That was one of Michael's pet projects."

"Was he in charge of it? Did he ever say anything to you about selling it?"

"What are you talking about? Clearwater Holdings was established to buy up land to protect it. To my knowledge, they never sell an inch of it."

"I don't know if you're aware of the article in today's *London Free Press* about the sale of Redcreek Forest to Danbury Homes. It's just gone through."

There was a startled pause, and then Andrea replied, her voice slightly shrill, "I was not aware of any such article. I don't believe it. He's not even cold in his grave yet, and they rush right out and sell it!"

"So you didn't know it was to be sold?"

"I didn't know. And I assure you, Michael would never have done such a thing."

"I'm sure it takes time to arrange a sale like this," I said slowly. "Could Clearwater have been planning this without your husband's knowledge?"

"Oh no. Anything to do with Redcreek would have had to go through Michael's hands, and I know he wouldn't have sold so much as a fig to that vile little Philip person."

"Do you mean Philip Lockerby?"

"That's the name. Michael had run-ins with him off and on over the years. He had a very poor opinion of him and of Danbury's business practices. They're the ones who bulldozed that endangered falcon's habitat to build a housing tract up by Georgian Bay. The fines were a mere slap on the wrist compared to the money they stood to make. I'm certain Michael would never have approved the sale of any land to that company, especially not Redcreek. The newspaper must be misinformed."

"Maybe so," I assured her. "I'll try to find out more. I'm sorry to have upset you."

"Michael loved Redcreek," she said, her voice dropping to a quieter level. "Once, he took me walking through it in the autumn when the leaves were turning. It was beautiful. It was the only time I remember seeing Michael so relaxed and happy. If he did sell it, Erin, I didn't know my husband at all."

Chapter Fifteen

I caught up with Theresa Bixby as she was about to leave for home. She was in the lobby, giving Dribbles a last fond scrub around the ears. I didn't mind him hanging around the center; he seemed to have a calming effect on the guests. But he could also be a bit distracting, so I shooed him away.

"Could I speak to you for just a minute?" I asked Theresa. We leaned against the front desk, and I got straight to the point. It was quitting time, after all, and she'd want to get home. And I certainly wasn't going to pay overtime.

"I wanted to ask you about Cathy Lewis," I said.

"What has she done now?" Theresa sighed, pushing her bangs out of her face.

"Nothing. I just wanted to know if she has ever told you the circumstances around her assault conviction."

Theresa blinked at me, and I thought I saw a wariness creep into her face.

"You want me to disclose what we've discussed in therapy?"

"It's hardly confidential, really," I protested. "Your clinical notes are all in the file, and I have access to the patient files. But I didn't want to plow through five weeks of notes. I thought it would be simpler and less invasive if I just asked you to elaborate. It's important. It . . . well, it might have to do with the murder."

Theresa considered this for a while, and I waited while she decided whether it was all right to talk.

"She's only mentioned it once," Theresa said at last. "About four years ago, she was rear-ended by another driver, and they got into an argument over whose fault it was. One thing led to another, the other driver got in her face, and Cathy grabbed the nearest thing she could, which happened to be an umbrella on her front seat, and clubbed the guy over the head with it. He had her charged with assault. Since the umbrella had a sharp steel tip, they called it assault with a weapon. I think she was given a fine and community service hours rather than jail time. That's all she told me. I can't see how it could have anything to do with Michael Fortier's murder. You don't think she was responsible, do you? That's ridiculous."

Okay, so it wasn't exactly murder material. But it did show a propensity for striking out in anger in the heat of the moment. I decided to keep Cathy on my list of possible suspects.

When she left, I went back to my desk in my office and looked under the stack of papers. My unfinished chocolate bar was gone.

* * *

Jason was discharged from the center on Friday morning, returning to his independent life. This time, he looked a little more sure of himself, ready to take this step. I had grown fond of him over the weeks he'd stayed with us, and I knew the rest of the staff felt the same. Without planning to, we ended up throwing him an impromptu party there in the lobby—staff and guests, with Dribbles milling around everybody's feet. Janet produced a strawberry shortcake (which also doubled as Grant's birthday cake), and Laura gave both of them presents. (Day planners. Not my first choice for someone like Jason, but perfectly appropriate coming from a secretary. And it was heartfelt.) Ten o'clock was a little early to be indulging in sugar, but we didn't let it bother us. Jason accepted our good wishes and farewell cheers with a red face. When Eva rose on tiptoe and kissed his cheek, he got tears in his eyes.

"I'm going to miss all of you," he declared. "I know I hardly know you, really, but I feel like you're family." He glanced painfully at Eva and away. I saw her slip her tiny hand into his great paw. I suspected she would be visiting him in his new life, and I was happy for them both.

When our guests left the center, they were carefully reintegrated into their community. Our occupational therapist helped them get settled, and we didn't completely step away until they had housing, employment, follow-up counseling, and other community supports arranged. Most of the time, I didn't hear from our guests once they left the center, unless they ended up falling off the wagon and being readmitted. But that had happened only a couple of times. The successful cases we rarely heard from again, other than, perhaps, a Christmas card. I hoped Jason would be one of the successful cases, but I also hoped he would keep in touch.

As we mingled, I noticed something strange about Dribbles's face. Bending down closer, I saw a smudge of chocolate caught in his woolly whiskers. Not strawberry shortcake or whipped cream. I frowned down at him, and he rolled his eyes guiltily at me—caught out.

"Shame on you," I said.

Dribbles hung his head and shamed himself further all over the floor.

I muttered as I stomped to the kitchen for a roll of paper towels. "I guess that solves one mystery, at any rate." I supposed I was relieved to find out Cathy had not reverted to petty theft.

After Jason had gone, I saw Grant wander out onto the back porch and went to join him, carrying my cake plate. Grant was standing at the railing, looking out at the garden. The police had given me permission to resume control of my vegetables, but in all honesty, I didn't have much heart for picking beans and caging tomatoes now.

"Happy birthday," I murmured, leaning against the railing beside Grant.

"Thank you."

We were quiet for a while, just looking out at the yard together. The song of the moment was "On This Day of Joy and Gladness," and after some thought, I decided it was appropriate. It *was* a joyful day, or at least a step toward joy. I caught myself before I actually started humming aloud.

"Do you think Jason will survive okay out in the world?" Grant asked a little worriedly.

"I'm sure he will. Eva will make sure of that. Though I'm not entirely sure she's completely in this world herself." I gave a wry smile. When he didn't return it, I added softly, "Is something bothering you, Grant?"

He gazed out over the yard, the weedy flowerbeds, the scraggly hedge, the sagging gate. I thought the lines around his eyes looked deeper today.

"You need a maintenance man around here," he said. "You should hire someone to help you."

"I agree completely," I said, "but I don't have the money, and Greg really can't take on more than he already does. It wouldn't be fair."

"I'm supposed to check out tomorrow," Grant said. "But if you need me to, I'd be happy to stay on a while longer and help get your poor yard back into order. The police really trampled it."

I studied him a moment, trying to read his serious face. "Cold feet?" I kept my tone light.

He looked at me then away, and a smile finally curled across his mouth. "I'm not afraid to leave. I'm not worried I'll relapse, if that's what you're asking. I've learned my lesson on that score."

"I'm glad."

"It was a bad time," he acknowledged. "A vulnerable time. I faced retirement and my wife's death all at once. My kids and I haven't been very close for a long time. Losing Annie, well, that kind of left me like a fish out of water. And not having my job to turn to . . ."

"Left you flopping on the riverbank, trying to breathe," I said, nodding. "I know what it's like, not being able to catch your breath—not knowing whether to keep swimming or just turn belly up. I've been feeling like that myself for the last few years."

"But you didn't turn to the bottle," he said with self-reproach.

"I also had Jennie and my religion to help me keep my head clear," I said. And I realized it was true. I'd been very lucky to have those supports already in place. I would have been lost without them.

"We all do what we can to get by," I told Grant gently. "Now maybe you're ready to try a different way."

"Yes. I definitely think I'm in a better position to make wiser choices now."

"So the idea of going back to the real world doesn't bother you?"

He paused then said slowly, "No, not in that way."

"What is it, then?" I asked quietly.

He gave a half shrug. "I—I don't have anywhere I need to be."

I set my plate down on the porch table and slipped my arm through his but said nothing. After a moment, Grant went on. "I don't know quite what to do next with my life. I have no job to go back to. My kids are independent and don't need me around."

"Have you talked to Theresa and Ethan about this?"

"Yes. We've made plans. I can keep busy. But I'm not *needed* anywhere, you know? That's all that lies ahead of me, just keeping busy. I want to be useful." He turned his steady gaze on me. "I've found this to be a beautiful and peaceful place, restorative even. But I'm not just clinging to this place. I really think I have something to offer, a way I can be useful. I'm a pretty good handyman around a house. I've even done a little carpentry. I'd enjoy helping you out. If you'd just think about it, I'd appreciate it."

"I'd be happy to have you stay, Grant," I said slowly. "You would be a real help to me, I admit it. But I can't pay you."

"I wouldn't expect pay. I have my pension to live on. It would be my hobby. Something to look forward to getting up and doing every day." He gave a rueful smile. "Something to put in my new day planner."

"I couldn't accept free help."

"You can give me meals, then, as a trade, if it makes you feel better. I'm a lousy cook."

"It's far for you to commute from Toronto."

"I'm not attached to my condo. And my grandkids are in Oakville, out this end of town. I've been thinking about it for a while now. I could sell my place and move closer. Maybe even live here somewhere on the grounds."

Something in his tone reminded me of Jason and made me look at him more closely. "You aren't afraid I need protection, are you? I mean, with the murder and all . . ."

"No, that isn't why I offered. I think you could take on ten murderers single-handedly with nothing but a broom." He chuckled, his eyes crinkling.

"Me?" This startled me. I didn't see myself that way at all.

"What do you say?" Grant asked quietly.

"I'd have to talk to Ethan and Theresa and see what they think about it," I said. "Our goal is to help you get back into your regular life whole and healthy. I'm not sure hanging around here is the best thing for you."

"But if they agree?"

Was I about to agree to welcoming a murderer into our little group? I studied his lined face and the look in his friendly eyes and hardly thought so. Surely you had to start trusting somewhere. He was being brave, facing his insecurities and finding workable and viable solutions to his fears, and I needed to do the same. So I smiled, gave his arm a little squeeze, and picked up my plate. "I'll be happy to have you."

He grinned. "Thank you."

"You might regret your offer," I warned him. "There's a lot to be done around here."

"Good. Set me to work."

"Not officially, not until I talk to the others. But if you really want something to do while you're waiting, you could have a look at the stuck closet door in room 403," I said.

He was laughing as I left him.

* * *

I introduced myself on the phone as a freelance writer doing an article on urban development. I knew I couldn't say I was with any particular newspaper because it could be too easily verified (or not). And it seemed wiser to give my name as Erin McIntosh, in case he Googled "Erin Kilpatrick" and found the newspaper articles about the murder at my wellness center. It wasn't technically a lie. My maiden name was McIntosh, though I hadn't used it in years; and, after all, I *could* write an article on urban development someday and submit it for publication, couldn't I? I hadn't said any paper had *asked* me to write it.

In any case, Lockerby sounded flattered and agreed to see me Saturday afternoon. I was envisioning a leisurely, much-needed drive through the countryside to London, but then Lockerby informed me his office was in Etobicoke, a disappointing fifteen minutes away. It took longer to locate the riding volunteers who had parked behind my car and get them to move their vehicle than it did to get to Danbury Homes.

His office was in a modern, bunkerlike concrete building with mirrored windows and an iron-rail fence, like some sort of compound. I walked up the sidewalk, past junipers and scabby-looking forsythia, and went into the cold marble lobby. A secretary in impossibly high heels met me at the desk.

"Erin McIntosh," I said. "I have an appointment with Mr. Lockerby."

"Yes. He's expecting you." The secretary pushed a button with her two-inch-long nail (How on earth did the woman type with those things?) and announced my arrival. An incomprehensible squawk responded, but apparently she understood the command. She gestured toward a far door.

"He'll see you now. Please go right in."

I had dressed as Junior Girl Reporter—sensible shoes and slacks, with a suit jacket over my silk blouse. I even carried a notebook and pen. Lockerby looked up from his desk as I entered. In the split second before he rose to his feet, his face was unguarded, and I was able to gauge his reaction and get my own impression of the man.

Flash. That was the only word that came to my mind. He was shorter than I expected, his plump figure smoothly disguised by a linen suit the color of warm sand. (Armani? I wasn't sure of such things, but the cut of it shouted money.) His dark hair was superbly coiffed to hide the fact that he was starting to bald. There was a thick gold ring on one of his fingers, and he made a show of popping his wrist from his sleeve to check his watch. No doubt he wanted me to notice it was a Rolex. The gesture also served to remind me that he was a busy man, pressed for time, so it was an honor that he had agreed to meet with me. My mind automatically registered *left wrist,* and I wondered how long it would be before I stopped noticing things like that.

Lockerby's office was the perfectly designed setting for him—vast, sleek, full of hard surfaces and angles. It was the latest in modern chrome and glass, but I found it too chilled by the air conditioning. I wondered if the Danbury condominiums would look the same. I much preferred my molting Victorian shambles of a house. It was decrepit but comfortable and welcoming. Lockerby's office said plainly, "You're underdressed." Lockerby's expression became indulgent, almost patronizing, and he shook my hand with overfamiliarity, giving it an extra-long little squeeze. He had the gesture down pat, but his palm was unpleasantly damp.

"Thank you for seeing me on short notice," I said.

"Not at all," he replied, ushering me into an orange bentwood chair before resuming his seat behind the desk. I sat with both feet pushed against the tile floor to keep myself from sliding off the slick seat. It was low enough to give him half a head advantage over me.

"I know you're a busy man, so I'll come right to the point, shall I?"

He waved his hands in a gracious "go ahead" sort of way, crossed his fingers on his stomach, and leaned back. "Fire away, Erin."

"I understand Danbury Homes recently acquired a parcel of land near London called Redcreek Forest."

"Yes. But that's not new news," he said. "We're planning to build some beautiful condos on it." He sounded ready to launch into a sales pitch, but I plowed on briskly to show him I wasn't there to scout out real estate.

"I'm hoping to find some new angles to write about," I said. "I understand you've been negotiating for that land for some time."

"We've had our eye on it for quite a while."

"But it wasn't possible to buy it until recently?"

"No. It was owned by Clearwater Holdings, as I'm sure you know. The full story was in the paper in London."

I smiled sweetly. "Yes. I understand Clearwater put up quite a fight to buy the land when it first came up for sale two years ago."

His smile remained serenely in place. "At that time, Clearwater managed to outbid us, that's true. They had some wealthy backers. We made sure we were in a better position to purchase when it came up for resale this time."

"But why would Clearwater sell it to you after working so hard to acquire it in the first place?" I persisted.

He arched one eyebrow, trying to look knowing, but on his pudgy face the effect was rather lost. "Well, I suppose you'd have to ask Clearwater that, but I'm sure it's no surprise to you to learn we've paid quite a bit more for it than Clearwater paid when they acquired it."

"So you're saying they made a good profit on it."

"Yes. That's fair to say."

"Do you think that was their motive all along, knowing you wanted it? To dangle it in front of you until you were able to offer a higher price?"

He shifted slightly in his chair, and I saw his fingertips tap together lightly, impatiently. "Again, if you want to know their motives, you'd have to ask them."

"Sure. Thank you," I said, switching my line of questioning. "Mr. Lockerby, when was it that you first learned Clearwater was putting Redcreek up for sale? I'm surprised the media didn't make more of a fuss about it when it came on the market."

"Well, it wasn't on the public market," Lockerby said.

"What do you mean? It wasn't offered for public sale?"

"No, it was a private sale. I mean, why advertise when you know you have an eager buyer already lined up?" He flashed his white teeth at me.

I could think of a couple of reasons, including attracting other interested buyers. "They didn't want to get a bidding war going?"

"I guess not. I don't know that anyone else was interested in that property."

I found this hard to believe, but I let it go for the moment. "I suppose less publicity also meant less hassle from environmentalists," I suggested helpfully. "I believe they raised a fuss two years ago when it first came up for sale."

Lockerby spread his hands, shrugged, and smiled again.

I remembered I was supposed to be taking notes and flipped open my notebook. And turned the top page so Lockerby couldn't see my Things to Tell Vinnie list.

"How did you come to know of its availability?" I persisted, scribbling briskly.

The smile didn't flinch. "The CEO phoned me personally. He knew we'd wanted it before, you see, and he wanted to know if we remained interested."

"That would be Mr. Michael Fortier?"

I thought the smile's wattage dimmed a little. "Yes."

"How long ago was this?"

"Several weeks ago. Months, maybe. I don't know for sure."

"Still, it was a pretty quick deal, wasn't it?" I asked.

There was a sound from the lobby, and the intercom on the desk bleeped like a distressed sheep, but before whoever was on the other end could say anything, the office door opened. Harris towered there, a thunderous look on his face.

Chapter Sixteen

Junior Girl Reporter felt her stomach slide into her sensible shoes. Behind the detective, the secretary was making apologetic grimaces at Lockerby and flapping her long-nailed hands ineffectually. Harris stepped inside the office and closed the door in the woman's face.

"Excuse me!" Lockerby protested, standing. Harris stepped forward, a good foot taller than Lockerby.

"Detective Liam Harris," he said abruptly, flashing his ID. The mystery of his first name was solved, at any rate. He turned those hazel eyes on me, and I managed a weak grin and a wave.

"Fancy meeting you here," I said.

"Detective!" Lockerby said, and the smile definitely slipped from his face. "What's this about?"

"I wanted to ask you some questions," Harris replied through clenched teeth. "But it appears my friend here has beaten me out of the gate."

"I'm writing an article on urban development," I informed him. "Mr. Lockerby was just telling me how Michael Fortier phoned him personally to let him know Redcreek was available to purchase."

I figured that was as far as I was going to be allowed to go, and Harris would now summarily dismiss me. Instead, he surprised me by dropping into the chair next to me and crossing his slim legs.

Lockerby's eyes scrolled over the detective's long, lean frame, and a look of wariness crossed his chubby face.

"By all means, do carry on," Harris said with an airy gesture. "You seem to be doing admirably."

I blinked at him. "But I—"

"I'm sure we are both interested in the same questions," Harris said, gazing straight ahead and not looking at me.

I swallowed and turned back to Lockerby, who slowly resumed his seat, looking at me with uncertainty.

"All right, then. Mr. Lockerby, were you surprised to learn Clearwater was now willing to sell?"

His eyes slid from me to Harris, who sat silently, enigmatically. I could tell Lockerby had no clue what was going on, but he answered gamely enough. "We were pleased. We didn't ask a lot of questions about their change of heart."

"And did you handle the purchase yourself, Mr. Lockerby?"

"Yes, I acquire the locations for all of our developments," he replied.

"Was Mr. Fortier the only one you dealt with at Clearwater Holdings?"

"Yes, I believe so. He was one of the partners, as you know, and CEO. I don't have to tell you it was a substantial amount of money. He wouldn't have put that large a deal in the hands of a subordinate. He handled it himself."

"Have you ever known Clearwater to sell land before? Aren't they solely in the business of acquiring it?"

"It wasn't for me to question their decision to sell," Lockerby said, sounding defensive. "Maybe they'd reconsidered the environmental value of the property. Or perhaps they'd overextended themselves. They rely on private money, you know, much of it belonging to the partners themselves. The economy being what it is, I thought they must have needed the cash, if I thought of it at all."

"Did you get the feeling that anyone else at Clearwater knew that Mr. Fortier was negotiating with you over that particular piece of land?"

This seemed to give him pause. He rubbed his hands together, smoothed his perfect hair, looked out the window at the cheerless parking lot, and rubbed his nose. After a moment, he said, "I don't see why they wouldn't. I mean, I dealt only with Mr. Fortier, but I assume his partners would have known all about it. Are you implying that they didn't?"

I glanced at Harris.

"I haven't spoken to them yet, but that's certainly one of the things I'll be asking them," Harris said. I couldn't help frowning, wondering what the police did with their time. That would have been one of the first questions I'd have asked. I tried not to look irritated. Then it occurred to me that Harris might very well know the answer but was playing his cards close to his chest.

"You think Fortier sold the land without their knowledge?" Lockerby looked a little green at this.

"It does seem odd that they would change their mind about protecting that forest," I noted. "And that if they *had* decided to sell, they wouldn't try to start a bidding war between buyers."

"We're the largest developer in the London area and one of the largest in Ontario. They likely wouldn't be able to find a better buyer than us."

"You said you didn't know of any other developer who was interested in that property," I said. "Is it because they would not be able to develop it? Are you certain *you* can develop it?"

Both men looked at me blankly.

"What do you mean?" Lockerby asked.

"Well, I imagine an environmental study will have to be done on the property," I pointed out. "The city wouldn't let you just build without a land-use study."

"An environmental study was done at the request of Clearwater Holdings several months ago," Lockerby said, looking more at ease. "I have a copy if you care to see it. It states very plainly that Redcreek Forest does not hold any particular value above comparable wooded areas in southern Ontario. No endangered species. No rare habitat."

I blinked. "But it's a Carolinian forest. There's almost none left."

"If there's none left, I expect that's because it's been cut down and built on," Lockerby said with a laugh. "It's nothing that special, Miss McIntosh."

At the name, Harris straightened and cast a look at me. I ignored him. I felt as if my feet were on shifting ground. Perhaps I should have done my own research instead of relying on Cathy Lewis's impassioned information.

"I was under the impression that it was a valuable and uncommon forest," I muttered.

"Well, what can I say?" Lockerby said, shrugging. "I foresee no problem getting a building permit."

I wondered if Fortier had somehow faked the study. Could someone do that? "I'd like a copy of that environmental assessment, please."

"Certainly. I have no objection."

Harris had apparently decided we'd talked trees long enough and smiled tightly. "Mr. Lockerby, could you please explain to me the exact transaction that occurred between you and Mr. Fortier?"

I hadn't thought of that question. I poised my pen over the notebook and looked expectant.

Lockerby licked his lips. "I offered him, through my lawyer, the amount of eight million dollars. For the amount of acreage, it was more than generous."

"And he accepted the offer straight out?"

"He talked me up to ten million, Detective."

"Through your lawyer," Harris said.

"Yes."

"And how much, Mr. Lockerby, did you offer him personally, not through your lawyer?"

Lockerby stared at him, his mouth opening and closing. Harris recrossed his legs, the picture of patience. He looked like George Plimpton about to announce the next Masterpiece. When Lockerby didn't answer, Harris added, "We do have access to Fortier's personal bank account and the full cooperation of his wife."

Lockerby sighed. "He wanted a million and a half to go into his account, off the books. Clearwater wouldn't know about that part of the offer, obviously."

"So you bribed him." I couldn't help saying it.

Lockerby spread his hands again. "More like, he suggested a certain sum. I just went along with it. It's what happens in this line of business. We all got what we wanted." His polished accent was starting to slip. I detected a note of New Jersey in his voice.

I couldn't keep quiet. "Clearwater didn't. The environment didn't. The citizens of London didn't." I waited for Harris to interrupt and shush me, but he didn't.

Lockerby's smile grated on me. "The citizens of London are going to get a very progressive, valuable, beautiful asset to their community, Miss McIntosh. The businessmen of London are one hundred percent behind this project, I can tell you that. And their city will approve the development because it brings much-needed dollars into their community. You know, the provincial government and the federal government have many ways to make money, including through sales tax and income tax. But municipalities can only get their money through property tax. So what it comes down to is, condominiums pay better than trees do."

"I want to be clear on this," Harris said quickly before I could reply. "Out of the blue, Fortier calls you and offers to make the deal happen if you'll give him a million and a half."

Lockerby coughed. "Yes, well, it took a little haggling, but I guess that's a fair summation."

"And he also mentions he has miraculously managed to obtain an environmental study that would support the development of the property—or at least not hinder it."

Lockerby pursed his lips and studied his hands, rolling his gold ring around his finger thoughtfully and not meeting Harris's eyes.

"Mr. Lockerby, when did you meet with Mr. Fortier to sign this deal?" Harris asked.

"Last Wednesday. That would have been June fourteenth. It was originally set for the fifteenth, but Fortier said he had a conflict and we needed to move it up a day."

I looked at Harris. He tented his fingers in front of his mouth, looking thoughtful. "Did you meet with him in person? Did he come here?"

"I met him at a restaurant in Mississauga," Lockerby said. "For discretion's sake, we chose not to meet in either of our offices. We didn't want the media getting wind of anything until it was finalized. We signed the papers Wednesday around one o'clock, and I had the money wired that afternoon to the account numbers he gave me. Ten to Clearwater, one and a half to his personal offshore account. I received the title the same day. Registered with the land office. All very slick."

"All very fast," Harris observed. "Offshore, you say?"

"Yes. The banks here report any deposit over ten thousand to the government." And Lockerby looked at me and winked, as if this were all a great game. I kept my expression stony.

"Well, we had been negotiating for a little while, as I said," he went on. "All we had left to do was tie up the formalities."

"And no lawyers were present?"

"My lawyer was there. He had drawn up the papers. But Fortier didn't have a lawyer with him."

"Your lawyer's name, please?"

"Ted Hollingshead. I can get you his number."

"Was Mr. Hollingshead aware of the extra million and a half going into Fortier's personal account?"

"No. That was between us." Lockerby was looking rather damp around the collar by this time. I saw him glance at his watch.

"When you say you had been negotiating, does that mean you had met with Mr. Fortier previously?"

"Not in person," Lockerby said. "We had been communicating primarily by phone. I sent an e-mail once, but he called to request that I not because it would be—" He stopped short, but I knew he had been about to say "traceable."

"Ah. Then it is reasonable to assume the others at Clearwater didn't know about the transaction."

He tipped his head from side to side, grimacing. "I couldn't say. But obviously, the one and a half million wasn't something he'd want his partners to know about. That was a little extra something between us. I guess he was afraid I'd mention it in an e-mail. So we stuck to the phone. Why? Do you think Clearwater is going to contest the sale? I'll see them in court if they do." New Jersey was out in full force now.

Harris waved a dismissive hand. "It isn't important to me one way or another who owns the land or whether the sale was legally binding. Your lawyers can fight that out with Clearwater's lawyers. I'm here to investigate a homicide."

Lockerby sobered, looking pale. "Yes, I heard about that. Poor guy, to get shot like that."

"And only hours after he sold the land to you," I added.

His eyes grew wide, and he looked wildly from me to Harris. "You don't think I had anything to do with that, do you? Why would I? I had what I wanted."

"Would you want the world to hear about the bribe you paid him?" I challenged.

"Who cares?" Lockerby retorted. "It wasn't shame on me for agreeing to it. That's done all the time. It was shame on him for asking for it. If I were you, I'd be questioning the other people at Clearwater who might have found out and been upset with him about it. But I was happy with him. I was happy with the whole deal. It was signed, sealed, and delivered."

"I want to go back to what I was asking earlier," Harris said and slid a disapproving look at me for getting sidetracked. "Are you telling me that you didn't meet with Fortier personally while negotiating this deal?"

"That's right. It was all done by phone."

"Did you ever meet him in person prior to last Wednesday?"

"No, I don't think so. I have never met him in person, no."

"But you've had other dealings with him in the past, and you're telling me you've never met with him personally?" Harris asked, leaning forward to stare at him intently.

"No. That's not how business is done these days, Detective," Lockerby said. "We keep a step back, if you see what I mean."

"I can certainly see why you would," I replied sourly.

"To your knowledge, did your lawyer meet with him during the negotiations?" Harris queried.

"I'd have to ask him, but I don't think so. I think it was all done long distance, right up until the signing of the actual papers."

"If you could supply me with the account numbers of the bank accounts you transferred the money to, I'd appreciate it," Harris said.

Lockerby licked his lips. "Sure. I'll just—it might take me a minute to find them."

"Thank you. We'll wait."

Lockerby managed a sickly smile. "Sure. Always happy to help."

* * *

As we left Lockerby's office and entered the parking lot, Harris turned to me.

"McIntosh?" he asked pointedly, glaring with one eyebrow arched.

"My maiden name." Figuring the best defense was a strong offense, I asked quickly, "What are you on to? You had an idea whirling around in your head back there. I could see it."

"It just occurred to me that there was very little person-to-person contact in Fortier's life. His own wife hardly ever saw him. His secretary didn't expect him to show up at the office half the time."

"You think he was a recluse?"

"I don't know. All I know is, other than Lockerby, no one actually saw Fortier in the flesh after Saturday morning when he left detox, until he showed up in your garden without his face."

I flinched, and Harris saw it. His eyes narrowed, and he looked down at me thoughtfully.

"So," I said, "it *was* the real Fortier at detox. Where are you going with this line of thought?"

Harris glanced over his shoulder. The secretary's sullen face was watching us through the glass door. Harris caught me by the elbow and propelled me into his car.

"We can't talk here," he said and shut the door on me. When he'd situated himself behind the wheel, I pointed out to him that my car was sitting beside his. But, of course, he knew that. No doubt he had recognized it the instant he'd arrived.

"We'll come back for it," he said briefly. He started the engine and pulled into the street. I reached resignedly for my seatbelt, glad that at least so far he hadn't bitten my head off for coming to see Lockerby.

"So did the others at Clearwater know about the sale?" I asked.

"No. They do say ten million dollars appeared in their account out of nowhere. So that part of the story lines up."

Ah, so he *had* spoken to them. "Now that you have the other account number, you can find out where the other million and a half went," I said.

Harris sighed. "Not likely, if it's an offshore account. I don't hold out much hope of finding out whose account it is. I'll get my detective constable to look into it anyway."

"How did Fortier think he was going to talk his way out of this, once his partners found out about the sale of Redcreek? How would he justify it to them?"

"I don't know. Maybe by using the phony environmental study."

"So you think it's phony too?"

"Or at least fudged. Gotta be. I could see him telling his partners that the land wasn't important environmentally after all and he'd decided to try to recoup the money they'd spent on it. Maybe even make a little profit. They were partners, but he was the main man running the organization. Lately, they'd left more and more of the business in his hands. They would believe him, and if they didn't, he could always say the thought of making a profit on their original purchase just proved to be too tempting for him. They'd fuss about it and maybe ask him to resign, and he'd retire in shame—with a nice, fat bank account."

Harris paused, and it was as if I could see his brain shift, turning over. A faraway look came into his eyes. He drove for a moment, and I kept quiet, waiting to see if whatever he was thinking would come out. When he spoke again, it sounded as if he'd forgotten I was there and he was merely musing aloud. "How does Lockerby know for sure that it was even Fortier who showed up at that restaurant and signed those papers?"

My mouth fell open, and I forgot about keeping quiet. "Do you think it wasn't?"

He looked at me then back at the road. "Think about it, Erin. Lockerby had never met him. He just assumed it was Fortier. The man introduced himself as Fortier; he showed up when they'd arranged to meet. But do we know it was actually Fortier?"

"As far as we know, nobody else even knew about the deal," I pointed out. "They'd spoken on the phone several times. Are you saying it wasn't Fortier? Then who did Lockerby make the deal with? Who did he transfer the money to? The title was real, wasn't it? He registered it at the land office without any trouble."

"We do have two Fortiers to choose from. I should compare the signature on the contract with Fortier's known handwriting."

"Good idea," I agreed. "And you could also compare it to the impostor's signature in my guest book."

"Right. You know, I should have asked Lockerby for the phone number where he contacted Fortier. Was it his office number or a cell phone?"

"Ah. Good question. Maybe it wasn't Fortier's number at all. If you can find out whose number it was, you'll have the impostor."

"On that same note," Harris said slowly, "how do we know it was Fortier who sent those e-mails to his wife from his Blackberry?" He shifted his eyes to look at me. "They were sent on Tuesday, just as Andrea claimed. I checked. They originated from Mississauga, not Sault Ste. Marie. You can tell by the tower that relayed the messages. He also e-mailed his office a couple of times on Monday and Tuesday. Nothing important, just normal business."

"No startling announcements like 'I'm about to sell Redcreek Forest to a developer'?"

Harris shook his head. "But there's no way to know if it was Fortier who sent them. Just that it was his Blackberry that was used."

"Go on, I'm following you," I prompted.

"He switched his appointment with Lockerby from Thursday to Wednesday. Is that significant? Why would he do that?" he mused.

"I can answer that one," I said. "Dr. Meacham was due to see Michael Fortier on Thursday for an appointment. Callum would have recognized right away that it was an impostor and not the same man who had been in his detox center. When the impostor found out Callum was coming on Thursday, he moved up the appointment with Lockerby so that the deal could be done and he could be far away before Callum could come and blow his cover."

Harris glanced thoughtfully at me and then nodded. "You think well," he said a little grudgingly. "You ask good questions."

"The questions are easy. It's the answers that are hard."

"Not at all," he replied. He glanced over his shoulder and merged the car smoothly into the steady stream of traffic on the Queensway. I wondered how far we were going to go before he returned me to my car. "The hardest part of this job is figuring out which questions to ask," he went on. "You can figure them out better than some I've seen in this job. And people seem to respond when you ask them."

If this was the reason he had let me remain at Lockerby's interview, he didn't say so, but I sat back in my seat, feeling a little smug. Harris was silent a moment, and then, as if driving and thinking were too difficult to do at the same time, he pulled the car over into the parking lot of a hamburger joint a few kilometers from Lockerby's office.

"I should throw you in jail for interfering with an investigation," he said conversationally. "But I'm not going to. In fact, I think I'm glad you were there today after all. You got Lockerby loosened up and talking before I got there, and since he was on a roll, he just kept talking, probably more than he would have if I had been the one to start the interrogation."

I felt ridiculously pleased at the praise but kept my face carefully expressionless.

He reached for his door handle. "All this thinking is making me hungry. Do you want a hamburger?"

"How can you think of food while there's a murderer running around out there?"

"Do you want a milkshake with it?"

"Strawberry."

Chapter Seventeen

When Harris returned me to my car half an hour later, I asked if he was heading back to Mississauga.

"Yes, why?"

"Can I sidetrack you for a little while?"

He shot me an enigmatic look. "So what's new?" he muttered.

"Just meet me at the Credit River Cemetery. I want to show you something."

* * *

He tailed me all the way back to town, and every time I looked at him in the rearview mirror, he made faces at me. Once, he stuck his thumbs in his ears and wiggled his fingers. He kept his customary solemn look on his face while he did it, and I couldn't help laughing. I couldn't quite figure this Liam Harris out, but it was fun trying. The song in my head was now "Father, This Hour Has Been One of Joy," and when I realized it, I was brought up a little short. Was that really how I was feeling? Bodies in the garden, a killer on the loose, and I was *enjoying* myself? Well, actually . . . yes. A little.

We parked in the cemetery parking lot and walked up the slope together. The heat of the day had faded, and a fresh breeze blew in from the river, bringing with it the scent of flowers. There were few people about, just a couple of black-dressed women by the war memorial and three or four people scattered around, paying their respects at different graves. None of them paid us any attention. I took Harris to the area where the marigolds were planted, one after the other. I pointed out the headstones.

"What about them?" he asked.

"It's another mystery for you to solve," I explained. "My neighbor is an elderly lady who lives alone—she never married. She comes here often, and she brings flowers to these eleven graves. I can't think why. I mean, they can't all be her relatives. If she just has a soft spot for children, there are children buried all over the cemetery. Why does she focus just on these?"

Harris put his hands in his pockets, considering the rows of small stones, all with their similar inscriptions. He walked slowly down the line, reading each one. A pensive look came over his face.

"None of them has others buried around them with the same surname. No parents, no siblings," he observed. He straightened and looked around, and I thought he was looking for landmarks, getting his bearings. Then he turned to me with a sad little nod.

"This is the Children's Services section."

"The what?"

"The Children's Aid Society has a section of the cemetery where they bury children who die while they're in their care. Technically, when the CAS has custody of a child, they are legally the child's parent. They're responsible for providing a burial place if that child dies while in their care."

I looked at the rows of stones, aghast. "They were all wards of CAS?"

"Yes, I think so."

"That's dreadful."

"Not really. I think it's kind of nice that they're here together."

I felt a funny prickle in the back of my throat. "I seem to remember someone once telling me Hilda Turner used to be a social worker when she was young. I guess she took on the task of caring for these graves as an act of service. I didn't know."

"Mystery solved?"

"Yes. But this is awful."

"Why?" Harris asked gently.

"Because Hilda is in the hospital with a bad heart, and I don't think she's expected to recover. I'm watching her dog for her. If she dies, who will take care of these children's graves?"

Harris stood looking at me for a moment, and then he surprised me by reaching out a lean arm and putting it around my shoulders. It was a light but comforting weight, his hand warm on my shoulder. As we turned and began walking away, he said in a low voice, "I guess we will."

We walked in silence a moment, and then I nodded at a spot ten feet away. "That's where my husband is buried."

Without speaking, Harris turned and went toward the spot, his arm still around me. We came to a stop in front of Robert's stone and stood looking at it a moment. I bent and removed the now-dead flowers I'd placed there a few weeks before, and Harris's arm slipped back to his side. It was a mild summer afternoon, but I felt suddenly cold without his touch.

"Jennie doesn't come here any more than she has to," I remarked, placing the flowers in the nearby trash can.

"It's hard for a kid to lose her parent. She was what, ten?"

"Yes. It's been three years, but she's still taking it hard."

"Can I ask what happened?"

I looked away, over at the pond with its musical fountain. There were pop cans floating at the edge of it. Had someone sat there and toasted a lost loved one? A midnight picnic, maybe?

"Jennie knows her father died in a car accident," I said slowly. "Someone ran a red light and T-boned his car. What Jennie doesn't know is that his girlfriend was in the car with him at the time."

Harris said nothing. I glanced at him but couldn't read the expression in his hazel eyes. I looked away again. "She had three cracked ribs and a broken wrist. He died instantly. She's living in Toronto now."

"Had you known?" Harris asked quietly.

"About the girlfriend? Yes, for a few weeks. She was someone we knew at church. Her husband had left her, and I guess she'd turned to mine for sympathy. And he was happy to play the rescuing hero. It's especially awful when you consider the emphasis our religion puts on marriage and family. It wasn't supposed to happen like that."

"No."

"I didn't clue in until it had been going on for a while." I scuffed the grass with the toe of my shoe. "I was still deciding what to do about it when the decision . . . became unnecessary."

"I'm sorry."

"Me too. Our marriage started off all right. We were happy for years. I'd rather Jennie remember that part."

"There's nothing to gain from telling her every detail," he agreed.

"If she ever looks it up, the newspaper account of the accident mentions that a woman was in the car with him. If Jennie ever asks me, I'll have to tell her. But she's still so young, and she loved her father. I don't think she could carry the whole burden yet." I hesitated then thought, *In for a penny, in for a pound.* "I think part of what went wrong between me and Robert is that when I had Jennie, there were problems with the delivery. I wasn't able to have any more children after her."

"And your husband took that hard?"

"Harder than I did, I think. I was just glad to have Jennie. Much as he loved her, she wasn't enough for Robert. *I* wasn't enough for Robert. I guess he felt he needed one more great adventure."

We were silent a minute, and then Harris cleared his throat as if he'd made a decision. He pronounced starkly, "Robert was an idiot."

I couldn't help smiling. "Thanks for that. I think I agree with you."

Harris reached out a slim finger and lightly touched the top of the stone, almost placatingly, as if apologizing for what he'd said. It was a surprisingly sweet gesture.

"So what about you?" I asked lightly. "Ever married?"

"I've come close once or twice," Harris said. It was his turn to look over at the shimmering pond. "Each time, I decided I liked the girl too much to inflict myself on her. A homicide detective is impossible to live with. What did your husband do for a living?"

"He was a high school science teacher and wrestling coach. Have you always wanted to be a detective?"

"Not always. Just since I was about three." He gave a slow half smile, self-deprecating, that didn't reach his eyes.

"You've found what you love to do, then."

"At least until a rich uncle leaves me his fortune and I can retire."

"Do you have any prospects?" I asked with a smile.

"None whatsoever. My only uncle is a ticket-taker on the Pittsburgh transit system. He lives with three cats in a one-room apartment above a laundromat. And have you always wanted to run a rehab center?"

I shook my head. "That's just a new venture since Robert died. I used to be a hospital social worker, helping patients find community resources, things like that. After the accident, I wanted something I could do at home so I could be near Jennie. I knew Callum from the hospital. He suggested there was a real need for inpatient addictions treatment. We bounced around the idea of opening detox and rehab programs in tandem. When I saw the real estate ad for a ramshackle, nineteenth-century convent in need of fixing up, I knew it was what I was supposed to do."

"That's brave."

"That's desperate," I corrected. "I've never done a brave thing in my life."

The look Harris turned on me was genuinely surprised. "What are you talking about? Everything you do is brave."

"I'm the least brave person I know," I protested. "I've never been fearless like Robert was. I feel like I'm forever sprinting from problem to problem, staying just one step ahead of catastrophe. Never solving anything. I'm terrified of failing. I worry constantly."

"The very fact that you keep moving is brave. A lot of other women would crawl under the bedcovers and never come out if they had to face what you face every day."

I felt tears forming a tight ache in my throat and shook my head, scowling to keep them back. Frankly, I wasn't used to gentle treatment, and his kindness, on top of the bishop's concern, threatened to reduce me to a puddle of self-pity. The thought of melting in front of Harris made my jaw tighten. In spite of my effort to hide it, Harris saw my struggle and put a warm, heavy hand on my shoulder.

"Look at what you've accomplished, Erin. Give yourself some credit. Do you honestly not see it?"

I couldn't speak—only shake my head. He sighed, sounding tired.

"You've renovated that place into a welcoming and beautiful home. You run your own business very capably—and not a comfortable little business, either, but a difficult and important one dealing with real issues. You're raising a daughter on your own, who seems to be turning out just fine. You handle everything in your path with ease, including dead bodies turning up in your yard."

I tossed my head and blurted out before I could stop myself, "Oh yeah, I'm really brave about that. I don't feel like I've slept since I found him."

There was a pause as he studied me. Why had I told him? I kept my eyes turned away, ashamed at my admission.

"The image will fade after awhile," he said softly. "Trust me. I know."

There wasn't pity in his voice or contempt for my weakness. He did know. And I did trust him. I dashed the back of my hand over my eyes, and Harris politely put his hands in his pockets and looked out over the hillside while I got myself under control again.

"Sorry about that," I muttered. "I'm okay now."

He gave a low chuckle. "No you aren't." Then he added, "But you will be."

I ran my fingers through my bangs and looked up at him. "Yeah, I will be. Thanks."

"Next time, say something sooner," Harris said. As if there would be a next time.

"Why? I'm not your problem."

He glanced sidelong at me and said dryly, "No?"

"Anyway, thanks for letting me drag you out here," I went on. "And for solving the mystery of Hilda Turner."

"It's what I'm best at," he replied.

Chapter Eighteen

When Harris showed up Monday morning, somehow I wasn't surprised. I'd had a restless night again but not for the usual reason this time. For once, I hadn't thought about the scene in the garden at all. My mind had been churning with ideas all night, and I'd hoped for the chance to talk to Harris about them.

"Jennie and I were just about to go riding," I told him by way of explaining my tall boots and hard black hat. "Want to come?"

"Yeah! Please do, Detective Harris!" Jennie chimed in. She looked especially pretty this morning with her hair in a long braid down her back and her new cream riding pants (a gift from her grandparents) still mercifully clean.

To his credit, Harris only hesitated for a second before agreeing. From the look on his face, I doubted he'd ever been on a horse, but I admired his pluck for trying. It took only a few moments to find him some boots and a protective hat that fit. We walked down to the stable together, feet crunching on gravel and Jennie bouncing ahead of us like an overjoyed puppy. Greg Ng saw us coming, and for a brief moment, I thought he would dart back into the stable. I was sorry to trouble him by invading his animals-only domain, but after all, it was what I'd hired him for, wasn't it? He glanced only once at Harris and then turned his attention solely to Jennie.

Jennie preferred Dancer, a placid Appaloosa that never lived up to her name. While Greg helped her with the tack, I walked down the aisle to a far stall, where my personal favorite stood watching alertly. Empress was a Paso Fino, a bit smaller than the other horses and a beautiful dappled gray. True to her breed, she had the smoothest gait in the world, ideal for therapeutic riding. She also had hard hooves that required no shoeing, a definite plus for a frugal owner. Willing and strong, she would be the perfect mount for Harris.

I selected a bay quarter horse for myself, named (by Jennie, with complete disregard for the mare's gender) Luke Skywalker. Harris managed to climb aboard Empress with a modicum of grace. Greg hid a definite grin as the detective settled himself into the saddle, and we were off.

The morning was clear and pleasant, the breeze light, and for a while, we rode in peace, just enjoying the outing. We kept to the pasture, since I wasn't sure if Harris had enough experience to chance riding on the road. For a while, Jennie stuck with us, casting approving looks at Harris from time to time, but after awhile, she grew bored with us old people and cantered ahead to do her own thing. Harris watched her go and then carefully pulled his mare closer to mine.

Once Jennie was out of earshot, he spoke.

"He'd cancelled them."

I looked at him. "What?"

"Fortier. He'd originally been scheduled to go on those business trips. But about a month before them, he cancelled. He told his secretary about going into rehab, and they agreed on how to cover it up. Make people—including his own wife—think the business meetings were still on, so no one would hear about rehab and judge him. And no one would expect to see him around the office for a while."

"I thought you said the secretary didn't know about detox."

"I sent my constable over to ask again, and the secretary broke down and confessed about the cover-up. It was done to protect the reputation of the CEO of the company, after all. It's understandable."

"So the secretary did know more about Fortier's life than his own wife did," I remarked sadly.

Harris nodded. "I have a theory," he said. "Hear me out before you laugh at me."

"Okay." Like I would say no? Like anyone would ever laugh at that grim, keen face?

"To recap: someone impersonated Michael Fortier at your center. It's not impossible to think that someone also impersonated Fortier when he met with Lockerby on Wednesday."

"I concede it's not impossible," I said.

"And if so, I think we can assume it would be the same person. I can't imagine two fake Fortiers running around."

"Agreed," I said. "That would be excessive. My fake Fortier was on the field trip to the waterfall Wednesday morning, but he was on his own briefly afterward. He told my staff he was going to the bank and would come straight back, but he didn't get back until an hour and fifteen minutes after everyone else. That's a long time to go banking. He could have gotten to his appointment with Lockerby by one o'clock, had a quick lunch, signed the papers, and returned to the center by two fifteen. Did you want to compare the signature on the contract to the signature in my logbook?"

"I'll take the book with me today, if I may," Harris said, nodding approvingly.

"Just the relevant page," I said. "There's no need to break the confidentiality of all my past patients, surely."

Harris sighed. "Just the relevant page," he agreed. "Now listen."

"I'm listening."

"The fake Fortier at your center made a point of being memorable. He made sure you would all remember he was there. He spoke to everyone, interacted with everyone, was very personable and chatty. He fought with one guest."

"And kissed another one," I added. "Remember Eva at the waterfall. She said it meant nothing, it was just friendly, but she certainly remembered it anyway."

"It just bolsters my theory," Harris said, looking pleased. "Fake Fortier made sure you wouldn't forget him, to the point of acting out of character. The real Fortier wasn't chatty and personable. And he wasn't prone to flirting with women, if we can believe his wife."

"I think if she says he wasn't, we can assume for the time being that he wasn't. And whether he actually was or not isn't germane to the point, is it?"

"No. The only reason I can think of for someone to make a point of being so memorable," Harris went on, "is so he could establish in your minds the very fact that he was there at that specific time."

"That thought had occurred to me too," I said.

"You, your staff, and your other guests are all his alibi. He could use you to prove that Fortier was alive and well on those dates, at that certain vital period of time."

"I see where you're going," I said. "And the one thing that was so vital about that particular time—"

"The only critical thing we know of that happened during that period of time was the finalization of the Redcreek sale."

I nodded enthusiastically. "And there's really no reason to be emphatic about the fact that Fortier was at the center—to make a point of it—unless it was to cover the fact that the real Fortier actually wasn't."

Harris inadvertently tightened his grip on the reins, and Empress obligingly came to a dead stop. He maintained his balance and looked down at her twitching ears, a little surprised.

"Did we run out of gas?" he asked mildly. "Was it something I said?"

"Relax your grip."

He did, and Empress calmly started forward again. Harris looked thoughtful. "If only my detective constable were that responsive," he mused. "You were saying?"

"I was saying we can plausibly conclude that this man was impersonating Fortier so that the world would think Fortier was still alive when he wasn't. So that the world would believe this land deal was signed by the real Fortier, when in fact it wasn't."

"But aren't you forgetting something?" I asked. "According to the coroner, Fortier *was* alive and well at that time. He was alive all week, up until late Wednesday or early Thursday."

We thought for a moment, the only sound the horses' feet plodding amiably along. Far ahead of us, Jennie turned and waved. We waved back.

"But what if he wasn't where people assumed he was? What if he was somewhere else, up to something else at the time, so he had someone else sign for him?"

"Are you saying Michael Fortier engineered this whole thing himself?" I asked. "If he couldn't make it to the appointment with Lockerby, he would have just said so and postponed the signing of the deal."

"Unless it had to be signed at a certain time," Harris pointed out.

"Why would it be? What restrictions were there? It hadn't gone public yet. There was no chance of it doing so until he and Lockerby announced it. Was there some other time constraint?"

"That's what I don't know," he said, deflated. We were silent again. When I looked up, he was looking at me. He really did have the most amazing eyes, close up.

"You have a quick eye for people and good instincts for what they're like," he said, nudging Empress with his knees so she moved closer to Skywalker. He was getting the hang of her smooth rhythm. If it weren't for his incongruous suit jacket, he'd look quite natural on horseback. "You met the fake Fortier. You interacted quite closely with him for a few days in your center. You've met all the principal players. So tell me what you're thinking. Are we on the wrong track? What other reason could this man have for impersonating Fortier?"

I studied Skywalker's bobbing head. "What if it wasn't that he was somewhere else, doing something else?" I said slowly. "What if Fortier was prohibited somehow from signing the deal himself?"

"Prohibited how?" he asked.

"Confined against his will?" I suggested. "You said it yourself: no one saw him in the flesh after he left detox that Saturday. And someone else could have been sending those e-mails with Fortier's Blackberry on Monday and Tuesday. Say, a rabid environmentalist like Cathy Lewis—"

"Cathy? Your patient? How did she get into this conversation?"

"Just hear me out." I glanced around, even though I knew full well that Cathy was currently in a session with Theresa and her sisters and couldn't possibly hear us out here in the field. "Cathy has a brief history of assault when she loses her temper. She once lived in London and is very opposed to the idea of condos being built practically in her old backyard. And she's anxious to preserve the Carolinian forest. So what if this environmentalist-who-may-or-may-not-be-Cathy gets wind of the deal and wants to stop it? She has means and motive. She kidnaps Fortier so he can't follow through with the deal."

"Wouldn't it be more effective to just expose the proposed deal to the media?"

I ignored his derisive tone. "But someone else who knows about it decides to take it upon himself to hide the kidnapping from the authorities, impersonate Fortier, and go through with the deal on his behalf."

"And pulls it all together within the hour after Fortier disappears? It's starting to sound like a Wagnerian opera." Harris shook his head. "Too many players. Too many unknowns. Too many people knowing about the land deal that hadn't been announced yet."

"If it weren't for the impostor, I think Cathy would fit the bill for the murder very well," I replied.

"Maybe so, but there are still too many questions." He held up one hand and ticked off each item on his fingers as he listed them. "How would she know about the land sale in the first place? How would she know to find Fortier as he was just coming out of detox on Saturday and no one knew he was there? Why would she have kept him alive until Wednesday night and then killed him? And we can't ignore the impostor. Whatever the solution, it has to take him into account."

"Well, true, but—"

"Cathy would know Fake Fortier was a fake, if she had kidnapped the real one. She'd have exposed him the minute he walked into the center."

"Not necessarily. To do so, she'd have to admit she knew the real Fortier. What would she say, 'I know you're a fake because I have the real one tied up in my basement'? Remember, she'd have to kill Fortier eventually; she could never let him just go free. He'd rat out the whole thing. And he could still sell the land the minute she released him."

"You're right; Fortier would have to die. But it's still overly complicated. And it isn't possible that it's Cathy because you would know if she'd left the center to do a spot of kidnapping. She didn't have Fortier tied up in *your* basement, did she?"

"Oh, all right," I said. "Not Cathy then. But someone."

"Why wouldn't the impostor just expose the kidnapping and rescue Fortier? Why go to the bother of impersonating him at all? All he would have had to do was tell the police what he knew, and eventually— hopefully— Fortier would have been rescued and been free to sign the deal himself."

"Okay, okay, what about this?" I said. "It's not that Fortier *couldn't* sign the deal. It's that he *wouldn't*."

I could see a spark light Harris's eyes. He gave his thigh a light punch, and Empress turned her head and blew through her lips at him.

"That makes sense," he said triumphantly. "It fits with what we know of Fortier's personality." He patted Empress on the neck.

"And it validates Andrea Fortier's opinion of him," I pointed out. "She said he'd never sell Redcreek. Maybe we should believe her. He wouldn't."

"So someone wants the deal to go through, but Fortier won't do it. That someone puts Fortier out of commission for a while and hires an actor to impersonate Fortier and sign the deal on his behalf. He couldn't kill the real Fortier right away because the coroner would be able to determine the time of death, and everyone would know he wasn't alive when the deal was signed. It would bring the validity of it into question. So he detained Fortier somehow. Abducted him, locked him up somewhere. Then once the deal went through, there was no choice but to kill Fortier at that point."

"So who is the somebody?" I asked.

"Who stood to benefit from this deal?" Harris asked.

"The other partners at Clearwater just got ten million dollars richer," I pointed out.

"They also have a nasty mess on their hands, trying to placate the hundreds of people who donated money two years ago so Clearwater could buy Redcreek in the first place. It's going to be a big headache for them. I can't see them bringing it on themselves voluntarily. We have someone looking into it to see if it also constitutes fraud."

"That's what I thought too. But the partners would have been in a position to know Fortier's movements, maybe even to swipe his Blackberry."

"All right, I won't dismiss them from the suspect list yet," Harris said. "Even though all three of them are over seventy-five."

"Who else would benefit? Obviously Lockerby and Danbury Homes," I said. "Lockerby would be high on my list."

"Mine too. If I were Lockerby, I wouldn't start cutting down trees just yet," Harris said with satisfaction.

"Do you think he gave you the real account number where he sent the million and a half?"

"Easy enough to find out. We're working on it. If it turns out to be bogus, he knows I'll be back to see him."

"If it isn't traceable—or if he thinks it isn't traceable . . ."

"What?" Harris was watching me closely.

"Maybe it belongs to Lockerby himself."

Harris looked surprised at my suggestion. "Redirecting company funds to pad his own wallet?"

"It's a possibility. It sweetens the deal a little and gives him all the more motive to see this deal through. He could say the money went to

Fortier when it didn't. Fortier isn't here to argue one way or another. But surely Lockerby wouldn't be that stupid. He's got to know he must be your top suspect."

We had reached the far end of the pasture and turned to follow the fence eastward. Jennie was in the center of the field now, trying to coax Dancer over a makeshift jump made from two buckets and a two-by-four. Dancer was sensibly having none of it, so I didn't fret over my daughter's safety.

"What was your impression of Lockerby?" Harris asked.

I turned back to him and shook my head. "Lockerby is all suit and no substance. No ethics, and I wouldn't trust him farther than I could throw him. But I don't get the impression he's a brilliant, devious mastermind. I think he's a pretty straightforward crook. Dishonest, yes, but clever, no."

Harris arched an eyebrow at me. "Your point being?"

"Bank accounts aside, a scheme like this would also involve finding a look-alike to impersonate Fortier and planting him at the center. It would take a lot of knowledge and a lot of guts, and Lockerby doesn't strike me as having either."

"True."

"And if Fortier's own wife didn't know he was going into detox, how would Lockerby know? I mean, it's a good ruse, to make the switch after detox on the way to my center. His wife wouldn't be expecting him home. As far as the world knew, Fortier was up north for business. And the staff and I hadn't ever met Fortier and wouldn't be able to tell the fake one from the real one. But how would Lockerby know all that to use it?"

"The whole idea is pretty daring, considering he didn't even personally know the man he needed to have impersonated," Harris pointed out.

"So he says. Anyway, it would be tricky for Lockerby to pull it off, especially in this way."

"Agreed," Harris said, and the corner of his lips twitched. "So what are you thinking?"

"If it wasn't Lockerby, who else wanted the deal to go through? Do we have anyone else? Who else stood to benefit from it?" I asked.

"The person who shared Fortier's bank account?" Harris suggested.

"You're still determined to pin this on Andrea Fortier, aren't you?" I accused. "But she didn't know he was going into detox. She thought he was on his business trips."

"So *she* says. She had access to everything: the bank account, the Blackberry—and through it, his e-mails, phone, and calendar. She could convince the world Fortier was alive and going on about his regular business, and no one would question it." Harris stopped, a sudden confused look on his face. He'd finally realized he had moved beyond theorizing and was discussing a case in detail with a member of the public. My heart sank when I saw that expression. I'd been having such fun too.

"I can't see any harm in bouncing theories around," I said quickly. "You're not *telling* me anything I don't already know."

Harris gave a low cough and shifted in the saddle. "Well . . ."

"Just tell me this," I went on. "If Andrea did know about detox and saw it as her chance to bump him off and make a packet, I could maybe understand it. But why not just call my center and say 'My husband decided he doesn't want to come after all,' instead of sending an impostor? Why not just send the impostor to the meeting with Lockerby and miss my center all together?"

"As we said, maybe it was to establish witnesses to the fact that he was 'alive and well' at that moment. I agree it does seem overly convoluted," Harris said.

"I thought the ruling principle of detective work was that the simple explanation is usually the true one. I don't think she did it. It would be too easy to point to the money in the bank account and say she had a motive. She's too smart to leave herself that wide open."

"All right, all right. Do you have a better suspect in mind?" Harris asked.

"No. I guess we're back to Lockerby again."

He let out a bark that I think was supposed to pass for a laugh and shook his head. He ran his free hand down his face and suddenly looked tired and much older. Without speaking, we turned the horses back toward the stable.

Chapter Nineteen

When Harris had driven off with the page from the guest log, I went back to my cottage to phone the hospital. The house was quiet; there was no sign—surprise, surprise—of the renovators. There was a message on my answering machine from Sister Watson, telling me that Hilda Turner had died that morning.

I had braced myself for that possibility, but it was still a shock to think she was gone so quickly. While I'd been plodding around the pasture with Harris, a woman had been breathing her last, alone. I suddenly felt bereft. I should have been there with her.

I phoned Sister Watson back to offer to help with the funeral. Jennie returned from her ride, and after my call, I found her in her room, listening to her stereo and rubbing Dribbles's ears as he lay sprawled on her bed. When I came in, she guiltily started to push him off the quilt, but I shook my head.

"He can stay there. In fact, it looks like he's here to stay, honey. Sister Turner passed away this morning."

"Oh no!" Jennie's mouth dropped open, and she curled her arms comfortingly around Dribbles's neck. "Oh, you poor boy. Do you think he understands she's gone, Mom?"

"I don't know." I sat on the edge of the bed and roughed the dog's woolly head. He gave me an enthusiastic lick. "But he does understand that he's in a safe, comfortable place, where people love him and will take care of him."

Jennie nodded, and I saw a tear slip down her cheek.

"We're going to keep him, then?"

"That's the plan, unless someone in her family wants him." I doubted it, since no one had inquired about him all this time. I hesitated, and then I told her what I had found out about Hilda Turner's ongoing act of compassion at the cemetery. Jennie thought about this a moment and then looked up at me with shining eyes.

"We'll have to take over doing it for her now," she said firmly.

"We?"

"Yes. I want to help."

"I thought you didn't like going to the cemetery, honey," I said, touched.

Jennie shook her head, her braid bouncing against her shoulders. "I don't. But I will for this. Somebody has to do it, Mom. I *want* to do it. It will be like saying thank you for Dribbles." She shot me a fierce look, the tears trembling on her lashes but not falling. "It's just a few flowers once in a while, right?"

"Yes," I said, pulling her into a hug. "Just a few flowers." But it meant so much more than that.

* * *

Monday morning, David Metcalfe was discharged from the center after completion of his program, returning to Windsor with promises to stay in touch with us. I doubted he would; I thought he would be one of our successful cases. Each time we discharged a patient, though, I couldn't help wondering if we were sending a murderer out into the community. I didn't think so, but could I be sure?

As soon as things had settled with the discharge and after a discussion with the therapists, I decided Grant could stay on as my handyman. I was glad I wasn't going to be losing touch with him too. My bookings were winding up for the summer, and I suggested to Jennie that we let Callum and the staff know we were going to close up for two weeks in August. I decided that was probably the best thing for our little family after everything that had been happening. I couldn't afford a trip to Nova Scotia to see Robert's parents, but I could manage Peterborough, three hours away, to see mine.

"Can Dribbles come too?" she asked immediately. "I don't want to go if it means putting him in a kennel."

"Yes, he can come too," I assured her. "Will it be good to get out of here for a while?"

"I don't know," she said, shrugging. "I like it here."

"It's been a pretty upsetting summer so far," I added, watching her reaction. But she only nodded.

"A lot has happened," she said. "But something good has come out of it, anyway."

"You mean Dribbles?"

"Well, yes, him. But also Detective Harris."

I frowned. "What do you mean, Jennie?"

My daughter merely grinned impishly back at me. Flipping her braid over her shoulder, she whistled to Dribbles and left the room.

Volunteers from the Therapeutic Riding Association arrived that morning. With much talking, laughing, and getting in everyone's way, they managed to get their riders into safety gear and out the door. They only took a few at a time, generally, and usually had at least two volunteers per rider—one to help guide the horse if needed and one to walk beside the rider's foot and offer encouragement and instruction. I'd seen the riding program instill confidence in timid patients, self-esteem in despairing ones, and a sense of purpose and usefulness in others. In Jason's case, it had also seemed to help with his coordination and balance. If nothing else, I figured the program reminded my guests that, if they were able to control a large, intimidating animal, such as a horse, they could surely control themselves as well. For many of them, it was the only experience they'd had in a long time with being in control of anything.

At ten o'clock, I found Jennie hovering near the front window, once again in her riding pants and hat. Before I had time to ask her what she was up to, the doorbell rang. Jennie jumped to answer it, and I knew, even before seeing the happiness on her face, that it was Ed.

"Hey, Jennie," he greeted her, blue-haired and bejangled with piercings as always. But today he wore a conservative polo shirt and ordinary jeans—no black, no rips, and only the requisite number of zippers. In fact, his clothes looked positively normal. He caught sight of me behind her and said cheerfully, "Hey, Mrs. Kilpatrick."

Jennie hadn't realized I was there. She started and looked up at me with a mixture of defensiveness and hope. I smiled. "Have fun, you two," I said.

Relief spread over her face. "We will." She grabbed Ed's arm and towed him to the back door and out.

I went into the backyard and watched them make their way to the barn. Greg Ng was standing by the paddock, watching the last of the volunteers get their rider up on a chestnut mare. As they moved away, Greg turned and saw Jennie and Ed coming. I watched with surprise as taciturn Greg broke into a broad grin, and I heard him call out, "Hi, Ed! You're back for another try?"

The two exchanged a high-five, and Greg punched Ed lightly in the shoulder.

"Sure am," Ed said. "Give me one with some spirit this time."

Greg went into the barn. Jennie and Ed bent their heads close together, talking in tones too low for me to overhear. They both laughed, and I saw Ed nudge Jennie gently with his elbow. After a few minutes, Greg reappeared, leading Thundercloud and our smallest mare, who had the unfortunate name of Buttercup (again, Jennie's doing, not mine).

"Good enough?" Greg asked. I was still startled to hear his voice. I'd grown accustomed to his silence.

"That'll do," Ed replied. He turned and cupped his hands together for Jennie to step into and helped her onto Buttercup then mounted Thundercloud himself. Greg went into the barn again and returned with Empress. I could see her dancing, eager to join the other horses. Greg mounted and rode ahead, with Ed and Jennie following behind at a circumspect walk, heading for the back pasture, where the other riders were getting underway with their exercises. I watched Ed and Jennie go, straight-backed, knees nearly touching with the nearness of their horses, the sun lighting their blue and gold hair.

Jennie probably finds the riding as therapeutic as Ed and the other patients do, I thought as I turned back toward the house. We could all find a little healing in nature. She and I both needed healing, I knew. And then the idea occurred to me that maybe Greg did too. I turned and looked back, but they'd already disappeared from view.

* * *

Now that there was a lull, I went back over to the cottage to see how Vinnie and his men were coming along with the kitchen. At least they'd shown up to work. Vinnie assured me with many smiles and expressive gestures that they would be finished within the week and I would have no more electrical problems whatsoever for the rest of my life, world without end, yada yada—all of which only told me that he had no clue what was wrong with my wiring, the kitchen would remain a war zone for at least another month, and he would likely be significantly over budget.

"I will do my best job for you," Vinnie vowed, one hand on his Roman heart. "I treat you like my own mother."

"This is the mother in a subsidized nursing home in Scarborough?" I pointed out. "This is the mother you haven't visited in six months?"

Vinnie's face took on a pained expression. "You question I know my job?"

I ran a hand through my bangs and let out a deep sigh. "No. I'm sorry, Vinnie. I know you are good at what you do. I'm just impatient. It feels like we've been renovating for years."

Vinnie tipped his head to one side and gave me a long, perceptive look. Then he reached out and very softly touched my cheek with one calloused finger. The gesture surprised me but warmed me too. "You work too hard. You have too many worries," he said.

"No, what I have is too much mess in my house," I said ruefully. "And not enough dollars in my bank account."

"What you need is a good man around to take care of you," he said, stepping closer. He drew his shoulders back to make himself look taller and looked down his prominent nose at me. His dark eyes glittered. I could smell paint thinner and chalk dust on his clothes. I was too taken aback to move right away, and Vinnie, taking this as an encouraging sign, put a none-too-clean hand on my shoulder and massaged it. "You need a man to take away all your worries."

I couldn't help laughing. "What I need is my kitchen back. I'm going squirrelly without it, Vinnie." And then I added for his benefit, "You know a woman can't be happy away from her oven for very long."

This, bless his male Italian heart, he understood. My contractor waved a hand airily, as if the unfinished drywall, doorless cupboards, empty window frame, and disassembled sink were a mere trifle. "You go have lunch, *bella*," he said gently. "When you come back this afternoon, you will have your kitchen back."

"Yes, well, that's a lovely thought, anyway," I sighed.

When I returned to the center, Callum had just arrived. He greeted me with a formal handshake as always, but when we went into my office, he closed the door behind us and gave me a swift kiss on the cheek. Bending down to my height, he looked me in the eye.

"How are you holding up, Erin?"

"Okay," I told him. "But I'm thinking of taking off the first two weeks of August. Things are slower then, and I think the place can get by without me for a few days. If there are no incoming guests, I'll shut the whole place down for a holiday and go see my parents."

"An excellent idea. You haven't taken a break since you opened Whole-Life."

"Look who's talking," I said. "You haven't taken a vacation since you started med school."

"Nonsense. There was that conference in New York."

"Two days in a hotel conference room doesn't count as a vacation," I said.

"Well then, I'll have to take a break too," Callum said, and his handsome face took on a speculative look. "Your parents are in Peterborough, aren't they? Do you think maybe they'd have room for one more? I could get in some hiking. I've heard it's a nice area. We could go boating one day."

As he spoke, he slowly moved closer to me, and now he stood mere inches away, looking down at me with half-lidded blue eyes. I suppose ordinarily I would have been surprised, maybe even pleased, at this obvious show of interest, but after my encounter only moments before with the amorous Vinnie, I wasn't in the mood for this sudden shift in Callum's attention. We'd always been friends, and I knew there'd been indications that Callum wanted to be more than friends, but I just wasn't in the frame of mind for it, nor was I sure I'd ever be. I stifled a sudden urge to giggle and cleared my throat.

"I could certainly ask Mom if she still has the hide-a-bed in the basement," I said brightly. "But Jennie and I will be too busy to go boating, I'm afraid. Now, tell me what you think of Grant Calderwood staying on. He said he'd told you about that."

A flicker of irritation crossed his face, but he recovered his usual good nature with effort and stepped back to a more comfortable distance. "Grant, yes," he said. "Um, yes, he told me about it, and I suppose it's a good move for him at this point. It gives him some focus and responsibility. He's the type of man who needs a defined role to play."

"Yes." I retreated behind my desk and sat down. "Goodness knows I can use the help because it's more property than Greg Ng can handle by himself. But I can't afford to pay for the work to be done, so Grant staying on is a blessing for me. I just wanted to make sure you agree that it's in his best interest and won't interfere with his progress. I don't want the center to be a crutch. Ethan and Theresa supported the idea."

"I don't think it will do any harm," Callum said, frowning. "He's right; he really has nowhere else to go where he's needed. But, Erin, if you give him a bed, that's one less patient you can accept. That's going to cost you a lot more in lost income than hiring a handyman would."

"Oh, I won't be giving up a patient's room. If he can't find an inexpensive apartment here in town, I'll turn the extra storage room in the barn into a bedroom. There's a bathroom and shower out there already, by the tack room, and if I have my contractor insulate it and maybe replace the window, it should do nicely. Grant can come to the center for his meals and to hang out in the evenings. He could even continue with outpatient therapy if you think that would be advisable."

"I guess that's better than putting him up in your cottage," Callum muttered.

I cocked my head to one side, looking at him. Did he see mild-mannered, elderly Grant as a rival? Surely not. But what else could explain his frown?

"No, I wouldn't do that. Jennie and I need our space," I assured him, my eyes steady on his. We looked at each other a moment. Then he nodded to show he got the point. Clearly unhappy, he turned the conversation to the other patients.

Janet tracked me down at lunch to inform me we were low on perishables. I did the main shopping for the center twice a month but sometimes had to run out between shopping trips for things such as milk or eggs.

"No problem," I told her. "I'll run and get stuff this afternoon. I need to do some grocery shopping for me and Jennie anyway." Not that I had cupboards to put groceries into, but still, I could grab some quick-prepare stuff that didn't require a kitchen. I was getting tired of eating at the center every day. I needed an occasional break from work, and sneaking over to my own cottage for a quick sandwich had always been a nice interlude. I knew Jennie felt the same way.

At that moment, a band of volunteers appeared in the dining room doorway, looking hopeful, and Janet hurried away to see if she could make lunch stretch to accommodate them. I hadn't seen Ed and Jennie come back yet, and I debated whether I should go find them and tell them lunch was ready. No, Jennie would think I was coming to check up on them. I'd send Rebecca.

Rebecca was upstairs, wailing over a plugged toilet on the third floor. Water had started to overflow onto the floor, and she stood with dripping towels in hand and tears of frustration on her cheeks.

"I don't know what else to try," she declared, dropping the sodden towels on the floor. "I used the Drano. I used the plunger."

"I'll take care of it," I told her. "I think I have one of those snake things in the garage."

"Thanks, Mrs. K," she said and fled.

I turned off the water to the toilet and surveyed the damage, wishing for the millionth time that I had a handyman.

And then I remembered that I did.

Hallelujah! I splashed to the door and ran down the stairs to find Grant.

By the time we found the snake and Grant had dealt efficiently and confidently with the offending plumbing, it was midafternoon. I was in much better spirits, having saved myself a plumber's bill, and Grant was feeling useful and needed. It was happiness all around. I washed up and set off for the grocery store.

I avoided the cheaper Food Basics down the street (neighbors tended to stop me and pump for updates on the murder investigation) and went to a Metro on the Parkway instead. I was less likely to run into anyone I knew there.

I had just finished loading my cart and was fishing for my credit card in my wallet when I looked up and saw Max Polinsky. He was browsing through the tabloids at the next checkout counter over. He seemed engrossed in a story ("Jealous Cow Attacks Farmer's Wife"), and I figured he hadn't seen me. I grabbed my cart, ducked out of line, and hurried down the nearest aisle to the back of the store. The last thing I wanted, after a pleasant morning with Ed, was to have a nasty encounter with his father. Ed had been in good spirits when he and Jennie had returned to the house, and he'd appeared healthy, both physically and mentally. Max, in the short glimpse I'd gotten, seemed the opposite. His hair was greasy, he hadn't shaved in a few days, and his eyes were bloodshot. Like any good ecologically concerned consumer, Max had brought his own plastic bags to the store. They'd been in the top of his cart, and I'd gotten a quick look at them. They were all from the beer store. Oh dear. So much for the effectiveness of outpatient therapy. Maybe I could have a quick word with Sam, who had been the Polinskys' therapist. Max Polinsky wouldn't speak to me, but maybe he'd listen to Sam. True, he was no longer our patient, and therefore not officially my concern, but I still cared what happened to him.

And maybe it wouldn't hurt to have Ed over casually now and then, just to keep tabs on things. I'd hate to see his progress hindered by a deteriorating home life. I had real hopes for that kid.

When I pulled into my driveway, Harris's car was there, and Harris was lounging on the front steps of the cottage, hands in his pockets.

Chapter Twenty

"They said at the center that you'd be back soon," he greeted me. He came to help me unload the grocery bags from the trunk. I always used reusable canvas bags instead of plastic, which were better for the environment and held more, but that meant they also weighed more. I was grateful for the help. Juggling two bags with one hand, I unlocked the front door with my other hand and stepped inside. The house was unusually quiet, no sign of workmen anywhere, and I realized Vinnie's truck was gone from out front. A stab of anger flashed through me. So I hadn't encouraged his advances this morning. Did he have to get back at me by walking off the job early?

Fuming, I stepped into the kitchen and stopped so suddenly that Harris, following me, bumped into me with his armload.

The kitchen was done.

I couldn't believe it. I flipped on the wall switch and watched in delight as the ceiling light came on. Setting my bags on the floor, I ran my hand along the countertop, touched the handles of the cupboard doors, caressed the faucet of the sink. It was all put back together, just the way it had been before the electrical nightmare, right down to the curtains framing the new window. No dust, no footprints on the floor, nothing to show that this morning the room had been a disaster area. Open-mouthed with amazement, I opened the cupboards above the counter and saw that all my things had been unloaded from their temporary places in laundry baskets on the floor and returned to their rightful spots. Rows of cans and jars faced me, tidy stacks of dishes, exactly where I'd originally had them. The dull drone in my head sprang brightly into "Joy to the World." I turned to Harris with a broad smile.

"I think I'm in love," I declared.

He looked startled. He set his bags on the table and turned to stare at me.

I waved a hand around, taking in the restored kitchen. "My contractor told me today before lunch that he'd have the room done by this afternoon. I didn't believe him. In fact, I laughed. But look!" I opened the fridge to look at the light inside. "It's all finished, the wiring works, and it's all put back together again just like he promised. I shouldn't have doubted him."

"And for this, you've fallen in love with him?" Harris asked dryly.

"Hey, a woman's kitchen isn't just a *room*, you know. This man has pulled off a miracle, big time. You should have seen it this morning."

"So that's all a fellow needs to do, eh? Pull off a miracle or two?" Harris shook his head and sat down at the table, leaning back in his chair while I put my purchases away. I would cook up a nice meal tonight for me and Jennie, here in our private, beautiful little kitchen, just the two of us. I glanced at Harris. Or maybe three.

While I worked, I told Harris about Hilda's death and Jennie's decision to care for the children's graves at the cemetery.

"That's a significant offer Jennie made," he commented. "That's very sweet of her."

"I thought so too. I admit I was surprised. Maybe she's starting to recover from what happened with her father. It's the first sign she's shown that she's willing to face the cemetery, anyway."

"That's good, then."

I stretched to put a bottle of olive oil in a high cupboard. Harris jumped to his feet. Taking the bottle, he stretched above me with his much taller frame and easily put it away. When he lowered his arms, we were standing just a few inches apart, and the nearness suddenly made my breathing go funny in a way it hadn't with Callum or Vinnie. I ducked away and reached into another bag for more groceries.

"So what brings you by today, anyway?"

Harris shrugged. "Janet said Monday was chicken pot pie night."

"Ah. And you were hoping I'd throw another free dinner at you." I put the apples in the crisper and closed the fridge.

"The possibility crossed my mind," he replied.

"You're welcome to stay. But I thought I'd cook something here for me and Jennie instead of going over to the center tonight. If you'd rather eat with us, we'd be glad to have you." He looked at me, and I felt suddenly embarrassed. "Or you can go to the center for pot pie. Either way," I added nonchalantly.

"Thank you. I'd be happy to join you." There was a small pause, and then he added, as if trying to find something to say, "By the way, about that bank account number. It's a private account in Antigua. Absolutely no way to trace whose it is."

I straightened and looked at him. "Could the police in Antigua find out for you?"

"No. The only way would be to get a court order and be able to prove a case of either money laundering, terrorism, or drug smuggling in Antigua itself. The account is set up with the banking company's name and not the individual's, and he can access the money online or withdraw it through any local ATM. No need to go to Antigua himself. So it's a dead end, just as I thought."

"But would the bank release the information if you proved to them Fortier's dead?" I asked, unwilling to let it just go. "It would become part of his estate, after all."

"Lockerby said it was Fortier's account. It might be, for all I know. But it is more likely the killer's personal account."

"Oh." I slumped. "Yeah. The killer would have to be able to access it. If it were Fortier's account, the fake Fortier wouldn't know the number to give Lockerby, and the killer wouldn't be able to get at the money once it was deposited. It had to be the killer's account to begin with."

"Right. I'm sure the password and all the other information he would need are highly secured."

"So we're back where we started," I sighed. "No doubt by now the killer is long gone, living it up in the Caymans or somewhere."

"On a million and a half dollars, you could live pretty comfortably," Harris agreed.

"I don't suppose he could have tortured the account information out of Fortier while he was holding him?" I added thoughtfully.

Harris shook his head. "No sign of torture on the body. No sign of injury other than the shot that killed him. In fact, the only significant or unusual thing we found was on the soles of his shoes. The lab found calcium carbonate, latex, formaldehyde, and titanium dioxide. Gesso,"

Harris added, seeing my blank look. "It's the recipe for the acrylic primer that artists use in oil painting."

"And you know this how?"

"Forensics has access to all kinds of databases. Do you have any gesso at your center?"

"We don't run an art therapy program per se, but we do have some art and hobby supplies for the guests' use. I don't know off the top of my head if we have any gesso, and I can't remember if there were any art projects going on that week."

"Check for me, will you?" Harris hesitated then added, "His blood alcohol level was through the roof when he died."

I felt a stab of sorrow. "The poor guy. After six weeks of detox, if he went back on the bottle that heavily, it would have had all the more effect on him."

"On the bright side, he was so blitzed he probably didn't have any idea what was coming," Harris said. "That's a mercy." He paused a moment then added, "Maybe that's how the kidnapper held him. Instead of under lock and key, maybe he just kept Fortier on a really good bender."

"If so, then my fake Fortier couldn't have been the kidnapper. He was here at the center the whole time. How could he be here and also be drowning Fortier with alcohol somewhere?"

"True. The mastermind who hired the fake is probably the actual kidnapper and likely the actual killer."

I shook my head. "I think we've been sidetracked. We've considered Lockerby, who isn't clever enough to pull it off, and Andrea Fortier, who wouldn't go about it in such a way. Since neither of those have seemed right, we've been searching for someone else who could have come up with the plan and hired the fake. But isn't the simplest explanation usually the correct one?"

"What do you mean?"

"Who says anyone hired him? Couldn't the fake Fortier himself be the mastermind? He may have needed an accomplice to watch Fortier for a few days, but other than that, who says there had to be a third party at all?"

"I suppose so," Harris said doubtfully. "So let's think about that. If the true motive for Fortier's death was to make sure the Redcreek sale went through, how would the fake Fortier have benefited from the actual sale?"

"Maybe he owned land nearby that he hoped would increase in value when the condos were built."

"Maybe he worked for Danbury Homes," Harris suggested. "That may explain how he came to find out about the land deal."

"Maybe he was a student desperate to find a condo near the university." I laughed.

"Housing is hard to come by, but surely that would be an extravagant way to go about securing a place." Harris shot me an admiring look. "Why don't you give up this rehab thing and take up sleuthing? You think well."

"No thanks. I wouldn't want to carry a gun," I said with a laugh. Harris's facial expression didn't change, but I thought a funny look came into his eyes, and he didn't say anything. Suddenly awkward, I turned back to the last forgotten groceries in my hands and said lightly, "So you're willing to give up Janet's pot pie for my cooking, huh?"

Was it relief I saw on his face? Harris resumed his seat and stretched his long legs out in front of him.

"Yep," he said.

"You're actually taking an hour off?" I teased. "What, not enough work to keep you busy today?"

Harris didn't reply right away but looked down at the kitchen floor as if inspecting it for crumbs. I wondered if Vinnie's housekeeping passed his inspection. Then he looked up at me, and his hazel eyes were intense, a light in them I hadn't seen before.

"Actually, I'm only on part time right now. I don't have a full caseload."

"Why?"

"They're easing me back into full time. I've been off for the last three months. This is actually the first case I was assigned after I came back to work."

"Oh." I felt stupid, as if I'd stepped in something I shouldn't have. "I didn't realize," I stammered. "I guess since your brother . . . you needed time off."

He shook his head, but his eyes didn't leave mine. "I wasn't allowed to work during the inquiry."

"What inquiry?"

"Looking into the circumstances of his death."

Something in his tone made shivers run up my arms. I slowly sat down in the chair opposite him, steadying myself under that burning gaze. "Can I ask what happened to your brother?" I asked quietly.

"He died in a drug deal gone bad."

"Oh. Was he a policeman too? Was he undercover?"

"No," Harris said slowly. "But there was an undercover cop involved."

"You said you always get your man. Will you find the man who killed him?"

"I killed him."

I blinked at him in stunned silence. After a moment, Harris looked away, and I suddenly felt it was easier to breathe once I was out from under that pinning stare.

"One of our boys was undercover, trying to infiltrate a drug ring in Mississauga," he said. His voice was low but steady. "It had been going on for several months, and we were getting close to finding the source of the drugs—the main dealer. One night, we got a distress call from the undercover officer, and I was the first to respond. It was a warehouse, and as I approached, I heard a shot. I knew our man was in there. Instead of waiting for more backup, I went in with my gun drawn. There was no one on the main floor, so I went up to the upper level, and just as I came out of the stairwell, I was fired on. I shot back blindly and rolled for cover behind a big metal drum. There was a volley of shots exchanged, and it was dark. I couldn't see who was shooting at me." Harris tipped his head back and closed his eyes as if reliving that terrible moment, the darkness, the blindness.

I swallowed hard and reached to put my hand on his arm. "You don't have to tell me," I said.

He shook his head and looked at me again, his expression bleak. "Finally, the shooting ended, the dust settled, and I found the officer wounded but alive behind a pile of debris. And I found my little brother, shot through the heart, with the hot gun still in his hand. I'd killed him."

Talk about horrible images in your head. "He was the one shooting at you?" I whispered.

"Yes."

"But you didn't know he was there."

"No. I didn't even know he was back in town. He'd always been . . . wayward, to put it nicely. I knew he'd dabbled in drugs. I should have known—I didn't know the extent of his involvement."

"With the dealer, you mean?"

His glance slid away from me. "He *was* the dealer. He was smuggling drugs in from Colombia."

I shook my head, wondering at the pain he must have felt, must still be feeling. "It wasn't your fault. You didn't know he was there. Do you think he knew it was you coming up the stairs?" I asked.

Harris ran his long fingers through his hair, mussing it. "I don't know. Probably not. He didn't wait to find out. He just started shooting."

"It was dark. He probably didn't know it was you."

He gave a low sound like a chuckle. "I'd like to think he wouldn't have shot if he *had* known."

"Of course, but, like you, he *didn't* know."

"Ah, but that's the difference," Harris said, and the look he gave me was hot and fierce. "I would have shot anyway."

"Well, sure," I stuttered. "It was your job. You had to save the undercover officer."

Harris let out a long breath. "Yes," he said. "But tell that to my parents."

I couldn't think what else to say. I stood and began folding up the canvas grocery bags, smoothing them flat. Part of me wanted to cry at the horribleness of it all. Part of me wished he hadn't told me. And part of me wanted to spin around and throw my arms around his neck, smooth his hair like I did Jennie's, and murmur assurances that everything would be all right. But it wouldn't be all right—ever again. Right or wrong, he would have to live with this the rest of his life. And I had dared whine to him about *my* nightmares? I stole a look at him, marveling that he could still be so keen, so strong. I imagined such a thing would have broken most men. And then I wondered how broken he was.

As if picking up on my thoughts, Harris came to stand beside me and fingered one of the folded bags. His voice was controlled and careful as he said, "I've given myself all of the speeches and assurances and arguments. I did the obligatory counseling sessions with the force's shrink. I tell myself it was unavoidable, it was my job, I didn't know it was him. I had a duty to my fellow officer. As if that makes it any easier."

"No, it doesn't. It's a terrible thing to have gone through, and it's awful that you were put in such a situation at all," I said forcefully. "Any way it turned out would have been impossible."

"That's what I told you," he replied quietly, shrugging, but his voice was sad. "Impossible to live with."

I did turn to him then and took his upper arms in my hands like I did with Jennie when I really wanted her to hear me. I had to tip my head back to look him sternly in the eye.

"The whole situation. The chain of events," I said. "*That's* what's impossible to live with. Not you."

He looked a bit startled.

I gave him a little shake to emphasize my point. "It happened. It's rotten. But your brother's choices brought it about. It wasn't your fault. Do you understand me?"

He blinked. "Yes ma'am."

I released him, picked up the grocery bags, and tossed them on a chair to take out to the car on my next trip. Behind me, Harris gave a faint chuckle.

"Yes, ma'am. I think I understand you," he repeated. His voice sank to a drawl. "If I hear you rightly, you're saying it wouldn't be impossible to live with me."

"Well—"

"In fact, it might be conceivable to live with me."

"That's not—"

"Are you saying you want to?"

"No!" My cheeks were burning.

"And here I was hoping."

I spun to stare at him. His lips were doing the twitching thing again. "I guess I'd better start thinking up a miracle or two to do," he murmured.

Chapter Twenty-One

Harris was a different person during dinner. It was as if he'd been carrying the story of his brother's death in a pack on his back and now he'd been allowed at last to set it down for a while. His manner was easier, his tone lighter, and he came closer to smiling than I'd ever seen before. He chatted through supper with Jennie, asking her about school, about Dribbles, and about the horses. Jennie got him to promise he'd come out for another horseback ride one day soon. With me, he kept the topics equally innocuous, but whenever our eyes happened to meet, there was a glint in them I wasn't sure I understood. I was always the first to look away.

After the meal, I cleaned up the kitchen (humming "Joy to the World" under my breath—it seemed determined to hang around) while Jennie and Harris went into the living room. I could hear them chatting cheerfully, though I couldn't tell what they were saying. From the banging and thumping, I could tell they were wrestling around with Dribbles, who barked once in a while in sheer joy. I was sure the dog hadn't had much rough-and-tumble at Hilda's house, and he was loving the attention. I suspected Jennie was too.

After dessert, Harris left, waving as he went down the driveway. I watched his taillights disappear as he turned onto Felicity Street, and then I went back into the kitchen to put away the leftover pie. Jennie snagged the last of the ice cream and went to watch TV. As she passed by me, carton and spoon in hand, she gave me a broad grin.

"I approve," she said.

I followed her into the living room. "What do you mean? Approve of what?"

Jennie wiggled her eyebrows at me in a Vinnie-like way. "Detective Harris, duh," she said, and took a bite of ice cream. "Or are we allowed to call him Liam now?" she asked with her mouth full.

"Certainly not," I replied. *Liam, indeed!* I hesitated, wondering if she was hoping for something—I hardly dared think what. I cleared my throat.

"You know, Jennie, we both think Detective Harris is a pretty nice guy. He's—I think he could be a good friend."

"Yeah." She plopped onto the couch and took another spoonful of ice cream.

"But there's a big leap between being a good friend and being . . . more than that. I'm not dating him. Remember all the talks we had about you dating Mormon boys when you're sixteen? Well, the same goes for me. Dating Mormons, I mean. Not that I'm dating anybody. I'd clear it with you first," I assured her. I was flubbing this up; I could tell by the wry look in her eyes, her indulgent smile. I coughed and took a different track. "If someday I decide I'm ready to date again, I'd only be interested in dating LDS men. I couldn't marry someone who wasn't. If—if I ever remarried, I mean." *Was* I thinking of remarrying? If so, it was news to me. Man, I was making a mess of this! But Jennie just chuckled.

"It's okay, Mom," she said, grinning. "I've explained all that to him."

"To whom?"

"Detective Harris. I told him all about us being Mormons and all that, and he's cool with it."

"You *what*?"

"Sure. He said he knew a few Church members and thought Mormons were nice people."

"Oh," I said. I started to turn away, but her next words brought me whipping around again.

"I explained how you married Daddy in the temple and how you can only do that once. But I told him if you ever got married again, I thought it would be important to you to marry someone who shared our beliefs. He said it sounded good to him. I think the word he used was 'reasonable.'"

"Just when did you two have this profound conversation?" I gasped.

"While you were doing the dishes and getting out the dessert." She grinned at me around her spoon. "He had some questions, but

I told him you and the missionaries would talk to him more about it someday. He was okay with that. So it's all good. He's open to it. You just have to make the appointment."

I stood there with my mouth opening and closing but no sounds coming out. I didn't know what to say. There wasn't anything to say to that, really. So I went back into the kitchen. There was nothing to clean, but I scrubbed at the countertops and table anyway. Good grief! Where did Jennie get such notions? Where had she gotten such daring tendencies? Not from me, surely. Was my growing interest in Harris so apparent—*did I have a growing interest in Harris?* She was jumping to conclusions all over the place. And what would Harris think now? I was mortified. *It was just a simple dinner, that was all,* I told myself. *Nothing but dinner.*

* * *

It was about three in the morning when I suddenly woke up with the word *gesso* in my head. It took me a moment to remember why. I had forgotten to find out if we had any at the center. I lay mulling over it for a while. If the impostor had been wearing the shoes at the center, walked through a hypothetical spill of art supplies, and then placed the shoes on the body later, that would be evidence tying him to the actual murder—provided we could match the gesso to a container of the stuff here at Whole-Life, that is. But if the real Fortier had been wearing the shoes all along, it didn't tie him to the impostor or Whole-Life. Where else could he have picked up artists' primer?

I found it impossible to go back to sleep, and once again, I got out of bed to look out the window at the moonlit yard. The trees cast everything in deep shadow. I couldn't see the garden from here, but my mind could easily envision it. However, I didn't want to entertain morbid thoughts tonight. Truth be told, I was getting impatient with my nightmares and imagination. I knew I needed to let it go. I yanked the curtains closed, flipped on the bedside light, and reached for my scriptures to see if I could read myself back to sleep.

* * *

The next morning was Hilda's funeral. It was a small service held in the chapel, with just a couple of speakers, some songs, and a violinist.

Hilda had few family members, and most of the congregation was made up of friends from church. Bishop Sand's talk about the promise of life after death hit me especially hard, and as we sang the final hymn, I found myself thinking about Harris and the story he'd told me. I couldn't seem to get his face out of my mind, his voice as he'd bantered with Jennie at the table. My heart ached when I thought of the burden he was carrying about his brother. The thought occurred to me that if any comfort was possible, he might find it in my religion's beliefs about life after death. About forgiveness and Christ's Atonement. I wondered if I had Jennie's nerve to talk to him about the concepts the Church taught. It was funny, really, to think I could yammer away with Harris without compunction about the lives and motives of strangers; I could even tell him about my husband's death and betrayal, something I'd never spoken of to anyone. And yet, I hesitated to speak to him about the truths I believed in, simple concepts that might ease his pain. Here I was, well beyond my teenage years, still hanging back, the self-conscious one at the party. Why hesitate? Was I just shy? No, not really. Was I afraid he'd dismiss me as a religious nut or a fool? Maybe. Why was it so easy for Jennie to approach the subject with him but so difficult for me? I thought of my daughter's matter-of-fact courage and felt ashamed. If Harris had needed help putting in a vegetable garden or caring for a horse, I would have been right in there, giving advice and sharing what I knew. Why was sharing my religious views any different? If I thought it could possibly help him, wouldn't I say something? Of course I would. I would do whatever I could to help him.

It shook me a little to realize how much I wanted to help him, how much I didn't want Liam Harris to be broken.

As we all stood for the small family to shuffle out of the chapel, my gaze drifted to the sleek white casket with its spray of flowers. It occurred to me that I was being rather pompous in my attitude. After all, I was sort of broken myself, wasn't I? It wasn't enough to share the things I professed to believe in. I needed to pay a little more attention to them. If faith could help Harris with his pain, couldn't it also help me with my fear?

There was a brunch after the funeral, for which I'd brought a fruit salad and croissants, but I just left the dishes for others to serve and drove home. Two funerals so close together were too much, and I had a lot to think about.

When I got home, I changed into jeans and a blouse and headed over to the center. As I crossed the driveway, I saw Vinnie pull up in his truck. I turned back and waited until he'd climbed out of the cab. He looked like he'd slept in his overalls. There was paint permanently ingrained into his hands, and he hadn't washed or shaved in several days. As I approached him, his face split into a broad, white-toothed grin. His hair blew messily into his eyes, and he smelled of bacon grease. To me, he was beautiful. The new, determined-to-be-courageous me marched straight up to him, took his head in my hands, and firmly planted a big Sicilian kiss on each of his bristly cheeks.

"You did a beautiful job putting my kitchen back together," I said. Never mind that he had been the one who'd taken it apart in the first place. I was sincerely grateful to have everything back to normal again and was in a mood to overlook irrelevant details. Vinnie laughed in delight and shook a finger an inch from my nose.

"I told you I would do it. You were not believing me, but I kept my promise. Vinnie always keeps his promise."

"Yes, he does," I agreed. "I'm sorry I didn't believe you. You're my hero."

"Wait until you see the good job I do on the bathroom," he said. "When you shower, you will think you are in paradise." Shouldering a sledgehammer, he winked at me and marched into the cottage.

I left him to it and went into the center.

* * *

Our art supplies, as it turned out, consisted of a set of watercolor paints, a box of Crayola crayons, some butcher paper on a roll, a set of pathetic plastic-handled brushes, and a self-inking stamp shaped like a paw print. Certainly no oil painting supplies, and not a bottle of gesso to be seen. I called to tell Harris, but he didn't answer, and I left a brief message telling him that wherever Fortier had picked up the substance on his shoes, it wasn't at our center.

Thursday evening was our Relief Society activity night, and I decided to treat myself to an evening out. Life had been altogether too stressful lately, and the idea of spending an evening in the company of other women, eating cookies and listening to a guest speaker, sounded like the pick-me-up I needed. But I'd forgotten that all the other women would want to talk about was either Fortier's death or Hilda's. I answered their questions with vague smiles and monosyllabic replies, and I was relieved when the Relief Society president finally rose to introduce the guest speaker.

It was Sister Clark tonight. She and her husband had recently returned from a mission to Romania, and she'd brought a slideshow of green countryside, quaint villages, majestic architecture, and smiling people. The Clarks had had a wonderful time and had enjoyed a lot of success teaching the people of Romania. They'd been confident, not shy about it at all. They'd set a goal of placing five copies of the Book of Mormon every day and had stuck to it their entire mission.

"Five?" someone in the audience gasped. I understood her amazement. To place that many, I'd have to wrap them around rocks and throw them through people's windows. How long had it been since I'd even tried to place *one*? Harris's face flickered across my thoughts again. Would I have the nerve to give him one? Did I *have* one to give? I would check. After all, Jennie had paved the way for me—plowed the way, more like it, like a tank crashing through thin trees. I would do it; I'd talk to Harris.

Placated by this resolve, I sank back to absorb the beauty of the rest of the slides. The thought of running off to another country for a few years, leaving everything behind, appealed to me . . . well, maybe not really. I wouldn't want to leave Jennie or my sweet cottage. And, I admitted, I would miss the work I'd come to love. I'd miss Bonnie and the staff and . . . um, other people. But it would be nice to disappear for just a *little* while and have someone else cover for me.

I sat up straight in my folding chair. *Cover.*

I blinked and realized everyone in the room was staring at me. Sister Clark had gone silent.

"What's the matter, dear?" Sister Watson asked.

"What?"

"You gave a little . . . squeak."

"Yelled, more like it," Sister Clark said. "Is something wrong?"

"I'm sorry," I said. "I didn't mean to interrupt. I—I just remembered something important. I need to go. Sorry."

I climbed over the other women in my row and exited. As soon as I was in the parking lot, I dashed to my car, strapped on my seatbelt, and headed for home.

If my theory was correct—that the fake Fortier was the mastermind and not just a hireling—then the whole case rested on his identity. We didn't know who he was, but he had to have known Fortier well enough to impersonate him. He also had to be in a position to *cover* for him, to make it appear Fortier was alive and well when he wasn't. He had to know Fortier sometimes sent virtual flowers to his wife. He had to be someone who could intercept Fortier's phone calls before the real Fortier heard them and also make calls from Fortier's phone, presumably over quite a long period of time. Lockerby had said they'd been negotiating awhile, and I assumed the real Fortier hadn't had any idea that this Redcreek thing was going to happen. While he was in detox, Fortier had phoned his wife from time to time. But after that Saturday when he'd left detox, he'd communicated only by e-mail. So we knew the impostor had Fortier's Blackberry. It had to be someone who could cover for Fortier without anyone questioning it.

I paused in my thought process, frowning, staring straight ahead. The murderer also had to be someone who could get his hands on the real title for the land—that would have been kept at Clearwater, probably in a vault or a locked filing cabinet. There was only one position someone could be in that would allow that much access.

* * *

It was too late that night to do anything about my suspicions. I spent a sleepless night. Friday morning, I slammed through breakfast and squirmed with impatience through staff meeting, hardly hearing anything my staff said to me. My mind was full, and I was eager to get on with the pursuit of my theory.

As I darted into the hallway after the meeting, Greg reached out and lightly touched my sleeve. It surprised me so much that I came to a dead halt.

"Sorry," he muttered. "I can see you're in a hurry, but I wondered if I could ask you . . ."

"Sure, it's okay," I said. I drew a deep breath and reminded myself what my first priorities were. He was my employee, after all, and more my business than Harris's investigation was (and Harris, I was sure, would prefer that I focus on my business and not his). When Greg hesitated, glancing at the others who were leaving the meeting, I suggested we go to my office. He gave a relieved half smile and followed me.

I didn't sit behind my desk because it looked too authoritarian, opting instead to sit casually on the edge of it. I motioned toward the chair, but Greg remained standing just inside the door.

"Sorry," he said again.

"Not at all," I said, using my most gentle voice, and it occurred to me I sounded as if I were trying to soothe a skittish horse. "What can I do for you, Greg?"

"I know I've only worked here a short time," he said, and I could see the effort it took for him to speak so much. "But I need to ask you for some time off. My grandmother needs my help. She's having a knee replaced at the end of the month. She—she doesn't have any other family to call on."

Which meant that *he* didn't have any other family either.

"Of course you need to look after her," I told him. "We can manage. Take whatever time you need. I imagine—is she back in China?" I tried to think how we would cope. It would mean at least a few weeks, likely more. Could I find a substitute student or riding volunteer to fill in? I couldn't picture Grant being able to manage the job, and I didn't think I had the time.

"Oh no, she's in Oakville," Greg said quickly. "She just needs someone to drive her and stay through the weekend. I'll be back the next Monday."

"Oh!" I felt foolish. "Well, sure. That's fine."

As he turned to leave the office, Greg paused and looked back at me over his shoulder. The smile he gave me was the first real warmth I'd seen from him besides what he'd shown Jennie and Ed, and it changed his whole appearance from furtive to friendly.

"My family's been in Canada since 1852," he said and laughed.

* * *

I made it over to the cottage without anyone else stopping me. Jennie was to spend the day at a friend's, so I bundled her and Dribbles into the car to drop them off. Then I kept going, down the Parkway onto the freeway, toward Toronto.

I'd looked up the address of Clearwater Holdings before leaving home—surreptitiously, with a feeling of guilt, as if I were looking up the address of a crack house instead of an environmental organization.

I felt my suspicions were correct, but that's all they were—suspicions. I wanted something more concrete to be able to hand to Harris. Clearwater was right downtown, so I opted to park at Islington and take the subway down instead of fighting traffic.

The station wasn't crowded at this time of day, and the trains weren't running at top frequency. I paced the platform, glancing from time to time at the electronic scrolling marquee that announced NEXT TRAIN ARRIVING IN TWO MINUTES. I strode up and down, considering what I was about to do and wondering how angry Harris would be with me for doing it. Another glance. NEXT TRAIN ARRIVING IN ONE MINUTE. I stopped and watched with interest as the amber words on the marquee changed to NEXT TRAIN IS IN THE STATION. The implication was, presumably, that if one was not certain that the great, massive, thousand-ton object hurtling past, six inches from one's fingertips, was in fact the train, one could look to the marquee for confirmation.

Musing, I stepped into the train. I have always liked the subway, the feeling of whooshing along at full speed, knowing that above you, cranky people in hot cars were honking at each other as they crawled along the streets. Speed was what I wanted right now. It being Toronto, I was the only white woman I could see in my train car, and other than a couple of men farther down, I was also the tallest person in the car. I felt very conspicuous.

When I got off to switch trains at St. George, there was a uniformed policeman standing on the platform. As I walked past, he gave me a cursory glance. I could feel my gait grow stiff and self-conscious. I imagined the officer grabbing his shoulder radio and telling dispatch to contact Harris. "She's at it again, sir!"

But he didn't, and no one stopped me. I got on the next train and went south three more stops. My destination was the top floor of a high-rise made of blue glass. I took the smooth chrome-interiored elevator up, and it opened directly across from glass doors with CLEARWATER HOLDINGS written across them in gold lettering.

Chapter Twenty-Two

I stepped inside and found myself facing a wall of tinted windows that provided a breathtaking view of downtown Toronto. Skyscrapers rose like canyon walls; below, tiny people filed silently along the sidewalk like a river in a gorge.

"May I help you?"

I pulled my eyes from the view and turned to face the receptionist, who sat at the long teak desk. Clearwater wasn't hurting for money, that was certain. But teak? It seemed a little tactless for an environmental conservation group to use wood from an endangered species. I gave the girl a polite smile and tried to sound businesslike.

"Hi," I said. "My name is Erin Kilpatrick. I'm a friend of Andrea Fortier's."

The girl nodded, indicating she knew who Andrea was. The receptionist didn't look much older than Jennie. Her blonde hair was pulled back with a pink scrunchie and—unlike Lockerby's assistant—I saw her nails were bitten short. She kept her hands on her keyboard as she looked at me, expectant, efficient. It was probably her first job, and she wanted to make a good impression.

"Would you happen to be Michael Fortier's secretary?" I asked, feeling doubtful. Certainly this blue-eyed teenager wasn't what I'd expected. I was looking for someone older, shiftier, perhaps, with a boyfriend who had unsavory connections and good impersonation skills . . .

"Oh no, I'm just the receptionist. I'm sorry, Mr. Fortier's secretary is no longer with us. Is there something I can help you with?"

"Oh!" I hadn't expected this either. "I hadn't heard."

"They let him go because, obviously, he wasn't needed anymore," the girl confided sadly.

"So they're not going to replace Mich—wait a minute. Did you say *he*?" I asked. I gripped the edge of the teak desk so hard I thought I'd leave indentations and leaned closer into her startled face. "Mr. Fortier's secretary was *male*?"

"Yes, didn't you know?" The receptionist drew back from me a little, not understanding my agitation. "His name was Trevor Murdock."

I let go of the desk and (letting myself indulge in a little theatrics) smacked my forehead with my open palm. I had suspected the secretary was the link through which the impostor accessed Fortier's personal information. It hadn't occurred to me that the secretary *was* the impostor. I had assumed the secretary was female, stereotyping based on occupation—I, who employed a male nurse, should have known better. I gave the receptionist a reassuring smile and tried to speak calmly.

"Could you please tell me about this Trevor person? Was he maybe six feet tall, dark hair, very personable, with a drop-dead gorgeous smile?"

The girl relaxed a little, and a wistful look came over her face. "That's a good way to describe him," she agreed. "You knew him too, then."

"Oh yes, I've met him," I said, scrambling for an idea of how to get the information I wanted. "I'd forgotten he was the secretary. I thought he was, um, a friend."

"Well, he was very friendly. You could make that mistake," the girl said, nodding.

I glanced at the placard on her desk. Carol Pond. "Carol, is it? Nice to meet you. Tell me, did Trevor work here long?"

"Two or three years, I think. Everybody liked him. We were sorry to see him go."

"Well, I'm sorry to hear it too. Andrea asked me to drop off a thank-you note to him for her, since I was going to be in the neighborhood today. For the flowers he sent to the funeral, you know."

"Oh, I see."

The girl apparently didn't pick up on the fact that if I'd had such a card, it would have had Trevor's name written on it and I would have known the secretary I sought was a male.

"But I guess she didn't know that he had already left Clearwater," I went on. "I guess he left, what, over a week ago?" And headed straight to the Caymans, no doubt.

"No, they just let him go a few days ago because he wasn't needed anymore. He'd just returned from vacation too. Can you imagine how shocked he must have been to get back into town and find out his boss had died while he was gone? It's just horrible."

"Trevor was out of town?"

"He was away for a couple of weeks. They hit him with the news the day he came back to work. Technically, yesterday was his last day of employment. We had a little party for him before he went."

I paused, taken aback. "He went on vacation and then he came back?" Of course. I'd forgotten the police had come to interview Fortier's secretary about the supposed business trips.

"Well, yes. He lives here in Toronto," she said, looking at me funnily, as though she were thinking, *After all, don't most people come back from vacations?*

"And his last day here was yesterday?"

"Yes. I felt so bad for him."

"I don't suppose there's any forwarding address for him?"

The sympathetic look intensified, but she shook her head firmly. "I can't give that out, I'm afraid. I suppose if Mrs. Fortier asked for it directly, that might be okay. Or, here, you can just leave the card with me, and I'll address it and forward it to him."

"Oh, thanks. I don't want to bother you with it," I said. "I'll just give it back to Andrea. She might want to speak to Trevor personally, you know, to express her sympathy that he's lost his job because of all this. I'll let her deal with it. Though, heaven knows, she has enough to deal with right now, doesn't she?"

"Yes, it's such a sad thing," the girl said, nodding. "We were all very sorry to hear about Mr. Fortier."

"I'm sure you were. Such a shock," I murmured, and we both nodded sympathetically at each other for a moment. "And so sad, that Andrea's last communication with her husband was by e-mail," I added.

"Oh, was it? How awful," the girl exclaimed. "That's so sad."

"Yes. She hadn't seen him in such a long time. I feel so bad for her."

"True. He was away on that business trip up north, wasn't he? And she hadn't seen him since he'd left?" the girl said.

So she didn't know about rehab either. I gave another sigh that I hoped wasn't too dramatic.

"When was the last time you heard from him?" I asked gently. "Was your last communication from him an e-mail too?"

The girl was looking teary-eyed now. "Yes," she said in a wobbly voice. "It's too bad that's the last memory you have of someone, isn't it? A silly old e-mail."

"When did yours come in?" I dabbed at my eyes with the back of my hand.

"Wednesday afternoon," the girl said, glancing at her monitor regretfully. "Just routine office stuff. Nothing important or urgent, really. It's so sad to think that . . . it must have been right before he died."

I shook my head in full sympathy. "Well, we can only hope he's happy wherever he is," I said comfortingly.

"Yes," the girl said, openly crying now. "Because he sure wasn't happy when he was here, was he?"

I saw a man down the hall put his head out of his office, looking toward the front desk, and I knew I needed to go before we made much more of a scene. I patted the girl's shoulder awkwardly.

"Thank you, dear," I murmured and turned to go.

I took the elevator down to the lobby, went out onto the sidewalk, and stood for a moment, thinking. I hadn't held out any hope that the impostor was here in Toronto. I figured he had withdrawn the money from his account and disappeared into an anonymous, comfortable life in a beach house somewhere. But he had come back to the office. Maybe he was trying to avoid the suspicion that would have fallen on him if he disappeared too soon after his boss's death. Or maybe he was so cocky and sure he'd gotten away with the scheme that he felt unthreatened and saw no need to leave town permanently at all. He could slip the money back into the country a little at a time without arousing curiosity.

What I needed was a phone book, but in this world of cell phones, a public pay phone was a rarity. I walked for three blocks before I managed to locate one and then found that the phone book had been ripped from its cord. Muttering under my breath about vandals and the sad state of the world, I walked another two blocks and found another booth. This time the phone book was intact.

There were two columns of Murdocks in the book, six entries for T Murdock. It was a long shot, but one of them might be Trevor. I copied the six addresses into the little chubby notebook I kept in my purse (*I wasn't a person who ripped phone books*) and then took myself to a Tim Horton's for soup and a sandwich for fortification. As I finished my chocolate doughnut (I decided chocolate was a must at this point), I debated over the list of addresses. Two, I recognized as being quite far away, a good half hour by bus or car. One was in a very ritzy part of town, probably beyond the budget of a secretary. That left three likely addresses. I wasn't positive where they were, so in the end, I scouted out an Internet café and looked them up on Mapquest.

One of them was on the subway route, as it turned out, and I decided to stop by that one on the way back to my car. I felt a little thrill go up my spine at my own daring. I knew I should probably just go to Harris with what I'd learned and let him check out the secretary. But what if I were wrong? What if Trevor Murdock wasn't the fake Fortier? The police had already interviewed him a couple of times, after all, and he hadn't raised any suspicions. I'd feel like an idiot sending the police yet again to check out an innocent person. I didn't want to go running to Harris with my theory until I was more sure of it. Truth be told, I'd rather face a murderer on his doorstep than look like an idiot in front of Harris.

And yet, I knew in my heart I had to be right. Only the secretary could have pulled it off, making everyone think Fortier was alive and wandering free when he wasn't. Only the secretary would have had the information he needed to send e-mails, intercept phone calls, and access the land title. No doubt he had Fortier's electronic signature and could have practiced signing it. It was a small matter for a good secretary to make the world think his employer was alive and well when in fact he wasn't.

So I took the train back to St. George then west to Dufferin. The address turned out to be a fourplex with crumbling cement front steps and rusting wrought-iron grills on the windows. There was no name on the one mailbox I could see. I didn't want to risk knocking on a door at random in case I came face to face with the impostor. To one side was an apartment building, but to the other side was a Subway sandwich shop. I stepped into it, bought a bottle of cold water, and stood at the window, drinking and watching next door. I'd finished my drink and the manager was starting to look at me funny by the time I finally saw someone approach the fourplex.

I stepped out of the restaurant and followed the man, catching up with him at the door as he dug for his key. He looked up as I approached—short, thickset, balding, with an earring and bad teeth.

"Sorry to bother you," I said briskly. "Could you tell me if a Trevor Murdock lives in this building?"

"There's a Timothy Murdock upstairs," the man said, puzzled. "Is that the name you want?"

"Oh, no, sorry. I must have the wrong person," I said. "Does he have anyone else living with him? A son, perhaps? I'm looking for a Trevor Murdock."

"No, he doesn't have any kids that I know of. I think he lives here alone."

"Tall, dark-haired, about forty?"

"Short, silver-haired, about fifty-five or sixty," the man replied.

"Thank you," I said and left before the conversation could go further.

Disappointed, I got back on the subway and continued out to Islington. I retrieved my car and, after some debate with myself, decided to check out one more address before heading home. The next address on the list proved to be an apartment building on the West Mall. I parked well back in the crowded lot. There was a dry fountain shaped like a mermaid in the courtyard and a swingset in a patch of grass that was fenced off with chain link, like a dog run. I sat studying the building for a minute but saw no one come in or out. Finally, I got out of the car and approached. The only way I knew of to make certain this was the right Murdock was to see him with my own eyes. But I had to do it in such a way that he wouldn't see me. There was a wall of buttons in the entry to summon the various residents, much the same way buttons made a vending machine spit out candy bars. I looked over the list and found T Murdock. My scalp began to prickle. Without giving myself time to hesitate, I pushed the button. And wondered if my impulsivity had gotten me into real trouble this time.

There was a buzz, and then a deep male voice said, "Yes?"

I swallowed hard. "Mr. Murdock, please," I said, pitching my voice a bit higher than usual. It wasn't hard to do in the circumstances.

"This is he."

I gripped my purse tightly in my hands. "Mr. Trevor Murdock?"

"Yes."

"PDF Deliveries. I have a delivery for you."

"What is it?"

"I don't know, sir. I just need you to sign for the box, please."

There was a pause and then the voice said, "I'm not expecting anything. Who's it from, can you tell?"

"Uh . . . Clearwater Holdings."

"Oh? Um . . . I'll buzz you in."

"Oh, would you mind coming down, please? I've left my delivery van running."

A pause. "Okay. I'll be right down."

The intercom went dead. I thrust open the door, dashed out of the entry, and raced for my car as if demons were on my heels. Once inside, I locked the doors and slid down low in the seat. I kept my eyes on the building doors and my key in the ignition in case I needed to make a fast getaway. My heart was pounding so hard I felt sick. There was an unbearable pause. Then I saw Trevor Murdock's head look out of the front doors, a puzzled expression on his handsome face. He stepped farther out, looking around, frowning. Even from a distance, I recognized that tennis-player body, the lean profile. My missing guest. The fake Fortier.

Gotcha.

I waited until Trevor shrugged and went back inside. I started the car and drove as unobtrusively as possible out of the full parking lot, in case he was watching from inside. Would he recognize my car? I wasn't observant about such things as cars, ordinarily, but he might be. I checked my rearview mirror for several blocks. No one appeared to be following me. He hadn't seen me, then.

Once on the freeway again, I gunned the motor and headed for Mississauga. My hands were shaking. I didn't know if it was from excitement or from dread of what Harris would say when he learned what I'd been up to.

Chapter Twenty-Three

I drove straight to the divisional office, parked, went in, and told the man at the front counter that I needed to see Detective Harris. He took my name, checked a clipboard, and picked up a phone. He turned away and spoke quietly so I couldn't hear him, but I took it as an encouraging sign that Harris was in. I waited impatiently, studying the posters and ads on the bulletin boards (police bike auction, towing service, missing cat) and trying to calm myself with "Be Still, My Soul." I didn't know all the words, though, and got rather caught, like a leaf in an eddy, with those four words repeating themselves over and over.

There was a buzz behind me, and the magnetic lock on the door released. I turned and saw an unfamiliar man standing in the doorway.

"Mrs. Kilpatrick?"

"Yes. I'm looking for Detective Harris."

"I'm Detective Constable Martin," he said. "Could you come this way, please?"

I followed him through the door, down a cold linoleum hallway, and past several closed doors. He turned right and opened a heavy wooden door then stepped back for me to enter first. It was a small waiting room, with the dismal generic look of all waiting rooms everywhere—a plastic-covered sofa, a '70s laminated coffee table, a water cooler, scuffed linoleum, and a spindly plastic fern in a blue pot.

"If you could wait here, please," the man said. "We told Detective Harris you were here, and he asked if you'd wait. He's on his way in. About ten minutes away."

"Okay, thank you."

He went out again, leaving the door open, and I sat swinging my leg and chewing a thumbnail, trying not to think about what Trevor was doing right now. Had I spooked him? Was he even now packing a bag for Argentina? I still couldn't believe I'd found him. If I had more than a million dollars waiting for me offshore, I doubt I would have hung around a dingy Toronto apartment for any longer than it would take me to pack my toothbrush.

There was the sound of footsteps coming briskly down the hallway, and suddenly I was frozen with nerves. I hadn't seen Harris since Jennie's infamous conversation with him about Mormons and marriage. How would he be toward me? I couldn't worry about it right now. There were other pressing matters at hand. I squared my shoulders and tried not to clench my teeth. I think I looked fairly normal by the time Harris came into the room.

He carried a paper bag in one hand and a cup with a straw in the other. He looked, I thought, somewhat pleased to see me.

"Root beer? Fries?" he asked.

"No thank you. I'm—"

"Wait. Come in here." He led the way down a short hall that continued through some glass doors into a large space filled with desks. Men and women, uniformed and plain-clothed, milled around, and there was the sound of phones ringing, computer keyboards rattling, and low, serious conversation. I followed Harris as he threaded his way through the room, ignoring and being ignored. We came to a smaller office with only four desks in it. No one was in this room, and Harris, looking satisfied, led me in and kicked the door closed behind us. He set his lunch on the desk nearest the door. It was by far the tidiest of the four, its Formica surface cleared of all but a neat inbox, a stapler, a cup of chewed pencils, and a computer. Compared to the other three desks, it looked practically unused. I assumed it was his.

"That's better. We can have some privacy in here," he said.

He dropped into his chair and nodded toward the chair at the next desk. I obediently pulled it over and sat down, facing him. I realized my feet were together, my back straight, and my hands in my lap, as if I were at a job interview. Or as if I'd been called to the headmistress's office for a reprimand. I forced myself to relax my hands and take a deep breath. But he spoke before I could.

"I'm glad you stopped by. I wanted to talk to you."

"Oh—"

"The other night, Jennie was telling me some pretty interesting things about your church. She said you'd be arranging some sort of meeting she wanted me to attend. Is this about that?"

"I'm sorry, I hope she wasn't too forward—" I began, disconcerted.

"Not at all. I thought that temple marriage thing sounded pretty intriguing. I wouldn't mind learning more about it." He raised his eyebrows at me. I stuttered a little, and Harris gave a barking laugh. He picked up his pop and took a long pull at the straw. His cheeks sucked in slightly to delineate his cheekbones. He really had quite nice bones.

"Um, yes, there are some things I'd like to tell you that I think could maybe help you. But I'll have to get back to you on that," I said. "Something more urgent has come up."

"Oh?"

"I've found the fake Fortier," I said.

He looked up sharply and caught me staring at his facial structure. I looked away.

"Say that again," he said.

"Well, I got to thinking. Who is the one person who would have access to Fortier's e-mail and phone and know that he sometimes sent virtual flowers—"

"His wife," Harris interrupted.

"—and had access to the land title for Redcreek."

"His partners."

"His secretary."

Harris froze for a moment, his drink halfway to his mouth, and then he set it down on the desk with a small splash.

I shrugged. "You're the one who said it: a secretary knows more about a man's life than his own wife. So I went to Clearwater Holdings this morning—"

His eyes (which really were quite beautiful) bugged out. "You *what?*"

I hurried on, not giving him a chance to yell. "The receptionist told me that his secretary had been let go because he wasn't needed anymore. He. The secretary was a guy."

"That doesn't mean anything," Harris said. "Lots of guys are admin professionals nowadays. It's not uncommon."

"Not all of them are gorgeous Fortier look-alikes with drop-dead smiles," I said. "And he'd been on vacation for a couple of weeks. When he came back to work, they told him his boss had died and they were letting him go because he wasn't needed anymore. The receptionist said they had a farewell party for him yesterday."

"Yesterday?" Harris tensed like a terrier spying his quarry in the underbrush.

"He's still in town. Maybe he felt it would be too suspicious to go off on 'vacation' and not return. He came back to the office. Yesterday was his last day."

"Incredible."

"I thought so too. Anyway, I tracked him down—it doesn't matter how, I'll tell you about that later—" Harris sighed, a look of resignation flitting across his face. "—but the thing is, I saw him, Liam. I staked out his apartment building not half an hour ago, and I saw him. It was the same guy who stayed at the center. I'm sure of it."

Harris stared at me in silence for a moment then shook his head and fished his car keys out of his pocket. "Right under my nose," he muttered. "Did he see you?"

"No, I'm pretty sure he didn't."

"Pretty sure?" His glare was fierce.

I squirmed. "Well, I had to lure him out of the building somehow, so I pretended to be a delivery person. I disguised my voice and spoke to him on the intercom. But, of course, I wasn't there waiting when he came down. I was hiding in my car in the parking lot. I don't think he would have recognized my car. But, um, there's a chance I might have spooked him a little."

Harris headed for the door. I jumped up and followed anxiously.

"I thought you checked out his secretary," I couldn't help remarking, jogging to keep up with his long strides.

"My partner Hawkins did—twice," Harris said with a scowl. "He just asked about Fortier's calendar and the business trips issue. He told me the basics of his report, but I didn't read it personally. Believe me, I'll have something to say about the fact that he never bothered to mention the secretary was a gorgeous guy."

"He might have felt a little funny saying it that way," I pointed out as we zipped down the hall. "That's what's wrong with the world today. There aren't enough meetings face to face."

Harris yanked open the glass doors and scowled at me over his shoulder.

"There's about to be one now," he said.

* * *

He snapped out short orders to several people, who jumped to do his bidding, and then he turned to me.

"What's his name and address?"

I gave them to him. Harris wasn't pleased to learn Trevor lived in Toronto. "We should bring the Toronto Police in on it, out of courtesy. But we can make the arrest, and I intend to be there when the boys pick this guy up."

He stopped at someone else's desk, reached over the startled-looking owner of the desk, and picked up the phone. I tried to look nonchalant and not listen in as he made a couple of calls, but I couldn't help hearing snatches. They weren't going to wait for the warrant, Harris told some unknown person. They were going to detain him right now. Flight risk. Enough time wasted. Marv (whoever Marv was) could work on the legalities.

Whoever he was talking to must have accepted this because Harris slammed the phone down. A frazzled-looking officer hurried up with a couple of papers that Harris thumbed through with a grim expression.

"Same name and address he gave when we interviewed him. Is Hawkins here?"

"Not on duty today."

"Rats. He could have identified him."

"No priors except one domestic call about a year ago," the officer said. "There's no photo."

"Tall, dark, and handsome," Harris said.

The officer jerked, startled. "Sir?"

"That's his description." Harris handed the papers back to the officer. "We don't have a photo, but we have a general description."

"Actually," I ventured, fighting the urge to raise my hand, "he isn't unusually tall. More average. Maybe six feet. Slightly tanned or olive complexion, maybe some Mediterranean heritage, but then, that could describe half of Toronto. Beautiful teeth," I added helpfully.

The officer blinked at me. Harris shot me a look, spun around, and headed for the parking lot. I followed. Two officers were getting into a patrol car. Harris got into another cruiser, and a different officer climbed into the passenger seat, leaving the one with the handful of papers standing on the sidewalk.

The hard part about being a civilian, I mused, was that you never got to see the wrapping up of the investigation, the excitement of the arrest. In the end, it's the police's job and, no matter how helpful you personally feel you have been, you have no place in—

The engine roared to life, and Harris stuck his head out the window.

"Are you going to stand there looking smug, or are you coming with us?"

"Coming!" I shouted, and climbed into the back seat.

The officer on the sidewalk coughed. Harris's partner looked horrified.

"You aren't taking her along, are you?"

"She's the only one who can identify him. She's the one who found him."

"Yes, but it might be—"

"She'll just follow us if we don't take her along."

The partner looked at me. I nodded and tried to look apologetic.

"It's better to keep an eye on her. I'll keep her out of the way when we get there," Harris added.

I wasn't sure I liked the sound of that, but I kept my mouth shut other than to give driving directions.

All the way to Toronto, Harris muttered to himself. I didn't catch all of it, but phrases like "distracting," "should have done it myself," "chicken pot pie," and "can't concentrate with you around" featured prominently. He spoke on his radio to someone, but I didn't follow everything I heard. Apparently, Marv wasn't happy about proceeding without a warrant. Harris replied with something about spooking the perp, flight risk again, and time being of the essence. Harris's companion, whom he introduced as Peterson, kept glancing at me over the back of the seat, through the grill, and looking unhappy. All hymns had flown out of my head, to be replaced inexplicably with the rousing brass of the theme from "Hawaii Five-O." I sat with my hands clenched between my knees, giddy with excitement and hoping no one I knew saw me being whisked along in the backseat of a police car. Heaven knows what conclusions they would jump to. Jennie would freak out when I told her.

"We can arrest him for forgery and selling property that didn't belong to him," Harris said to his partner as we zipped across the border into

Etobicoke. "Lockerby can ID him from a lineup. We've got the signature in the guest book that matches the signature on the sales documents."

"If we can confiscate Murdock's computer, it might link us to the Antigua account. I'll get Saul on it," Peterson suggested.

"Wait, aren't you arresting him for murder?" I asked, leaning forward. I wished the grill weren't there so I could see Harris's face more clearly in the rearview mirror.

"We don't have enough to link him to it," Harris said briefly. "Not yet, anyway." He spun the car around a corner, tires singing.

"But he was impersonating Fortier. You could prove it by comparing his fingerprints to the ones you found in his bedroom at the wellness center. And on my testimony."

"Yes," Harris murmured, and I suspected he was fighting a smile again.

"We know he must have kidnapped Fortier first before coming to my center," I persevered. "And then Fortier ended up dead. Isn't that good enough?"

"There's enough to justify a warrant to search his car," Harris said. "Something might turn up there. There were fibers on Fortier's clothes that might link him to Murdock's trunk. But that still only indicates complicity in the kidnapping, not murder."

Peterson said something sharp and low, but Harris waved a hand at him. "She knows more about this case than we do," he said, sounding weary.

"If his body was in the trunk and fibers were able to rub off, that means he wasn't wrapped up. He was dead for two hours before he was put in my garden. He'd probably stopped bleeding by the time he was put in the trunk, or the murderer would have wrapped the body," I pointed out. "But you may still find some blood rubbed off in the trunk. There was a lot of it—" I stopped, feeling suddenly ill.

Harris shot his partner a grim look. "You see what I mean?" he said. To me, he added, "It's still circumstantial. We can't tie Murdock directly to the murder. He could argue someone else drove his car while he was at the center. The only thing we have on him is impersonation and forging Fortier's signature on that land sale. We don't know where he kept Fortier all that time. We don't have a weapon. No forensic evidence."

"Well, he doesn't know that," I pointed out. "If you act like you have more, he might crumple and talk."

"Crumple?" Peterson muttered.

"I think the word you're looking for is 'fold,'" Harris said, but I actually saw his lips twitch this time.

When we neared the apartment building, I got to see the real advantage to being with a policeman. Instead of spending ten minutes searching futilely for a visitor parking space in the crowded lot, Harris simply stopped the car in the middle of the street in front of the building and left the lights spinning. We got out of the car, Harris holding my door for me. He gave me a look that brooked no argument.

"You wait here by the car. Do not come any closer."

"I thought I was supposed to identify him," I protested.

"Later. We'll bring him to you. I don't want you anywhere nearby if he decides not to come quietly."

Did people really say *come quietly*? Fascinated, I waited by the car while Harris and the three other officers advanced on the building. Then I noticed a third police car, this one from the Toronto Police, pulling into the parking lot. Two officers got out and approached Harris and his group. There seemed to be an awful lot of talking going on, and then Harris's group stepped back while the Toronto officers moved into the entry. There was a long pause, and then I saw a small man in a red sweater come to the door. The manager, I surmised, coming to let them in. *They wouldn't just ring Trevor's doorbell and ask to come up,* I mused.

The Toronto police officers disappeared inside, and Harris's group hovered, two at the front door and two easing toward the side door, in case Trevor made a break for it by that route. It seemed to be taking a long time to me, though in reality it was probably only a minute or two. I leaned against the car, ready to duck behind it in case of a rain of gunfire—and then I saw movement from the corner of my eye.

A car door closing. A car starting to pull out of a parking spot halfway across the lot. I hadn't seen anyone walking toward it. The driver must have already been getting into the car and had paused to watch the police deploy. The car backed up slowly, casually, and began to make its way through the lot at a decorous pace. It was a dark blue Chevy Cavalier with a ski rack on top.

"Harris!" I shrieked.

All heads turned toward me, and before I could finish shouting "There he is! He's getting away!" Harris was sprinting toward me.

He wasn't going to get there in time. The Chevy driver saw him coming and stomped on the gas. There was a screech of tires, and the car whipped around the end of the row of cars and headed straight for the exit. I was still in the street, the police cruiser at my back, and the only hope of creating an obstacle between the Chevy and freedom.

Admittedly, I'm not a cautious sort of person. I freely confess I sometimes act before thinking, or without thinking at all. But throwing myself in front of a moving car was a bit extreme, even for me. I heard a shout from Harris, the roar of an engine, and my only thought was, *At least he hasn't had room to build up much speed.*

But the car didn't hit me. At the last second, Trevor saw me, and his own instinctual reaction overrode his nastier personality. He swerved to the right, bumped up over the curb, and snagged a heavy metal newspaper box with the front corner of his car. It slowed him down just long enough for Harris to reach him.

Trevor tried to put the car in reverse, but it was too late. In a move that looked choreographed, Harris yanked open his door, spun him out of the driver's seat, and had Trevor's arms spread over the top of the car before the rest of the officers swarmed in. And it *was* Trevor too. Now that I could get a proper look at his face, I knew him instantly as my cheerful, charming guest. He wasn't cheerful or charming now—his hands tied behind his back with a strip of plastic, his face flushed red and twisted into an angry scowl. Harris, leaning over Trevor's shoulder, spoke in a low voice into his ear. Probably telling him his rights. Thank goodness I had been right and we hadn't captured a perfectly innocent tenant. The relief hit me like a wave, and I sat down on the curb and hugged my knees.

Then there was more standing around and talking. Officers spoke into radios. A small crowd of onlookers gathered on the lawn. The Chevy's engine idly ticked over. It was all rather anticlimactic in my opinion.

After awhile, I grew tired of waiting, stood, and sidled closer. I guess Trevor was getting bored too because after awhile, he interrupted the officers with a loud voice.

"I really don't know why you're bothering with any of this. It's ridiculous. Sure I worked for Mr. Fortier. But I didn't forge anything."

Someone made a low comment I didn't catch.

Trevor shook his head. "I don't need a lawyer 'cause this is all a mistake. I'm innocent."

"Sure looked innocent, didn't you? What were you going, fifty?" One of the officers laughed.

Harris squinted casually up at the sun, as if he were judging the time. "Murdock, you know Philip Lockerby can identify you as the man who signed the land sale contract."

Trevor licked his lips. "It was on Mr. Fortier's behalf. He authorized me to sign for him."

"Oh? He told you to impersonate him and sign his signature?"

"Yeah. He was in rehab. I already told you guys he was. So he couldn't be there himself to meet with Lockerby. He told me to go. He didn't want word to get out that he was in treatment."

"Ah." Harris looked intrigued by this news. "Too bad Fortier can't verify that for us himself."

"I have a document signed by Mr. Fortier authorizing me to conduct his business for him. It's at the office." Trevor was looking a little more confident now. I pictured him carrying Fortier over his shoulder through the gate and dropping him in the dark of the garden. My stomach churned.

"Another forgery, no doubt," Peterson interjected.

"Did he authorize you to impersonate him at rehab too?" Harris asked mildly.

"I don't know what you're talk—"

"I suppose he authorized you to kill him too," Peterson suggested.

"What? I don't know anything about his murder. Is that what this is about?"

"If I were impersonating a man who wound up dead, I might be a little nervous," Peterson said. One of the Toronto officers gave a snort.

"This is all a dumb mistake," Trevor protested. "Why would I kill my boss? I'm out of a job because someone killed him. I wouldn't do that to myself, now, would I? I wasn't even in town when it happened."

"That's right, you weren't in town. You were in Mississauga, leaving your fingerprints all over your room at the wellness center," Harris told Trevor and jerked a thumb toward me. Drat. He knew I'd moved closer. And I thought I'd kept out of his line of vision.

The man in restraints threw his head back to say something more. Then he caught sight of me. Apparently, he hadn't registered who I was when he'd swerved to avoid me. He'd only been aware of a human figure jumping out in front of him. Now he recognized me. His jaw went slack, and his eyes widened. He made a gurgling sound, and then he fell abruptly silent. If I could have taken his picture and hung it in a gallery, I would have entitled it "Man Scrambling for Words."

"You almost got it right," Harris told Trevor cheerfully. "Tough luck that of all the rehab centers in the province, Fortier had to choose the one this lady runs. You might have gotten away with it with somebody else."

"You don't have a case. You can't prove anything," Trevor said sullenly.

"We'll see what the judge has to say about that." Harris looked over his shoulder at me. "Is this the man who stayed at your center?"

"Yes. Definitely." I went ahead and stepped closer. "Nice to meet you again, Trevor." I saw the Toronto officers exchange looks, wondering why this civilian was there. I pressed on. "You left a lot of your stuff in your room at the center. Oh, but I guess it wasn't your room, was it? It was reserved for Michael Fortier."

He shot me a wary look, a warning behind his eyes. For an instant, it chilled me, until I reminded myself I was surrounded by big, burly policemen.

"I suppose this is the car you left parked at the library, isn't it?" I added. "You know, the library parking lot has pretty bright lights at night."

A sick look came over Trevor's face, and his shoulders sagged.

"You left quite a trail behind you, Mr. Murdock," Harris said. "It was only a matter of time before we caught up with you. I'm surprised you didn't take that million and a half and make a run for it before now. You left it a little late, didn't you?"

Trevor's eyes began to shift from side to side, looking for a way out. I could practically hear his brain churning. I felt a surge of anger.

"Bad enough you had to shoot the man. Did you have to ply him with alcohol too? That alone could have killed him," I scolded. "And while I'm at it, did you really think it wise to kiss Eva Stortini? I mean, she's at a vulnerable point in her life right now. It really upset Jason."

Harris gave a low chuckle. "Give it up, Mr. Murdock. Your life is an open book."

Again, Trevor didn't reply. I could see him putting together excuses, reasons, and I was having none of it. Wanting to push him over the edge, I leaned close and played my trump card.

"Next time, choose a better accomplice. Candace was sloppy."

Trevor's head snapped up. Beyond him, Harris's did the same. They both goggled at me, and then Trevor's face was suffused with anger, the change as sudden as if a windshield wiper had swept over it. He swore viciously.

"She told you! I can't believe it! I should have known not to trust that airheaded idiot!" He swung around to face the nearest officer. "I want that lawyer now. I'm not saying another word until I talk to a lawyer."

"Pack him up," Harris said, and the men led Trevor away to a patrol car and bundled him into it. Harris gave the top of the car a slap. Trevor sat with head bowed and eyes closed, his face tense, anger warring with defeat. I thought about Andrea Fortier and didn't feel the least bit sorry for him.

Over the top of the car, Harris and I exchanged smiles.

I stopped and looked again. Harris really was smiling. Not a twitching of the lips, not a sardonic half smile, but a broad, curving grin that split his handsome face ear to ear and made his eyes light up like LED bulbs. And I knew Jennie was right. Something good *had* come out of this.

As the car pulled away, Harris came over and pulled me aside. The other officers were talking in low voices, and the crowd of watchers began to disperse. Harris turned me around to face him.

"Candace?" he asked.

"Andrea Fortier's niece."

"That wasn't just a shot in the dark," Harris said. "How did you know?"

"I didn't know. But I couldn't think of any other reason Fortier would have had gesso on the bottoms of his shoes." When he continued to look blank, I went on. "We knew Trevor Murdock wasn't looking after Fortier if he was at the center the whole time. He had to have had an accomplice. Who would he have involved? The more I thought about it, Candace seemed to fit the bill. She's an art student, an oil painter. She'd use gesso. She would have been in a position to cross paths with her uncle's secretary at some point, and as I said, he was gorgeous—I mean, he would have appealed to an impressionable young woman. She'd probably have been willing to do anything for him. And to be fair, she might not have known at first that Murdock was planning to kill her uncle."

I could see Harris warm to this scenario. "Say Murdock, the faithful secretary, picked Fortier up from the detox center. Told him there was a change of plans and the wellness center couldn't take him quite yet after all. They had to kill some time. He drove Fortier to Candace's place, wherever she lives. Fortier would trust her. Sit and yack. She could convince him to have a few drinks."

I nodded. "That's what I'm imagining. Once he'd had a drink or two, it would have been almost impossible for him to stop. All she had to do was keep him quietly soused for a few days." Another thought hit me. "If there was any evidence left on the body tracing back to where he had been, well, that evidence would have pointed to Candace. The police might have blamed the whole thing on her. Fortier was childless. Maybe she stood to inherit or something."

"Pretty slick reasoning," Harris said with approval.

"I'm sure you would have figured it out, too, if you'd had time," I said. "I wasn't sure, but I thought I'd toss it out there and see if Trevor reacted to it. And he did."

"Yes, he did," Harris said, pleased.

"He should have waited for a lawyer," I added. "I assume you were reading him his rights when you were speaking in his ear up against the car."

"Among other things," Harris said.

"Other things?" I asked.

"I also told him he was very, very lucky he didn't hit you with that car." "Ah."

He shot me a bemused look. "Well, now maybe my boss will trust my instincts more."

"Why? What do you mean?"

Harris reached out and gave a stray wisp of my hair a gentle tug. "He told me to keep an eye on you. He thought you were nosing in on the investigation to lead us on a goose chase."

"Why would I do that?" I asked, astonished. At the look on his face, my eyes widened. "Was I really a suspect?"

He scooped his hand under my elbow and headed back toward the car. I could see him trying to hide that fabulous smile again. Peterson was standing there, waiting for us, looking grumpy, but I stopped short and pulled Harris around to face me in turn.

"Your instincts told you not to suspect me," I said. "Why?"

He shrugged, but his eyes were twinkling. "I've been doing this job for years. In spite of everything, I'm good at it," he replied airily.

I grinned. "You always get your man."

"Or in this case, woman," Harris agreed, and wrapping his long arms around me, he kissed me in front of everybody.

And for once, I had no song going through my head, no sound at all—only blessed, blessed peace.

Author Bio

Kristen Garner McKendry began writing in her teens, and her work has been published in Canada and the U.S. She received a bachelor's degree in linguistics from Brigham Young University and has always been a voracious reader. Kristen has a strong interest in urban agriculture, sustainable living, and environmental issues. She enjoys playing the bagpipes, learning dead languages, growing wheat in the backyard, and making cheese. A native of Utah, she now resides with her family in Canada. The idea for this book came out of a real estate ad for an old convent in need of fixing up and the thought, "What could I do with it if it were mine?"